# If You Are There

A NOVEL

## SUSAN SHERMAN

COUNTERPOINT
BERKELEY

Library of Congress Cataloging-in-Publication Data is Available

Names: Sherman, Susan, author.
Title: If you are there / Susan Sherman.
Description: Berkeley, CA : Counterpoint Press, [2017]
Identifiers: LCCN 2016040260 | ISBN 9781619028456 (hardback)
Subjects: | BISAC: FICTION / Literary.
Classification: LCC PS3619.H4676 I34 2017 | DDC 813/.6--dc23
LC record available at https://lccn.loc.gov/2016040260

Cover design by Jarrod Taylor
Interior design by Tabitha Lahr

ISBN 978-1-61902-845-6

COUNTERPOINT
2560 Ninth Street, Suite 318
Berkeley, CA 94710
www.counterpointpress.com

Printed in the United States of America
Distributed by Publishers Group West

10 9 8 7 6 5 4 3 2 1

For my brilliant everything
Lloyd Michael Peckner
1956–2015

*It matters little what god one believes in: It is the faith and not the god that makes miracles.*

—Henri Poincaré, April 1906

I.

# Warsaw, December 1901

I t was uncommon for a girl from the slums of Warsaw to escape the mills. There were some who married a good earner, more that died, but no one Lucia Rutkowska ever knew went off to Paris. To her way of thinking, just purchasing a ticket made her somebody, or nearly so, and she hadn't even gotten started yet.

On the morning she left, Lucia walked all the way from Babusia's house to the railway station in her new boots. They were her first pair of new shoes—truly new—had not been worn by another soul. On good days, when she was hopeful of making something of her life, she thought of them as a symbol of a bright future to come. On those days she saw nothing but fresh possibilities: a situation in a respectable house, money in her pocket, and a new dress to go with her new boots.

When they were leaving the shop with the boots still in the box, Babusia told her to give them to the boy to break them in. Lucia had no intention of doing so. When she told Babusia as much, her grandmother turned on her in annoyance. "So willful. Just like your mother." But Lucia heard the familiar stitch in her grandmother's voice. It had been eleven years, yet Babusia still felt the keen loss of her daughter, Lucia's mother, the brightest angel in heaven.

As it turned out, the boots were scuffed by the time Lucia reached the station; her heels were rubbed raw just as Babusia said they would be. A ferocious blister had formed on her right heel and another was threatening on her left, making every step a trial. She prayed to Mary the Blessed Mother to ease her suffering, to make her shoes more comfortable. However, the Holy Mother must have been busy with other, more deserving requests, for she got no relief.

Lucia tramped up the front steps of the columned portico, dragging a folding chair behind her, bumping it from one step to the next, wishing she could afford the fare for the omnibus. Even though it was only five grosze, Babusia had already given her all she could. Every expenditure had been accounted for, items added and subtracted, the list often copied fresh on a new piece of paper: so much for sausages and a loaf of bread; so much for a warm coat from the rag dealer that cost a little more because the stain was in the back; so much for a blanket, for a folding chair, for a warm pair of stockings; and all the rest for her ticket to Paris.

Lucia was so impressed by the train station that she had to stop by the door to take it all in. She crossed herself twice, fingering the rosary in her hand. Even though she had lived in Warsaw all her life, the only train station she had ever seen was the old tottery platform down the road from Babusia's house. This was something else. On the outside, the Vienna Station looked like a palace with its stone façade, wide colonnades, and two soaring clock towers at either end, each flying the Russian flag, but on the inside it looked like a cathedral with high windows and shafts of light pouring in through the clerestory. It reminded her of the painting of the Holy Mother and Child that hung in the Church of Mary Magdalene near Babusia's house. She imagined angels floating down on the light and stepping over to the counter to buy a ticket to Vienna or Skierniewice. It was a blasphemous thought; she felt a stab of remorse for having it. She offered a quick prayer of contrition to Saint Lucyna, her patron saint, who was by now used to her heretical imaginings.

She found a bench behind a pillar that had a good view of the doors. Babusia had warned that she wouldn't be safe until she was on the train, so she had to be careful. Stay alert. She put her bundles down and leaned the folding chair up against the bench. She noted the location of all the gates, just in case. Across the way at the railway restaurant, she spotted a table that sat in deep shadow half hidden behind a column. She thought that if the worst happened, if he came for her and she couldn't make it to the gates, she could hide there. She stuck her hand in a bundle and groped around for the medallion of Saint Ursula. She brought the little saint along for companionship, Saint Christopher for protection, and Saint Lucyna for everything else.

After that she relaxed some, unlaced her boot, and lifted her heel out to let it breathe through her stocking. She knew she still had to buy a ticket, but she had come such a long way that even Babusia would give her a little time to rest. Besides, the train didn't leave for hours, and looking around at her fellow travelers, well-dressed gentlemen and ladies coming and going in their furs flecked with snow, she couldn't believe there'd be much call for a place in a freezing fourth-class carriage, where you were expected to sit on your own folding chair and shiver under your own blanket.

Two girls, perhaps a year or two older than Lucia, came in through the big double doors, laughing at some private joke and stumbling over each other in their haste to get out of the cold. They weren't Poles. They were too well dressed in their fur coats and hats and expensive leather boots. The taller one had a matching muff that she carelessly tossed on a bench before collapsing on it and pulling her friend down to whisper in her ear. They were Russians—too noisy, too grand, their gestures too large and careless. Poles moved about in their own country as if they were in someone else's parlor. Russians made themselves at home, spreading out, claiming the most comfortable chairs.

Lucia tried to ignore them while keeping an eye on the door, but her attention kept straying back. She hated to admit that she envied those girls. After they removed their coats, she noticed that the thinner one, the one with the full mouth and almond eyes, wore a tailored skirt with braiding all around the useless little pockets. The same braiding on her gloves and on her boots. Lucia wanted to spend her time worrying about braiding, not about keeping warm and getting enough to eat, not of head lice and ruinous work in the factories, of cholera and typhus, of criminals in the streets. She wanted to be Russian, as shameful as that sounded. She wanted Russian worries.

Suddenly, the Russian girls rose up and headed toward the restaurant. As they passed, the taller one stumbled over Lucia's bundles, even though they were well out of the way. In that instant Lucia heard something break, a muffled snap like the delicate bone of a bird. They heard it too, for they hesitated, only for a moment, before going on without a word of apology or glance back.

Lucia opened the bundle and hunted around until she found the gromnica, the thunder candle that Babusia had given her when her mother died. It was in pieces. It had been a beautiful candle with her mother's name inscribed in gold at the base and decorated with a white ribbon and paper lilies. It was supposed to keep Lucia safe from lightning and flooding. At first she was furious, but then she hoped that God would strike them down, as every Pole knew he would, when he got as fed up with the Russians as she and her people were. She knew that things were not right in Poland. She also knew in her heart that God would put things right again as soon as he found the time.

Lucia was grateful for the many gifts that God had given her. Among them was her hair, which she wore in a thick braid down her back. Sometimes she would pile it on top of her head like a grand lady, but only when Irina wasn't around to scold her for acting above her station. She could cook and do complicated sums. People said her embroidery was accomplished. But her greatest gift of all was her vocabulary. It was nothing to use big words almost every day of the week. She had learned these words and many more in a dictionary that she had won at school for being an exemplary student. Exemplary.

She went to an underground school for the poor that had no name. They had to stay hidden because they spoke Polish and read Polish history and literature and wouldn't bow to the czar even if he were in front of them. Although, Lucia supposed Mademoiselle Wolfowicz would have told them to bow out of courtesy. Their teacher was exceedingly polite, even to her servants, even to the peddlers and beggars on the street.

The school was always on the move from back rooms to basements to the dark recesses of warehouses. They had to be careful not to get caught. Mademoiselle Wolfowicz would certainly be sent to Siberia. She was brave to run the school. She wasn't even paid, and she bought all the supplies herself. It was true that her father owned a big department store and they lived in a fine house on Nalewki Street, in the good section where all the rich Jews lived. Still, she spent a lot of her own money on the children, many of whom were not even Jewish. Once she even invited them to her house for little cakes and sandwiches. They were allowed to eat all they wanted and when the food ran out, she rang for more.

Mademoiselle Wolfowicz was the nicest lady Lucia had ever met. That's why whenever Tata or Irina called Mademoiselle the little *zhyd* or asked about her tail or her horns, Lucia wouldn't answer. She would just escape to Babusia's house. She always tried to respect her father and her stepmother, but sometimes it was a prodigious task.

"Prodigious," she whispered under her breath as she wrapped up the pieces of her broken thunder candle.

· · ·

Lucia and her best friend, Ania Brodowska, lived on Dobra Street in tenements that looked very much alike. Both buildings had the same rundown rooms, the same rubbish in the courtyard, the tap in front where everyone lined up for water, and the wrought iron balconies that occasionally gave way under the weight of a tenant. To the south, across Krakowskie Przedmieście and Nowy Świat, were the fine shops, houses, and government buildings. But this was Powiśle, a poor section of Warsaw, located along the river. Here the rutted streets lay mired in mud, the taverns stayed open late, and the occasional cry for help went unheeded. This is where the mill workers lived in a collection of doleful shacks that miraculously survived each passing winter despite their crumbling walls and patched roofs.

Every morning Lucia would stop under Ania's window and call up to her. One particular morning, they walked down Dobra Street to the square on Bednarska. It had snowed the night before, but the morning was bright under a clear sky. It was during Advent, right after Saint Barbara's feast, and here and there in sunny windows they could see bare cherry branches poking out of jam jars filled with water. Usually they made fun of the older girls who put them there hoping they would flower on Christmas Eve so they would find husbands on *zapusty*. At fourteen they were still too young to think of hanging their hopes on cherry branches, but they weren't so young that they didn't devour the latest romantic serials in the illustrated weeklies.

On most days Lucia and Ania made it a habit of stopping in Saxony Square at the obelisk erected by Czar Alexander II. It had been a gift to his Polish subjects. These were the same Poles who betrayed their countrymen and fought on the side of the tyrant, so spitting on the monument was something of a tradition among patriots. Lucia always spit first, because Ania needed time to screw up her courage. Generally, Ania was too scared to get up much spit. She had good reason to be scared. Spies were everywhere: the street cleaner on the corner, the waiter taking an order, even the fine-looking greengrocer's son, who teased them about being late for school. They could all be spies and you'd never know, until it was too late.

This time Ania didn't even try to spit, because she didn't like the look of the barber, who was watching them from the doorway of his shop. Instead she pulled on Lucia's sleeve and they walked on together, plowing through a deep pile of snow, letting it come all the way up to the tops of their boots.

•    •    •

Now that Lucia was at the ticket window, she hunted through her bundles for the coin purse. The clerk watched with growing impatience, his eyes drifting to the few respectable travelers waiting behind her with an undisguised look of contempt.

"I have it right here," she said, her anxiety growing. For one frantic moment she rummaged through her linens until her fingers clutched the little embroidered bag beneath the copy of *Madame Bovary* that Babusia had given her as a reward for improving her French. "Here. Here it is," she said with some relief. The clerk exchanged a knowing look with a well-dressed matron standing directly behind Lucia.

Lucia counted out the bills and offered them, shoving them through the window on the counter. He hesitated, regarding them with a look of disgust because they were dirty from Babusia's hiding place behind the hearth. Finally, he held them gingerly by a corner and counted them out again. Satisfied, he handed her a ticket and called to the next person in line without waiting for her to collect her things.

She took the ticket back to her bench and shoved it into one of her bundles. Then she sat down and unlaced her boot to check on the blister. It had begun to drain and the stocking was damp, sticking to the wound. She worked it free and held the stocking above the ankle to let it dry. She was just thinking that she could roll down her stocking to get a better look—it would have been gruesome, but also interesting in a strange way—when, with an icy thrill, she realized that crowds had been coming and going and she hadn't been paying attention. She bolted upright and surveyed the room: Two gentlemen stood checking the boards; an older couple sat hunched over the paper; a line of bored travelers stretched from the ticket counter.

She let out a breath and made a solemn promise to Saint Lucyna that she wouldn't let her mind wander again. A few minutes later when passengers came flooding in from an arriving train, she searched their faces, even though she couldn't believe he would be coming from the tracks and not through the front door. And yet, there in the crowd, among the wool *papakhi* and the fur hats, she spotted a man wearing a visor cap. The cap alone wouldn't have set off an alarm; most of the workers at the station wore them. But when she saw that he was also wearing a long dirty apron that covered his shirt and pants and an old cloth jacket with a torn hem, her chest went cold.

She jumped up, nearly tripping over her bootlace. With so many escape routes to choose from, she couldn't make up her mind. Finally she crossed to the restaurant, dragging her unlaced boot along, and took the table of last resort. There she crouched down in the chair, drawing herself in, becoming as small as possible.

She laced up her boot, unconsciously tying it into a pretty bow, while she tracked the man's progress across the crowded station. She couldn't see his face, only the cap, the apron, and the jacket, and that lumbering walk she knew so well.

A Polish boy carrying a tray full of dirty dishes stopped by her table. "What are you doing there?" he asked. He kept his voice down as he glanced around to make sure they weren't being watched.

"Nothing," she said.

His red hair was shorn at the sides making the crown of his head look like the comb of a rooster. She kept her eyes on the man in the apron. He was coming closer, but his features were still hidden under his hat. She couldn't be certain if she could not see his face. It felt like cold fingers were poking around in her stomach. "You can't sit there, you know," the boy said impatiently.

"I'm not bothering anybody." She was surprised at how unperturbed she sounded even though she could barely breathe.

"You have to order something. They won't let you just sit there."

"I'll have some tea."

He gave her an appraising look and shook his head. "You couldn't afford it."

She watched while a well-dressed gentleman surrounded by luggage, a wife, and four children stopped the man in the apron.

They conferred and after a moment the man in the apron began loading their luggage onto the cart. In her fright she hadn't seen the cart, even though it had been there the whole time. When it was fully loaded the man followed the gentleman and his family back through the gate and down to the platform.

The boy was still talking to her, although she hadn't been listening to a word. He had put a dirty teapot and teacup in front of her, along with a plate with a half-eaten pastry. "Don't look at anybody," he said in a whisper. He kept his eye on a waiter across the way, who was serving borscht to a Russian couple.

When she realized he was trying to help her, she gave him a grateful smile and thanked him. He looked a little like her cousin Czeslaw, the one who was always trying to kiss her, surely a sign from Saint Christopher that the saint was protecting her.

Then she remembered.

She had left everything on the bench: the book, the broken thunder candle, her precious bundles—all her things, including her money and her ticket.

•   •   •

On the last school day before Christmas, Lucia walked alone looking for signs from God. Lucia often looked for signs from God. Babusia had taught her it was just a matter of keeping your eyes open and your mind alert. Babusia always said that his signs were everywhere, and in this way he made his presence known.

On this particular morning she watched a rook linger over a smashed winter squash in the roadway. She wouldn't have taken this as a sign. Babusia taught her to be particular and not think every ray of sunshine filtering through the trees was the word of God. But this rook cocked his head and leveled his yellow eye so it looked directly into hers. It was as if he were saying: *Listen to me. I have a message for you.*

She was late that morning because she had stayed with Babusia in Praga. She was just coming over the bridge when she passed an old woman standing beside a fire burning in a rusty drum. A grate over the opening held a layer of roasting nuts, which the old lady stirred from time to time so they wouldn't burn. "*Kasztany, gorące kasztany . . .*" the crone called out in a reedy voice. She didn't put much into her call—some of the other peddlers were full throated and sounded like opera singers—but then she didn't have to. The smell alone was her best advertisement.

"*Kasztany,*" she called out to the crowd, holding out a steamy paper cone of nuts. Behind her the Vistula River flowed under a thick layer of blue-green ice. Along the western bank stood the slums of Dobra Street where rows of shacks seemed to be dissolving back into the snow-covered embankment.

"Hey, little swallow. You want to buy?"

And there it was. Another sign. *Little swallow.* She could have called Lucia a hundred endearments: little frog, sunshine, kitty, but instead she called her *mała jaskółka.* It fit with the rook. Maybe God was trying to tell her something about birds.

Later that day, just before school let out, Mademoiselle clapped her hands to get their attention. "Lucyna Rutkowska! Come up to my desk this instant." Mademoiselle was the only one in the world who called her Lucyna. Lucia rose with anticipation, flushing with pride even though she knew pride was a sin.

The class had been meeting for the last several months in the back room of Pani corset maker Alicja Jaworska's. She took the risk because her daughter went to the school. So far no one had given them away, and they had set up quite a nice place among the bolts of fabric, shelves of whalebone, and sewing supplies. They hardly noticed the clatter of the sewing machines up front or the little bell that announced the arrival of a customer.

After Mademoiselle presented Lucia with a dictionary, cookies were passed around along with glasses of milk. Of course the Polish children had to give their milk to the Jewish children on account of Advent, but nobody held that against Mademoiselle; she was a Jew and didn't know about the rules of Advent. In fact that's how Lucia got her final sign. For along with the usual Christmas cookies there were also butter cookies with blue icing in the shape of bluebirds. *Bluebird,* now who could ignore that sign? Everyone knew it was the bird of happiness and prosperity. Sitting in the back of the corset shop, biting the head off her first bluebird, she saw with surprising clarity that something was about to take flight.

On the way home Lucia held her dictionary under her coat so it wouldn't get wet and told Ania about the signs from God. It had just begun to snow, careless feathers floating out of a dull sky. Already she could hear the *ligawke* blowing from the different quarters of the city—the great wooden horns announcing evening Mass during Advent.

"Maybe it wasn't about flying away," Ania remarked as she pulled up the strap of her satchel. "Maybe he was trying to tell you that Mademoiselle was about to give you the dictionary and that you should celebrate tonight by cooking a bird."

Ania's mind worked in peculiar ways. Her mother was odd too, in her own way. It was a known fact that she didn't like to wear shoes, even though she owned a perfectly good pair. She preferred to go barefoot, even around horses, even in cold weather, but not in the snow, of course. She was peculiar, not insane.

Even though Ania's idea was a little absurd, it did get Lucia thinking. By the time she got home, she had all but decided to buy a duck for supper. It would be an extravagance, but she would tell Tata she had saved for it out of the food money. That was a lie of course, and she would have to go to confession, but it might be worth it, considering they all loved duck.

Lucia cooked all the meals in the house because Tata and Irina both worked in the mill. Since Irina rarely left enough to feed the six of them, Lucia was in the habit of taking a grosz or two from the tobacco tin hidden under the floorboards. She took only what she needed and replaced it the next day. Babusia always gave it to her, despite the fact that she didn't have much, only her husband's pension and a bit in savings. Still she didn't want to see her grandchildren go hungry, even though Babusia wasn't allowed to come to their rooms anymore, not even on feast days, not since Irina had come to live with them.

Lucia knew that their flat was the best in the building, not because it was finer than the others, but because it was on the first floor right behind the tap. Everyone else had to haul their water up the stairs. They had two bedrooms instead of the usual one and their front room was a little larger than the others, but it was still just as threadbare.

When Lucia got home, she found the kitchen nearly as cold as the courtyard outside. The porridge still sat in the pot left over from breakfast, only now it was covered with a thin crust of ice. Lacy ice patterns clung to the inside of the windows, and the washrag that hung on a hook next to the sink was stiff with frost.

"Emila!" She cried out for her younger sister, who took care of the baby. "You let the fire go." The baby was Irina's, their half brother, although they loved him all the same.

Lucia stood at the window in the front room looking for her sister in the courtyard. It wasn't as if the girl had so much to do that she couldn't find time to clean the house and keep the fire going. She would say she was only eleven and did the best she could. Lucia would say by eleven Bede was already at the mill, so she had no excuse. Bede was their brother, their whole brother. He was a roving boy and had to carry heavy cans from the carding room to the drawing room. It was hard work for any man, and Bede was only thirteen. But at least it was a safe job. Pani Kowalska's son got his fingers chopped off in the lapping house feeding cotton into the hopper of one of those big open feeders.

Emila was nowhere to be seen among the children playing hoops along the black-and-white fence that fronted their courtyard. Across the road was a chocolate-colored house with a sagging porch that had come off its supports. Up the lane were other houses: yellow, green, and orange shacks with peeling paint, broken windows stuffed with newspapers, and mossy roofs half buried under snow.

Since Emila wasn't home, Lucia took the opportunity to help herself to a little more from the tin. She took the money down to the market square, which was nearly empty this late in the afternoon. The sellers were packing up their crates, hurrying to bury their vegetables in straw before it began to snow again. She walked down an aisle littered with cabbage leaves until she came to the poultry stall. She kept an eye on the poultry man as she examined the ducks hanging on hooks, limp and lifeless. She waited until he was busy with another customer before calling his boy over. The boy had been waiting for her, had been watching her. She knew this about him, which is why she always dealt with him and not his father. It wasn't only because he gave her a better price. She liked him. He was different from the other boys: shy, searching, and greedy. Her eyes settled on him and she gave him a half smile that he could have taken any number of ways. It was the kind of inviting look she imagined the poor but deserving governesses gave to the handsome noblemen in the illustrated weeklies.

It was dark by the time she got home and still she had to pluck the bird out in the courtyard. She sat on a crate struggling to see by the stray light coming from the nearby windows. She pulled out a handful of feathers and let the wind carry them off to the corners of the yard. She had to work fast to keep her fingers from freezing. Snow drifted out of a black sky and mixed with the feathers until it was impossible to tell them apart.

That evening Bede bounded in first, wearing a long mill apron and two coats to keep warm. His hair fell in a greasy thicket about his face and his hands were red and chapped. He took after Tata with his long, thoughtful face and deep-set black eyes. His arms had been sticks a year ago and now they were thick and ropy from hauling the cans around all day. "What is that smell?" he asked in wonder.

"We're celebrating," Emila said, without looking up. She was on the floor changing Lucjan. The baby was on a blanket staring up at a ceiling mottled with mold. He had just been given his supper and now he was sleepy and relaxed. "She won a dictionary at school.

And she got a cookie too, in the shape of a bluebird." Lately Emila had been asking to go to school. No one took her seriously, however, since she was needed at home and an education was a waste anyway, especially for girls. The only reason Lucia got to go was because Babusia paid for it.

Bede ran a finger along the greasy wall of the pan and licked it. "We're eating duck for that? For a dictionary?"

Just then they heard Tata and Irina in the courtyard and a moment later their wooden clogs on the stairs. When their father pushed open the door he was still wearing his long apron and work pants and came inside without bothering to take off his visor cap, which was lightly dusted with snow. He muttered something about the smell and clomped over to the stove to take a look. His clogs were so loud on the wooden planks that they woke up Lucjan, who wailed in protest. Tata ignored his crying son because he could. He was the man, the head of the household, the *głowa rodziny*, and he didn't need to concern himself with a crying baby.

Irina slipped off her shawl at the door and stepped out of her muddy clogs. She picked up the baby and ambled over to the stove. "Is that a duck?"

Lucia didn't respond at first. Instead she poured the boiled potatoes into the colander to let them drain. There were a few green ones, but no one would mind. "I saved for it," she said. Lucia liked to think of herself as an honest person, one who didn't lie easily and always went to confession afterward. But God must realize that lying to Irina hardly counted.

Irina stood in the kitchen and followed Lucia with her eyes, back and forth from stove to table. Lucia could see that Irina's mind was working and that could prove troublesome. Finally she said: "You didn't save for it, did you? The old woman gave it to you." She always called Babusia the old woman.

Lucia dismissed the idea with annoyance. "I told you, I bought it with the food money."

"What food money?" Irina asked, her eyes narrowing in disbelief.

Her lips brushed the top of Lucjan's head as she absently gave him several kisses.

When Tata married Irina and brought her home to live, he told his children that she would be like a mother to them. She was only a few years older than Lucia and certainly no mother to her, although she had been a friend once when she first arrived. In those days she braided Lucia's hair and helped her with the sewing. Sometimes they would go to the market and Irina would buy her a sweet or a ribbon. She taught Lucia how to fix her hair so she looked older.

Then when Lucjan was born everything changed. Now, sometimes late at night, Lucia could hear Irina talking to Tata in their room. She would often complain that she wanted to stay home and be a proper mother to Lucjan. She would say that she didn't want to go to the mill anymore, that it was time for Lucia to take her place.

"If you do not want to eat it, then don't eat it," Lucia said testily. "No one is forcing you."

Everyone was used to their sparring. At best their exchanges were short and prickly. Tata usually abdicated his role as referee, choosing to ignore the tension in the room. If forced to take a side, he always took his wife's, still believing, or at least wanting to believe, that she deserved respect and obedience.

Tata tore off a piece of bread and slathered it with lard. "That's enough, Lucia. Irina is right. If it came from the old woman, then I do not want it either. I don't even want it in the house. So if it belongs to her, then you will have to take it back."

"It belongs to us, Tata. It's our duck." This was mostly true, so it didn't count as a lie. But she did blame Irina for making trouble and putting her in a position where a real lie might crop up at any moment.

"She saved for it," Emila said with some urgency. "She saved for a long time. Look Tata, here is the dictionary she won." She put it on the table in front of him. Perhaps Emila thought that if he held the dictionary, he might forget about the bird or at least the source of it and let it stay. By now all the other smells in the tenement had given way to it and the idea that it might go away, that it might be sent away, would have broken Emila's heart. At eleven, her heart was often getting broken.

Before the argument could escalate, Lucia scooped the potatoes into a bowl and set them down on the table. She surrounded the bird on the platter with roasted beets and turnips still in their skins. If she had had a bit of greenery or a piece of fruit, she would have put that on the platter as well to make it look more festive.

Tata took most of the crispy breast for himself and piled on the vegetables. Then, gripping the fork as if it were a knife, he began to shovel the food into his mouth. They had stopped saying grace shortly after Lucia's mother died. Once, all the feast days had been observed, Mass had been regularly attended, there was always a grosz or two for candles both at home and at the shrine of the Blessed Virgin Mary. She died shortly after giving birth to Emila, after taking her last breath in a bed soaked in sweat and blood. At the end she was delirious with fever calling out for Babusia, who was there by her side, holding her hand. After the funeral he never went to church again, preferring instead to take his grief down the road to the tavern. For all the days that followed he would ask nothing of God.

After dinner they were all a little reluctant to leave the table even though the plates were bare. The duck had been so unexpected, such a benediction, that, like mourners at a grave, they were unwilling to let it go.

Lucia rose and gathered up the bones for soup, dumping them into the pail along with the onion peelings and beet tops. Tata rolled a cigarette and gave it to Bede. Then Tata rolled one for himself, making a neat trough with the paper and filling it with tobacco. He lit it and breathed in the smoke, holding it in his lungs before letting it out in a cloud. For a brief moment he closed his eyes in relief and then opened them again.

"Lucia, come over here. I have something to tell you."

"I have to help Emila with the dishes."

"Leave them."

Lucia took a seat but did not like this development. Ordinarily, Tata did not have much to say, so when he made a special effort to do so, it was often a sign of trouble. Across the table, he sucked on his cigarette and it flared momentarily. Irina had taken Lucjan and gone into the bedroom. Another bad sign.

"So now you have two dictionaries and school is on holiday," he said, tapping the ash into his cupped palm. His voice sounded thick with fatigue. "Tomorrow I want you to tell your *babka* that you will no longer be going to school. You are done with all that."

Lucia's stomach lurched. "But I'm not finished yet. I've barely started."

"You know how to read and write. What more do you need?"

She felt dizzy. "But I want to be a teacher like Mademoiselle."

"And end up in Siberia? No, it is time you went into the mill."

"The *mill*," she said desperately.

"You are old enough now. It is time."

Lucia started to protest but thought better of it. Instead, she sat there for a moment collecting her thoughts, fingering the thick granules of salt on the oilcloth, while she struggled to control her feelings. Above all, she did not want to cry. She knew that tears only made Tata frantic. He didn't know what to do with them. He grew impatient, then frustrated, and finally angry, and she did not want him to get angry. Anything could happen if he lost his temper.

"Maybe I could do something else, Tata?" she asked hopefully. "I could work in a shop or be a clerk in an office. I could make more money that way. Just a few more years of schooling. And then I could go to work and bring home every grosz."

Tata dismissed her idea with a wave. "You will get used to it." Here his voice softened a bit. "I know you are disappointed, but there is nothing for it. Sooner or later we all go. This is what we do. All of us. Even you, Lucia."

Just this little bit of sympathy brought on the tears. Somehow she had to make him understand that a mistake was being made.

She was trying to sound reasonable, like an adult, but her voice thinned, became desperate and rushed. She tried to explain about what school meant to her, about all the things she was learning, but Tata only looked away, embarrassed by her tears.

It seemed that Bede too was uncomfortable, for he got up and moved off into the front room to smoke his cigarette in peace.

Without looking at her, Tata went on: "You will start out in carding. Maybe as a scavenger or a piecer. Maybe a doffer, but I doubt it, you being a girl and all." He said this more to himself than to her. "It'll be hard at first, no doubt, but in time you will know what to do."

Now she was crying in earnest.

He lifted his head and gazed at her. "Well, what did you expect, Lucia? That you were going to be a lady? Is that what your *babka* has been telling you? She doesn't do you any good filling your head with smoke. We are millworkers. We have always worked the looms. You knew that. You have always known."

It was true that Tata told her she would be a millworker, but she hadn't believed him. She thought something would come along to change all that; that it was only a matter of time. God would provide for her. Babusia had always told her that her destiny lay elsewhere, although she had always been vague about exactly where that was. Lucia knew that destiny wasn't something that could be changed. It was predetermined. She had looked it up.

That night Lucia crept out of the flat and into the yard where the snow had been falling for hours, obliterating the cart tracks in the road. Without the tracks to follow, she knew the going would be hard. Drawing her coat in, bending her head against the wind, she trudged through the fresh drifts. The road was deserted, but old warnings of evil on the prowl kept her on edge. She kept turning to peer down the alleyways and the side roads to make sure that nobody was lurking there to grab her.

The bridge was icy and buried under a fresh shroud of snow. At first she thought it was deserted, but then from out of the flurries she saw a figure plodding toward her. As he got closer she saw that he was a heavyset man plunging through the snow with the wind at his back, while one hand held the brim of his hat to keep it from blowing away.

She slowed her pace and hung back against the parapet to put as much distance between them as she could. His form shimmered fat and thin in the swirling eddies. Even over the wind she could hear the pulse in her ears and thought he could be anything: a robber, a thief, a murderer, or a tortured soul roaming with the devil himself. Then he was there, nearly upon her, and in the next instant he was traipsing past her on into the storm. It took only a few seconds for her to register the dog collar, the dark coat, and the look of grim forbearance that belonged to Father Tomaszewski. By the time she recognized him he was already gone, probably off to the bedside of a dying parishioner, leaving her on her own again.

Praga was like a remote village that had somehow gotten stuck to the heel of a large city. The modest framed cottages were set far apart with empty fields between them. What was left of the corn rows could be seen undulating under the snow. Babusia's cottage was down a lane off the main road, which was hard to find in the storm without a signpost to show the way. For a brief time Lucia thought she was lost. She imagined freezing to death just yards from the cottage. She searched for landmarks but found only windswept fields and humps of snow that had once been hayricks or low-lying bushes. Then she saw a familiar house and beside it the skeletal limbs of an old elm she liked to climb when she was younger. A few minutes later she caught sight of Babusia's house, and something broke free inside of her. She ran full tilt through the snow.

"What are you doing out there?" Babusia asked in alarm as she slid back the bolt and flung open the door. "What is it? What is wrong?" She pulled Lucia inside, wrapping her shawl around her granddaughter's shoulders, rubbing her arms to get the blood moving again. Lucia's teeth were chattering, while her lips were too numb for her to speak.

"Was there an accident? Is it Bede? I told them he was too young for the mill." Babusia was dressed in her long white night-gown yellowed with age. Her hair was mostly gray and hung like cobwebs about her shoulders.

"It's not Bede. Everyone is fine," Lucia managed to say.

Babusia helped Lucia into the kitchen, shuffling along beside her in her dead husband's slippers. "What is it then? Why are you out so late? Have you lost your mind?" She sat Lucia down in a chair, covered her in a blanket, and added a few sticks to the fire, all the while chiding her for being out on a night like this with the wind and the snow, and the white slavers hunting the lanes for young girls.

Lucia didn't hear a word of it. Instead she dropped her face in hands and began to cry.

Babusia's voice immediately rose an octave. "What is it, *mój aniele*?" She leaned over, put an ample arm around her grand-daughter's shoulders, and hugged her close while she let Lucia cry. "Ah, such tears. Tell me. What is so terrible that it drove you out on a night like this?"

When Lucia told her all about the dictionary, the duck, and Tata, about how she was going to have quit school and work in the mill, Babusia sat back in her chair and snorted a laugh. "So that is what he told you, eh?" She kissed the top of Lucia's head and stepped to the stove where the kettle had begun to sing. "Now you listen to me," she said, pouring steaming water into the mugs. "You are not going to work in any mill."

"But he said . . ."

"Ach, he knows nothing. He's a serf. What have I always told you, Lucynka?" She brought the tea over and took a seat.

Lucia shrugged and picked up the mug, holding it between her hands for warmth.

"You are a Sanguszko. Have you forgotten? You have Sanguszko blood in your veins. It is an old family with a proud name. Older than the hills. We are *szlachta*." She meant noblemen. "And *szlachta* do not work in the mills."

"But Mama . . ."

"If your *matka* had done right by her family and married a man of property, then you would not be in this predicament. When I think my own daughter married a serf I want to lie down in a coffin and pull the dirt over my head."

Ever since she was a little girl, Lucia had heard the stories about Babusia's life on her father's estate. Her grandmother was sixteen when the Russians came and took everything. Still she managed to save a few things that were scattered about her little house: the gilt chair with clawed feet in the parlor, the inlaid card table, and the line of empty perfume bottles on the shelf in the bedroom. Sometimes Lucia would take one down, pry open the stopper, and breathe in the lingering scent of happier times.

"But what about Bede? He's in the mill."

"He takes after him. I love the boy, but I don't see your mother in him. Not at all. You, you are different. You will have a different kind of life. God has ordained it. I have seen the signs." Here, she patted Lucia's hand and stroked her head. Then she got up and put her cup in the sink. "Come, it is late. Finish your tea and we will go to bed."

Lucia and her grandmother lay under a pile of old quilts listening to the fire dying in the stove. Over the next several hours the storm would stealthily deposit mounds of snow up against the door and windows. In the morning they would have to dig themselves out, but for now they could lay safe and warm in the old feather bed.

Lucia knew she would not be going to the mill. Babusia had said as much, and that was enough for her. Even so, great changes were coming. She clutched the edge of the quilt and pulled it up under her chin. She lay there in the dark thinking about the upending of her life, trying to imagine what it would be like. It was an enormous undertaking. It was like trying to imagine a vast, limitless plain or the edge of the universe. The effort made her dizzy, and she soon gave it up.

"Babusia?" she whispered.

"Mmm." By now her grandmother was half asleep.

"I can't remember what Mama looked like."

Babusia gave her a sleepy, halfhearted snort. "Not to worry, *dziewczyna*. Whenever you want to see your mama, just look in the mirror. That is exactly what she looked like."

Then Babusia sat up, reached behind her, and took down the cross that hung over the bed. She handed it to Lucia, saying: "This was your *matka*'s cross. Keep it with you. Hang it on the wall above your bed, and in that way she will always be with you. You will not be alone."

Lucia put the cross beneath her pillow and closed her eyes. In that drowsy, hypnotic state just before sleep, she was down by the river again washing clothes with her mother. She was only three or four, trying to help her with the wet clothes. It was a hot summer and they had waded out into the water. Their skirts hiked up and tucked into their waistbands, squinting into the sunlight. The light off the water was dazzling, blinding if you looked at it too long. It was so bright that she couldn't see her mother's face, only the halo of light around her hair, her features cast in shadow. Brightly colored rowboats dotted the river, blue, red, and green, bobbing in the water like buttons. Her mother lifted her up, kissing her neck and face, tickling and delighting her. Lucia snuggled down with her legs curling over the round pregnant belly. Then it came, that moment, a brief stillness, and she could see her mother's face looking at her, audacious, exuberant, and sturdy.

•    •    •

Lucia returned to her bench and found all her belongings just as she'd left them. After that she did not allow her attention to waver. She kept a stern eye on the station and the ramps leading into it, until it was announced that her train had arrived and was ready for boarding. She slid a folded handkerchief behind her heel to cushion it from the stiff leather, gathered up her bundles and folding chair, and followed the crowd down to the platform where the train sat waiting. It was late afternoon and she had been at the station for nearly eight hours. The crowd was moving slowly along the platform despite the wind and driving snow. She limped around a raft of ladies in fur coats and muffs and officers in greatcoats and *papakhi*. The air smelled of coal dust and perfume and then just coal dust and machine oil as she walked further down the train. Here the Polish workers struggled with their bundles of clothing and food, dragging their children along while they searched for their carriages.

Lucia's carriage was made of rough planks that did little to keep the weather out. A few hard benches sat under the windows and faced an old stove in the middle that didn't give off much heat. This was the women's carriage. Women from the factories and peasant girls from the countryside sat on the benches or on folding chairs or stools, huddled in their shawls and blankets, holding their hands out to catch whatever warmth was coming off the stove. Lucia set her chair down near the stove, careful not to block anyone's heat. She turned to an old grandmother, who sat shivering on the bench. "*Babka*, may I put a few sticks on the fire?" A small pile of wood was stacked nearby.

"Do what you like, *panienka*," said the old babka. "But remember, that is all we have, and it will be worse for us when we are in the mountains."

Lucia frowned at her, because that's not what she wanted to hear. But she knew the old woman was right, so she left the wood alone. Instead, she gathered up her bundles and wrapped them around her legs for warmth and safekeeping. She wrapped the blanket around her shoulders and drew it in under her chin. She watched the crowd outside on the platform, mindful of Babusia's warning about not being safe until the train had left the station.

The whistle blew and the train belched great geysers of steam into the frigid air. The last of the passengers climbed aboard, the stationmaster gave his signal to the brakeman, the whistle blew twice, and the train started to roll away, leaving only a few porters on the platform. One of those left behind wore a visor cap and a long apron like the porter before. He was hurrying past the others, going the wrong way, heading toward the end of the train instead of back up to the station. Even though he wore a coat with fraying cuffs and a torn hem, Lucia still wasn't alarmed until he had almost reached her carriage and she could see his face.

At that moment Tata spotted her too and ran for the carriage door. The other women held it closed and shouted at him to go away; that he wasn't allowed; that this was the women's carriage. The stationmaster ran over and pulled him off.

As the train continued to roll away by inches, she could see Tata arguing with the stationmaster. He struggled to get away, trying to make the man understand that his daughter was on the train; that he was about to lose her; that if he didn't get her back, she would be gone forever. When the train started to pick up speed, he wrenched his arm free and ran alongside the women's carriage. He urged her to get off, to come home, not to leave. She belonged with her family.

At the last minute she jumped to her feet and slapped her hands against the glass. "Tata!" she cried out. If she could, she probably would have gotten off right there, but in the next instant they left him behind and, with a clank of the wheels, changed tracks and headed out of the station.

# CHAPTER TWO

# Paris, September 1902

G abriel Richet had never before been invited to one of his brother's séances, although he tried not to take it personally. Charles rarely invited anyone who didn't have a scientific interest in his "experiments." He generally invited like-minded men of science, but on occasion he would include a skeptic or two as long they had some connection to the scientific community.

Charles lived in a large apartment off the rue de Médicis, a short walk to his laboratory at the Sorbonne. It was a sprawling home that took up four floors, packed with his wife's heavy horsehair furniture and the detritus of five nearly grown boys. It was a far cry from Gabriel's flat over a falafel stand in the rue Ferdinand-Duval in the Marais. He had two rooms on what they called the Street of the Jews, named for the Jews who had returned early in the century when they were once again tolerated in the city. Even though his rooms contained only a small painted table, a couple of chairs, and an iron-framed bed with a mattress that listed dangerously to one side; even though the cupboards were littered with rodent droppings and roach carcasses, and the window in the kitchen refused to close all the way; even with all these inconveniences and the one toilet in the hall that he shared with two families, he considered himself the king of the Marais. He had two whole rooms to himself in a section of the city where it was common for large families to cram into one.

There may have been another reason why Gabriel had not been invited to his brother's séances. He didn't like to consider this one, even though it was always there on the periphery, his thoughts snagging on it like a broken fingernail. Charles may not have wanted to introduce him to that mighty circle of great minds, the famous and not-so-famous men of science who regularly attended his brother's séances. Even though Gabriel knew he was being too sensitive, that his brother did not worry about status and rank, still Gabriel found himself wondering if his brother wasn't a little ashamed of him.

Gabriel stood outside the door of his brother's apartment and cleaned his boots on the iron scraper. He took time scraping the mud off from around the base of his heel, first one shoe, then the other, even stopping to shine them up a little with his handkerchief. It might have been the light from the lamppost, but he had to admit they looked fairly scruffy. He should have spent a few sous getting them shined. It might have put him more at ease.

He knew his coat looked shabby. It was worn at the elbows and the sleeves were dirty. Charles would say nothing, of course. He would not want to embarrass Gabriel. Later, when the evening was over and Gabriel was heading out the door, Charles might hold him back a moment and press a few francs in his palm. Gabriel would protest of course, but his brother would insist. He would say that it was time for a new coat or a pair of boots, and that it would make him happy if Gabriel took the money. The sad part was that Gabriel would take it; he always did, because he needed it.

Gabriel was met at the door by the new parlor maid, a friendly, open-faced girl from the countryside who fussed over him, taking his coat and hat, and kindly displayed no surprise that he didn't have gloves to give her. She showed him up to the third floor where he found Charles in the séance room, hunched over a camera affixed to a tripod.

Charles looked up when Gabriel walked in. "You're here, thank God. So you got my *bleu.*" Gabriel didn't even have to open it to know it was from Charles. No one in Gabriel's set ever spent money on a message sent by pneumatic tube. In Gabriel's world, if you wanted to summon a friend, you just stood under his window and shouted up.

When Charles hugged Gabriel he could smell the familiar scent of his brother, of good living, of cigars and fresh laundry.

"It's cold. Are you cold?" his brother asked. To the girl he said: "Get him something hot. Some tea or coffee." Then back to Gabriel, "Would you like a whiskey?"

"No, I'm fine."

"Get him a whiskey, Inès. That's a good girl."

She curtsied and hurried out.

"I'm not taking you away from anything, am I? I didn't mean to make it sound like an emergency. Nobody is dying or anything. Although, I suppose it's a bit of an emergency to me."

He seemed on edge, not able to sit still. This wasn't like Charles. He was usually calm and filled with confidence. Some thought him arrogant, but Gabriel always admired his equanimity. It was the kind of self-assurance that came with success. His brother was a well-respected physiologist, the editor of *Revue Scientifique*, and coeditor of the *Journal de Physiologie et de Pathologie Générale*. He had published papers on physiology, physiological chemistry, experimental pathology, and normal and pathological psychology. His recent work on the mechanism of regulating body heat in animals had garnered him praise and there was even talk of a Nobel Prize. Gabriel, on the other hand, had dropped out of medical school to become a writer. He was fifteen years his brother's junior and a catastrophic disappointment to their father.

"What is it, Charles? What's wrong?" Gabriel didn't like to think it was Amélie or the boys.

"You know how to work these cameras?"

Gabriel looked around at the five cameras situated around the room. He went over to examine the closest one. "This one looks simple enough. Why?"

His brother sank down in one of the chairs that surrounded a large round table that stood in the center of the room. It was a simply furnished room, probably because Amélie had not been allowed to decorate it. It didn't have the fussiness of the rest of the house, no cloche jars protecting miniature tropical glades, no soothing watercolors of Dinard or Saint-Tropez on the overmantel, nothing to suggest the determined will of a woman with a generous allowance and too much time on her hands.

"The photographer came down with a fever and there's no one to man the cameras. You know how to work a twelve-shot Facile?" He looked hopeful, but it was a fragile hope. Gabriel thought that his brother was preparing himself for disappointment.

Charles was an older version of Gabriel, the same blond hair closely cropped; only his was nearly gray. They had similar moustaches like twin sheaves of wheat over their upper lip. Gabriel was thinner than Charles, yet more solid, with strong arms and legs from his recent passion for cycling. They both had their father's long, horsey face, Charles's becoming more equine with worry. Clearly, he was worried now. And he had a right to be. The Facile was a complicated camera that took twelve dry plates at once and so could capture twelve shots without reloading. Nevertheless, it was tricky to reload if more shots were needed. Gabriel wasn't a photographer, only a Sunday enthusiast, but as a journalist for Le Matin he had access to exotic equipment and had even used the camera once.

"It shouldn't be a problem," he said, moving to the back of the room where the Facile sat perched on its tripod.

Charles's face lit up. "Really?" he said, combing his fingers through his hair and smiling at his brother. "I have six sitters coming in less than an hour for a new medium. I didn't want to have to cancel." Then he stopped, his grin fading, "What about the flash lamp? It's complicated I hear."

It was lying on its side on the table, a metal tube attached to a smaller tube with a horizontal arm at one end to hold the magnesium powder. Gabriel had never used one before, but just the other day a photographer at the paper was going on about them. Apparently, they were electrical now, using dry batteries to create a spark to ignite the magnesium. Push a button and the magnesium exploded into a bright white light.

"I think I can manage."

"You're sure?"

Gabriel nodded. At this Charles's features softened and his shoulders relaxed.

Gabriel knew that something of note had just taken place. His brother had come to *him* for help. Charles had thought enough of Gabriel to ask for his aid at a time when he needed it most. For a moment Gabriel felt as if he had just taken a sip of fine whiskey. A warm rush coursed through him, giving him a sense of well-being, a light-headed expansiveness. For one brief moment he had expertise in an arcane field. He was valued, perhaps even respected.

Unfortunately, the feeling left him all too quickly, before he could even commit it to memory. The truth was he wasn't an expert in photography. He had never used the flash lamp before and wasn't at all sure he could reload the twelve-shot Facile. Soon he would be asked to produce results or disappoint his brother, embarrass himself in his brother's circle, and experience yet another failure that his brother would avoid mentioning.

·   ·   ·

Gabriel had spent too much time in the café-concerts, the brothels, and the *brasseries de filles* of Pigalle and Montmartre not to be suspicious of his brother's séances. As a journalist he was often in the company of con men, pimps, and *grisettes*, working-class women who worked on the laundry boats, in the bakeries, and in the small factories during the day but at night occasionally prostituted themselves.

A few passed themselves off as fortune-tellers or mediums. Fewer still acquired regulars for their séances and built a reputation. He knew them. Mostly they were guarded when it came to the secrets of their trade, but there was one who, given enough whiskey, liked to brag about her tricks. She told him enough to make him suspicious of the whole field that his brother and the other scientists found so fascinating and investigated with such vigor.

The medium that night held no resemblance to the *grisettes* of Pigalle. She was from a world away. Charles said that she grew up in Algiers, where her father was an official in the Foreign Service. He said that she had been discovered there by Éléonore Bonnard, the wife of Colonel Bonnard, that she had sat for them on many occasions, and that they swore she had a genuine gift.

The medium, Alais Bonnet, arrived with her companion, Juliette Denis, the widow of Bernard Denis, the well-known sculptor. He had died recently and left his wife a large flat in the rue Soufflot in the Latin Quarter that was always filled with artists and writers, a boisterous crowd who typically came for an evening and stayed through to the morning. Gabriel had been there a number of times, although he doubted if she would remember him. He had even spent a night on her floor once, passed out in front of the French doors that looked out on the Panthéon.

"So where do you want us?" Juliette asked, after she introduced herself and Mademoiselle Bonnet. "I expect you'll want to examine her."

Juliette Denis was truly a beautiful woman. Gabriel surmised that she was perhaps ten years older than the medium, probably closer to Charles's age than to his own. She wore her hair long in a mass of different lengths down her back. He supposed that she wore the style of a young girl because she considered herself to be one. She was wild and reckless, still looking for surprises, still eager to be shocked.

"Will she submit to a search of her clothing?" Charles asked, his eyes briefly straying to Alais. The medium remained behind her companion, content to let Juliette proceed on her behalf.

"Of course," Juliette replied, without hesitation.

"And her body."

"A thorough search, you mean."

Charles nodded. He was careful. The controls he used in his experiments were as rigid as any he used in his laboratory. He always made sure the medium was thoroughly searched before, during, and even after the séance, so there would be no question as to whether she smuggled in any tricks: thread, hooks, bits of netting, masks, or devices of any kind that could aid in creating illusions. Of course, there were always questions, especially in the press. There had even been a few cartoons in *Punch* that a colleague had sent to Gabriel from across the channel, and one or two in his own paper that he had no power to stop. They were a satirical look at séances in general and Charles in particular. One showed a caricature of Charles holding a butterfly net chasing a figure wearing a bedsheet. No one in the family made mention of it.

Gabriel glanced at Alais Bonnet, whose features had stiffened at the suggestion that her body be searched. He could not tell if she was blushing or not. She was dark, an exotic-looking woman, not attractive like Juliette, but boxy and ungraceful with muddy brown eyes and a layer of down on her upper lip. She wasn't young, perhaps thirty or so, and did not carry herself well. She stood with her head slightly forward on her neck, shoulders rounded, her body heavy, unyielding, and defenseless. Her whole attitude telegraphed a life full of small disappointments.

Juliette whispered into Alais's ear and took her arm. Alais shrank into herself and shook her head. She was shy if fierce in her objection. A hurried exchange passed between them. After that the medium seem to relax a little, to give in, however reluctantly.

Juliette looked over at them. "Yes, it will be all right," she said, still holding the medium's arm. "She asks only that I am allowed to be with her."

There had been talk about these two women. Alais had moved in with Juliette a few months after her husband died. No one was quite sure what to make of their relationship, except that Alais was devoted to Juliette and content to follow her everywhere. She even drove with her in her phaeton, and no one ever did that. Juliette was a crazy driver, who often gave her horse its head. Once she nearly got them killed when the carriage careened around a corner and collided with a steamroller. A picture of it had run in Gabriel's paper.

Gabriel took great care with the cameras, setting them up properly, each with their own tray of magnesium. He positioned them in the adjoining room, keeping the door open. He made sure they were focused on various points around the room to satisfy his brother's obsession with recording every detail. He pointed one at the sitter's table, another at the medium's cabinet, and still another at a little table that held a bugle, a guitar, and a small bell, essential accoutrements to any materializing séance.

The medium's cabinet was nothing more than a corner of the room draped off by black curtains. A chair had been placed inside the space for the medium's comfort and to give her the privacy she needed to gather her psychic powers. There, she would sit with the curtains closed, sometimes for an hour or two, until the manifestations began to appear. At that point the curtains could be opened or remain closed depending on the wishes of the medium.

Gabriel didn't think much of the idea of a space where the medium could remain hidden from view while she conjured up her spooks. He thought that tricks of all kinds could be performed behind those curtains, and the sitters would never know it. He brought up his objections to his brother once a few summers back, while they were staying at Charles's house on Île Roubaud, a tiny island he owned off the coast of Hyères in the Mediterranean. The pink stucco house with its red tile roof and blue shutters sat wedged in a niche halfway up a craggy hillside dotted with pines, oaks, and scrub. They sat under the grape arbor next to the house looking out at the fishing boats anchored in the bay. The water was a patchwork of turquoise and azure, so clear that the shadows of the boats could be seen all the way to the bottom.

Gabriel hadn't planned on voicing his objections. He was sensitive to his brother's opinion of the press, and since Gabriel had just been hired on at the paper, he supposed he could be considered one of *them*. Charles was the one who brought up the recent experiments at his house. Gabriel only wondered out loud if the cabinet might not nullify the controls by keeping the medium hidden from view.

Charles let his eyes drift out over the water as he listened to his brother's objections. "Yes, I suppose ordinarily that would be a problem," Charles said, making an effort to sound unruffled and reasonable. "But you've seen my records. Maybe there is something I'm missing, but I've always thought my controls were rather complete."

Gabriel smiled uncomfortably and shifted in his chair, causing the brown wicker to creak under his weight. He wasn't used to questioning his brother's methods. Charles was so much older, more like a father than a brother. Their own father was a surgeon at Hôpital Pitié-Salpêtrière; he had already spent whatever paternal energy he had on his two older sons. So it was Charles who helped Gabriel with his studies, took him boating, and shared his interests in poetry, novels, and gyroplanes.

"Keep in mind that I examine their bodies, every inch of them inside and out. Even the women. I don't see how they could manage to smuggle in tricks without my knowledge, even from behind a curtain."

"Yes, of course," Gabriel said, wishing that he hadn't brought it up.

Charles wasn't listening, however. He had slipped away into his thoughts, his gaze still on the boats in the bay. "Still, I suppose it is possible." He turned to his brother. "Have you heard of a way? Do you have something in mind?" Charles knew the kind of places his brother frequented.

Gabriel shook his head, wishing he had something to offer. A warm tide of blood rushed to his scalp as he took another sip from his glass. He felt foolish bringing up his reservations without anything to back them up.

"There is nothing wrong with questioning my methods, Gabriel," his brother said. "I don't mean to imply that. I question them all the time and so do my colleagues. We take great care with the controls. Otherwise our experiments wouldn't be of much use."

A little later their brother Etienne arrived and the conversation was forgotten. A chair was brought out to the arbor and a new bottle was opened. The talk soon turned to flying machines and the family of anti-Dreyfusards, who had just bought the hotel on the neighboring island where Gabriel and his brothers liked to go for oysters. Of course, no one mentioned their younger brother, Victor, who always came to mind at the mention of oysters. Victor, who at twelve bragged that he could eat three dozen and at fourteen had died in agony when typhus desiccated his body. Now, it was just the three of them. Etienne was a bacteriologist working at the Pasteur Institute. He was only a few years older than Gabriel and already he was the leader of a team working on antitoxins for snakebites. Gabriel was the only member of the family who was not a surgeon or a researcher—a fact his father never failed to bring up at family gatherings.

•    •    •

Gabriel watched Juliette Denis lead Alais back into the room and help her into the chair that stood in front of the cabinet. Alais had shed her clothes and was now wearing a leotard that hugged her body, concealing nothing. Over the leotard she wore a pair of overalls like those worn by schoolboys in the countryside. The sitters took their places at the table. They were scientists from different disciplines: a mathematician, a chemist, two psychologists, and a physicist; most were well known in their fields and even somewhat known by the general public, especially in Paris. The gas was turned down and two candles were lit, one for the table and one for the volunteer stenographer: a physicist, a gangly fellow with closely cropped hair whose long, tender fingers kept combing the thick beard on his chin. The only other light came from a high window that captured the flickering gaslight from the street below.

Juliette Denis took up the candle on the table and held it up for Alais to see, instructing her to concentrate on it, to let her mind go quiet, to watch the glimmering light, now the only bright spot in the room. Juliette's voice soon matched the rhythm of Alais's breathing, urging the medium to give in to the heaviness, to let her eyelids close, to relax her body: her feet first, then her legs, pelvis, stomach, chest, and finally her head. Alais's eyelids flickered and closed. Her breathing became regular. Juliette urged her to go deeper still, to let herself drift down into the well. She described the well as a warm, safe place overgrown with vines and brightly colored tropical flowers. She urged Alais to go deeper yet, past the water, past the vegetation to its velvety inner core, which she described as a fur-lined bed.

Finally when Juliette was satisfied that Alais was in a deep trance, she asked Gabriel to help her settle the medium in the chair behind the curtains. He took one arm and Juliette took the other, and together they lifted her up and walked her over to the cabinet. As soon as she was settled, her head slumped forward on her chest and a thin line of drool ran down her chin. Juliette wiped it off with her handkerchief. She did it in such a perfunctory way that Gabriel got the impression it was a common occurrence during their séances.

Charles tied the medium to the chair with a new rope, making sure it was taut and secured with heavy knots. When he was done, he called up the sitters to test the bonds. They tugged on the ropes, examined the chair, and once they were satisfied, returned to their seats where they took up hands. Juliette closed the curtains around Alais and joined the others at the table. Gabriel stood in the doorway by the cameras, fingering the ignition button on the flash lamp, peering into the gloom with equal parts of hope and dread.

For an hour nothing happened.

Gabriel grew tired of holding the flash lamp and put it down. He brought over a chair and sat down, wondering how long until

Charles gave up and sent them all home. Several times over the course of the hour, Juliette Denis led the sitters in "Chez Nous, Soyez Reine," and "J'irai la Voir un Jour!" She said these hymns were a particular favorite of the spirits and singing them would help them come through.

Gabriel remembered these hymns from his childhood but didn't join in. He was bored and tired and just wanted it to be over. His mind kept wandering to a girl he had met at a party the other night. She fancied herself an anarchist and a painter, although his friends said she had money and belonged to an old family from the *faubourg*. He was thinking about running into her again and wondering how he could accomplish this when his brother suddenly shouted, "Camera!"

Gabriel jumped to his feet and grabbed the flash lamp. He swung the Facile around searching in the dark for his subject, until he found it—the guitar floating about twelve inches above the table. He didn't even have time to react. The hairs on his arms were standing straight up as he held the flash lamp and pushed the ignition button. Instantly the room exploded into a bright white light and the air filled with fumes from the burning magnesium. As the light began to fade Gabriel realized that he had forgotten to press the shutter button. By the time he remembered the light had faded considerably. In a panic he pushed the ignition button again and the flash exploded, only this time the guitar was gone. In the time it took him to realize he had forgotten to take the picture, the guitar had floated back down to the little table and now lay inert next to the bugle.

"Did you get it?" Charles asked anxiously.

"Yes."

"You're sure?"

"Yes, yes, I got it." Gabriel sounded impatient. Actually, he was suffocating under the certain knowledge that he had failed.

Another hymn, "Reine de France," and this time Gabriel joined in, not quite believing that it would usher in the spirits, but singing out all the same.

A groan drifted out from the cabinet, soft at first, then punctuated by weighty sighs. More groans. They sounded erotic to him and eerie, as if they were very close and yet far away—an icy whisper in his ear. The others shifted uncomfortably in their seats and avoided each other's eyes. Only Madame Denis seemed unaffected. At first Gabriel thought the noises heralded a new manifestation, but when they grew louder he recognized them as decidedly human. Finally he assigned them properly to Alais Bonnet.

Over time, Mademoiselle Bonnet's breathing became more pronounced and her groans began to grow in intensity. Sometimes she would cry out as if caught in the throes of a voluptuous fever, panting like an animal in heat and moaning with pleasure. It lent the séance a voyeuristic quality, launching it from the realm of scientific inquiry into something more elastic.

"It won't be long now," Juliette said, still unfazed by the display.

Alais Bonnet called out to her friend from behind the curtain. She urged Juliette to examine her.

"Shall I go in?" Juliette asked.

"Yes, go to her," Charles replied urgently.

Juliette got up and parted the curtain. "I'm here, my darling girl."

"Show them," panted Alais.

Juliette parted the curtain to show the sitters that Alais was still bound up with the ropes. She was writhing in the chair now, thrusting her breasts out and then her pelvis, moving to the limits of her constraints. "Examine me," she gasped, pushing her pelvis against the ropes. "Show them there are no tricks. Hurry, my love, before it is too late."

Juliette stepped into the medium's cabinet and closed the curtains—a shuffling of garments, whispered assurances, and the moaning began again. This time the pitch gradually climbed higher and higher while the volume intensified. The men kept their eyes averted. Perhaps if Alais Bonnet had been an attractive woman like Juliette Denis, their reaction might have been different. As it was, there was probably more than one who thought of escape that night, although no one made a move to leave. Finally Alais reached a kind of crisis, crying out as if startled by the intensity of her passion.

Then nothing.

In the ensuing silence an expectation seemed to take hold in the room. The men hardly moved in their seats. Outside they could hear a distant clatter of hooves retreating down the street. Juliette returned to the table, but not before closing the curtains behind her. After a moment something moved above the cabinet. Something was floating there, giving off a faint luminescence like a distant lamp. This time Gabriel was ready. He grabbed the Facile and the flash lamp and began to take pictures. By the light of the flash he was able to tell that it was the face of a woman wearing a hat, though her features were difficult to discern. The face shimmered like heat off pavement. The mouth opened slightly, showing sharp white teeth neatly spaced. Someone or something was singing an eerie melody in a child's voice. The words made him shudder. It was a lullaby for a dead child, a call to return from the grave. A light wind blew through him and chilled him from the inside.

When the singing stopped, the face began to fade.

During the subsequent calm Gabriel was able to check the focus of the camera. Despite his trembling fingers he made sure that the Facile had been trained on the right spot. Everything seemed in order and he began to relax, to reflect on the wonder of it all. It all seemed so unbelievable. Yet, he had seen it, photographed it. He was not a religious man, nor was anyone in his family, but the idea that spirits existed in this world, in the world of the concrete, of boulevards and crowds, motorcars and electricity, fascinated and frightened him. He didn't think much about death. Of course he knew that he was going to die, his brothers were going to die, and his parents and everyone he ever loved would die someday, just as Victor had. But maybe death wasn't so final, only a transformation they had yet to understand and document.

Gabriel remained alert to every sound: a rustling in the corner, a cool breeze on his cheek—something was waiting just out of sight. An orb began to materialize over the cabinet. It hung there, glowing like the moon behind the clouds. While the physicist wrote down every detail in his gray laboratory notebook, Gabriel took pictures from several angles. He was not so blinded by the flash that he couldn't make out the spirit's features: his well-tended beard, crooked nose, and shroud. His eyes were white without pupils and so brilliant they seemed to glow in the dark. They caught and held Gabriel, fearsome and penetrating. The spirit looked worried, as if he were about to voice some concern, but before he could say a word he disappeared.

The room fell silent after that except for the hiss of the radiator. When the candles began to gutter again, Gabriel grew tense, his hand ready on the flash. Gradually, he became aware of muttering in the room. It was a male voice, deep and strangely matter-of-fact, like a member of an audience making an aside to his companion during a play. Gabriel knew it wasn't one of the sitters. He could see them clearly and they were listening too. Charles silently signaled to the physicist and Gabriel could see him checking his pocket watch and marking down the time next to the entry. The muttering seemed to move around the room, the voice rising and falling, sounding ordinary and chilling. Then it began to grow louder; it sounded harsh, the words hard to make out. They seemed to come from another language, not Indo-European, perhaps Arabic. The sitters twisted in their seats, trying to locate the voice.

From behind the curtain Alais began to whimper. "Turn up the lamps," she cried. She screamed and everyone jumped.

Juliette sprang to her feet. "Turn them up! Quick!" She took two long strides and whipped back the curtain. Charles rushed to the lamps and turned up the gas.

"It's him. He's back." Alais sobbed, struggling to get free.

"Get her out of this," Juliette said, fighting with the rope.

Charles and another sitter worked as quickly as they could. Juliette talked to her in a soothing voice, stroking her head and eventually calming her down. When Alais was free Juliette held her while she explained to the sitters that a specter had been following them around, harassing Alais and disrupting the sittings.

"He is such a nasty fellow. Died on the river. For some reason he has a grudge against her. He says he's a relative, but she doesn't believe him."

"He is horrible," Alais said, her eyes filling with tears.

"Don't upset yourself, mouse," Juliette murmured. She offered a hand to her companion. "Come along. It's late. We have to get you home."

By the time the séance broke up, the trams had stopped running and the only way home was to walk or take a taxi. Since it was a cold September night, Charles offered to give Gabriel a room. Gabriel declined, saying he wanted to go home and develop the plates. So instead, Charles offered to pay for the taxi.

Charles didn't seem to notice Gabriel's struggle as he shoved several coins into his brother's palm, thanking him for his help. Charles was obviously pleased with the sitting; he said he was too excited to sleep that night and would probably wait up for the prints. Gabriel left his brother at the door, promising he would return in the morning as soon as he finished.

There was the usual flurry when Gabriel got home that night and turned up the gas: Cockroaches scurried across the floor to the baseboards and disappeared into the walls. He was so used to them by now that he didn't even bother smashing the slower ones. Instead he stepped over to the sideboard where photographic trays and bottles of chemicals sat among a chaotic jumble of books, paper, lumps of chalk, rulers, and mat knives. He shoved them all aside and got to work.

While he measured out the chemicals for the developer and stop bath, he thought about what he had seen that night. It all seemed too histrionic to be real, and yet he couldn't imagine how it was done. The medium seemed honest enough. Her performance, if that's what it was called, seemed genuine. And he knew Juliette Denis. Yes, she was impulsive and frivolous, and might want to fool the scientists on a lark, but he doubted if she had the skill to put on a performance like that.

Moreover, he wanted to believe in what he had seen. He wanted it to be true for selfish reasons. It would make a sensational story, it might even make a book, and he knew for a fact that Charles was looking for credibility for his new science. An article in *Le Matin* would go a long way in accomplishing that.

Gabriel mixed the developer, measuring out the potassium bromide and the sodium hydroxide and then the acetic acid for the stop bath. After completing a series of test strips, he inserted a sheet of gaslight paper into the printing frame, laid the first plate on top emulsion side down, and turned up the gas to expose it for five seconds. After he developed the paper, stopped and fixed it, he held it with tongs and turned up the gas to get a good look. It was the face of a woman theatrically made up with a painted mouth and dark eyes outlined in heavy pencil. The features looked asymmetrical and flat, one eye was higher than the other and the mouth was unnaturally thin as if stretched too tight. Even in the photograph the skin looked incandescent. He was examining her hat, a cloche decorated with gold tassels, when he noticed two small letters just to the right of one of the tassels, *LM*.

•     •     •

Charles picked up the first photograph and examined it carefully. Here was the woman in her cloche hat; here were the letters. Gabriel stood at his elbow admiring the photographs. He had to admit the print was technically good, the image was sharp, and the contrast couldn't have been better considering the lack of available light.

They were in Charles's front parlor—an overstuffed affair with tasseled sofas, Japanese silk pillows, and a Chinese screen or two. Outside, the sun was high enough to make long shadows of the trees that lined the street; inside, the crisp morning light lit up the peacocks on the satin wallpaper.

Charles brought the print over to the French doors to get a better look. "Oh yes, this is fine," he said, holding it up. "This is good work." It was still early and the family wasn't yet awake. He looked tired and his clothes were rumpled for having slept in them. Gabriel felt the familiar tide of warmth that came with Charles's praise; it was a heady sense of well-being that lasted only a moment but would be remembered long afterward.

"What is this?" asked Charles, indicating the letters. "A watermark?"

"It stands for *Le Matin*."

"Your newspaper?"

Gabriel nodded. "It's the exact image from last Tuesday's paper. The morning edition. That is Edna Manning."

"The American actress?"

"Yes. She's here in Paris playing the Odéon. And she is very much alive. And here, look at this one." Gabriel handed Charles the print of the old gentleman. "This is George I, king of Greece. Here is the original. I borrowed it from the paper's archives on the way over."

Charles took the print and held it up to the other one.

Gabriel pointed to the newspaper print. "See? The same two letters."

"But this one is different," Charles said, referring to Gabriel's print.

"Yes, a shroud has been added, the features have been altered slightly. A kind of collage has been made of it and then another picture taken. Even with the changes you can see it's the same image. Look at the mouth and the beard. It's the same man."

Charles peered at the two prints, his eyes moving back and forth, his mind whirring. Then he stopped and lifted his head. "That explains it."

"Explains what?"

"The medium must have seen the photographs in the paper. They must have been in her mind during the experiment and then, somehow, she projected them into reality."

"Projected?"

"She is a sensitive, after all. She has a developed sixth sense. Most of them do. They have the ability to make a physical image out of a mental one. They are sensitive to the vibrations of reality, but they can also, in some cases, project these vibrations. Think of it like a telegraph. They are both receptors and transmitters."

Gabriel gazed at his brother with a mixture of confusion and disappointment.

"I know it sounds improbable," Charles said, patiently, "but it is far more likely than the spiritistic hypothesis of the dead coming back to haunt us."

"Charles, they altered the photographs. They altered them and presented them as spirits in an effort to fool you."

"That may well be. Still, one has to look beyond the obvious and take an imaginative leap now and then."

"Not if it takes you out of the realm of reality."

"What is so incredible about the sixth sense?" Charles asked. "The existence of ghosts is far more problematic, because it contradicts all that we know about physiology. On the other hand, the hypothesis of the sixth sense, another sense that gives the medium the ability to perceive previously undetected vibrations emanating from reality, contradicts nothing we know about physiology. It is simply another sense like that of touch, sight, or smell. Only this one gives the sensitive the ability to perceive an array of vibrations, previously unknown to us, but that come from the real world. These mediums think they are gaining their knowledge from spirit guides or from the dead, but in reality it's their ability to pick up on these vibrations, to read minds, if you will, to receive mental image pictures sent out by people halfway around the world, or to hear messages that may have been drifting in the ether for centuries that gives them their unique ability. These are not messages from the dead, but particle waves that are as real as the Hertzian waves that give us our telegrams. They are not the product of ghostly emanations, but mechanical in nature, and will someday be measured and catalogued like any other real-world phenomena."

Gabriel didn't know what to say. Across the way a girl was watering geraniums on a balcony. The water cascaded down through the grate, sending two maids with market baskets on their arms scurrying out into the street to avoid the deluge. He stood there not seeing any of it. He was thinking about the two women, Juliette and Alais Bonnet. He was thinking they were probably having a good laugh at his brother's expense and at the expense of his brother's colleagues, these men of science, who were so high-minded they couldn't see what was plainly in front of them.

"We all have our theories, Gabriel," his brother went on. "Crookes is a chemist, so he sees it as a question of a psychic force akin to the natural laws of conservation of energy and mass. Lombroso, a physician, sees the production of ectoplasm as a function of the psychic body attempting to manifest. William Crawford, an engineer, sees psychic phenomena in terms of psychical structures and talks about cantilevers and structural force."

Charles collapsed on the sofa and stretched out with a sigh. "All these theories have some validity, I suppose," he said, reaching for a pillow. He laid his head back and closed his eyes and then added dreamily: "Of course, none of them explain the phenomena as completely as the sixth sense. Wouldn't you agree?"

Up to now, Gabriel had always respected Charles. He knew him to be a man of solid convictions, especially about something that had taken up so much of his life for the past five years. Charles was not usually wrong about such matters. And yet, Gabriel knew the kind of people who came to his brother's séance room. Gabriel lived in their world and knew a thing or two about their tricks. They were cunning, often ruthless. His brother, even with his extensive knowledge of the body, was an innocent. The fact that he was eager to prove his theories and to justify all the years spent on this new "science" made him an easy mark.

So now it was Gabriel's turn to take care of his brother. He would protect him. He would bring him proof and make him see clearly that he had been duped. He would go to the brothels and the café-concerts in Pigalle and Montmartre, he would talk to his contacts, bribe the *grisettes*, investigate rumors, follow leads, in short, ply his craft as a journalist. In this way he would save his brother's reputation, his position in the scientific community, and finally do something right. In return his brother would be grateful and proud of him. He might even mention it to their father. In any case, it would restore Gabriel's confidence in his brother's judgment, a strength he had come to rely on all of his life.

# CHAPTER 3

# Paris, March 1902

Lucia learned early on that everyone in Monsieur Babineaux's house had their place. Monsieur Babineaux sat at the head of the table and went off to the law courts every morning. Madame Babineaux sat at the foot, gave orders to the cook, and was *at home* every Thursday. The nursemaid had her meals in the nursery with the children, the cook cooked, and the housemaid made up the rooms.

Lucia's place was on her knees washing the kitchen floor, cleaning the ovens, and scrubbing the front steps. She was the kitchen maid, responsible for all the tasks that required soap and soda, black lead and polish, emery powder for the knives, bootblack for the boots, and a strong back for the coal chute. The worst job was polishing the marble threshold at the top of the front steps because she had to stoop at a certain angle, which put her backside on display for any passing tradesman. For this reason she tried to get this chore done early, before they arrived, so she wouldn't have to endure their hoots and hollers.

Even so, she was lucky to have the situation. Babusia had said as much when she sent her to the agency in Senatorska Street. There she was told that Monsieur Babineaux was a famous lawyer and that Madame Babineaux a renowned beauty, and if Lucia worked hard and was a good girl, she would enjoy the respect that comes from working in such a household. Lucia felt honored to be working for such a venerated family.

Venerated.

It was a testimony of sorts to Lucia's faith in God that she abandoned her folding chair at the railway station on the morning she arrived in Paris. It was true that she was too exhausted and hungry to drag it through the city and this more than anything may have caused her to lean it up against a pillar and walk away. Still, she liked to think that God had a plan for her, that she was about to make something of herself.

A determined rain had been falling all that morning, flooding the street corners and causing at least one traffic accident. When the rain stopped, umbrellas were lowered and men in homburgs and ladies in large hats hurried past Lucia without a glance. She did not know where to look first: at the street full of people; at the passing carriages, belching automobiles, and clanging omnibuses; at the dairyman on the corner; or the dog barber with his tub and brushes. The city was a wave of sight and sound, a consuming presence, clamorous and frightening, a vibrant organism that was set to absorb her and transform her into what she did not know.

Babusia had told her to stop a policeman and ask for directions, warning her against asking strangers, who could be white slavers. Lucia had been on the lookout for one for the last quarter of an hour, but so far hadn't had any luck. She was just about to go back to the station to find help when she happened to spot an old man shambling up the street with her chair.

He didn't seem to be in much of a hurry. Sometimes he even stopped to scratch his crotch. Never mind that she had abandoned the chair; now that it was going away, she wanted it back. It didn't take her long to catch up with him. When she told him straight out that he was stealing her chair, he didn't seem to understand her at first, even though she was speaking perfectly good French. So she repeated herself and this time she tried to grab it away from him. He looked shocked and insulted; nevertheless, he held on to it. He was surprisingly strong.

Once he understood that the chair was hers he gave it up with an apology. She understood him even though he spoke rapidly. He assumed the chair had been abandoned. Many chairs had been abandoned at the station in this way and over the years he had claimed them for his collection. He apologized for causing her any inconvenience.

She said that it was an honest mistake. She understood that now and no harm was done. She apologized for shouting at him. He smiled at her, even though she could tell he didn't understand a word she was saying.

He appeared to be such a nice man that she thought she could ask him for directions. She showed him the address and he understood immediately what she wanted. He told her that it was a fancy address, that most anybody in the city would know how to get there. He took a pencil stub from his pocket and tore off a flyer from a lamppost. It was a notice about a carriage accident looking for a witness.

He drew a little map on the back of the flyer, all the while describing the journey she was about to take. She was to wait across the street where a small crowd had been gathering and take the B omnibus, the brown one. He told her about the transfer at Malesherbes and a walk by a lake in a park. Outside the park gate there would be another boulevard and finally she would find her street on the left or maybe it would be on the right. She was to look for it. It wouldn't be hard to find.

When he finished he handed over the map and she thanked him. Before he turned to go she handed him the chair. He lit up when he understood that it was to be his, then patted her elbow and wished her well.

In the three months that Lucia had been working in rue de Logelbach she had not once seen the inside of the house. She was allowed only in the basement kitchen, on the back stairs, and in the attic, but never where the family resided. Judging by the kitchen, the rest of the house must have been a marvel. A cold cupboard stood against one wall, valiantly keeping the butter and cream fresh. Against the opposite wall stood a gas stove, a stalwart monster of iron and chrome with four ovens, a griddle, and eight burners. Since the kitchen had only one window, a battalion of gaslight sconces ran all the way around the room and was kept burning day and night. The everyday dishes were kept in a cupboard that stretched from floor to ceiling. It was large enough to house the entire set of 126 pieces. Lucia knew the exact number because she had to wash every plate, bowl, cup, and saucer once a week whether they needed it or not.

It was the cook's habit to emerge from her bedroom every morning at six o'clock and inspect Lucia's work. Madame Clos was an attractive woman, a newcomer to middle age, whose features had been fresh and gauzy once but had since hardened like a butter cookie left in the oven a second too long. Lucia had just finished polishing the family's boots and was ironing the laces when the cook appeared. Without a word of greeting she went about her business, peering up the flue and examining the stove to make sure it had been blacked properly. She checked the floor, particularly in the corners, and opened the cupboards. Lucia knew that the cook was satisfied when, without a word, she went to put on her hat by the back door. She adjusted it in the little mirror that hung over the coatrack, took up her umbrella, and left. Lucia knew that silence was Madame Clos's highest compliment.

That afternoon Madame Clos called Lucia over to the chopping block where four dead hares lay with their eyes open and vacant. The animals had gray fur and black paws, and seemed to be from the same litter, although Lucia didn't like to think of such things.

Madame Clos picked up a cleaver from a line of knives laid out on the table. "It's not difficult if you know what you are doing. But it must be done with precision. These are special hares that deserve nothing less than our respect and our consideration."

Lucia had noticed over the months that Madame Clos had the disconcerting habit of referring to the animals they were about to cook as if they were still alive and could get their feelings hurt. In any case, these *were* special hares and Lucia understood their importance. The other day she had witnessed an altercation between Madame Clos and Moreau, the hare lady, that had been so alarming Lucia had even written home to Babusia about it. This was the same hare lady who had been supplying the house for nearly a decade. They were the finest hares in all of Paris. She raised them on the slopes of Montmartre and fed them carrot tops and potato peelings from the best restaurants. But that was not the issue, as Madame Clos made abundantly clear on that eventful day when tempers flared and words were exchanged over two francs. Moreau protested, saying that the bill was correct and that she had never cheated anybody in her whole life, especially not the kindhearted Madame Babineaux, who had the misfortune of having a rodent for a cook. Needless to say, the woman was immediately banned from the kitchen.

After that Madame Clos could have gotten her hares at the covered market in boulevard des Batignolles near Place Clichy. It was close and it would have been nearly as convenient as having them delivered. Instead, she insisted on going all the way to les Halles, which meant she had to take two omnibuses and do a great deal of walking. Because she refused to waste even a sou of Madame Babineaux's money, she always sat up on top in the imperial. That morning it had rained, so even though she came home with fine hares, she was soaked through and chilled to the bone. "If I catch a cold and die, you can tell Moreau she will burn in hell for it."

Madame Clos hacked the head off the first hare and hung the carcass on a meat hook over the sink. While she worked she explained to Lucia the importance of a clean cut, a sharp knife, and how much force to use. Even though Lucia's French had been passable from the start and getting better every day, Madame Clos spoke to her as if she didn't understand, raising her voice unnecessarily

and enunciating every word. She did this in protest to what she saw
as an affront to her authority. Madame Clos would never have hired
a foreigner and if she did, she would have paid her next to nothing, instead of the wage that Madame Babineaux insisted on. It was
shameful to waste money on foreigners. You hired them only for
cheap labor. In Madame Clos's mind, Lucia was taking advantage of
Madame Babineaux, probably laughing at her behind her back, and
deserved nothing less than to be sent packing.

"It's your accent," Iris said, as they were getting ready for bed
one night. Iris was the housemaid and knew practically everything
there was to know about living in Paris. They shared a room in the
attic up under the eaves.

"My accent?"

"You have a thick one, didn't you know?"

"You understand me."

"Most of the time. Sometimes I don't. Sometimes I haven't a
clue what you are saying."

"And for this I will see the door?"

"*Be shown* the door," she corrected. "See what I mean?"

They climbed into the bed they shared and pulled the quilt up to
their chins. It was late April and Paris was still cold and rainy. They
could hear the fat drops falling on the rooftops and on the chimney
pots outside their window, and the fancy carriages clopping down
the cobblestones on their way home from the boulevards.

"She won't let you go," Iris said, yawning. She was small like a
child, with dark frizzy hair that she wore in a bun under her cap.
She had a pixie's face that should have been pretty, except that her
ears stuck out like vestigial bat wings. "She always talks that way.
She's been threatening to send me packing for years and I'm not
even a foreigner."

Iris was a funny girl. Sometimes she would give Lucia valuable advice and treat her as a friend. She taught her how to secure
her cap so it wouldn't slide down and how to pin up her hair. She
took her around on the omnibuses and showed her the city on

their afternoons off. She warned her not to speak to the dairyman because he might try and put his hands on her, but to be nice to the iceman, as he was a relation of Madame Clos and might put in a good word. At other times she pulled rank. She was the housemaid, after all, and Lucia was only the kitchen maid, nothing more than a servant to the servants. That meant that Lucia was expected to fetch hot water for Iris's stand-up wash and was not allowed to use the armoire, making do with hooks on the wall.

Lucia wished she had a real friend, someone who didn't mind she was a foreigner, who understood her despite her accent. She felt it more acutely at night, lying under her mother's cross, listening to the creaks and groans of a sleeping house. She ached for Babusia and Tata, Bede and the baby. She missed Warsaw and the crowds that spoke Polish and everything that was familiar and safe. If she had a friend, she would tell her about walking to school with Ania and how she discussed books with Mademoiselle, and about all the unimportant, mundane ingredients of her life in Powiśle. Her months of loneliness and isolation had softened her memories of Dobra Street. She no longer thought of it as a life of deprivation and uncertainty, a future of unfulfilled potential, but simply as home.

Going to Mass for solace was out of the question, except on Thursdays when she had the afternoon off and could attend vespers. The rest of the week she would wait until Iris was asleep, until her breathing was quiet and regular, and then she would creep out of bed, kneel by the bedside, and pray to Mary the Holy Mother and to God Almighty Himself for comfort and relief. She always felt better for it, certain that her prayers were heard. Afterward, she would kiss her fingertips, touch her mother's cross, and climb back into bed, sometimes muttering a good-night to Babusia, who was so far away.

Madame Clos had just cut the tail off at the base of the hares and was working on the forefeet. When she removed them she cut the pelt around the hock joints and severed one of the legs. She sliced the pelt away from the inside of the thigh and ran a cut all the way to the base of the tail. She did the same on the other leg until the two cuts joined up. Then she gripped the skin and pulled the fur away from the flesh like she was peeling off a glove. When she was done she handed the carcass to Lucia to wash thoroughly and told her to finish the rest.

The hares were full of blood, so it took a long time for them to drain. The worst part was pulling off the pelts. They were much harder to remove than rabbit pelts and Lucia had to be careful and not tear them so Madame Clos could sell them to the rag and bone man along with the ashes and cooking fat. As cook, it was Madame Clos's right to earn a little pocket money on the side.

Later Madame Clos came to inspect Lucia's work. "You have done this before?" she asked, running her fingers through the soft fur.

"Not hares. Only rabbits."

The cook merely grunted in reply. She regarded the pelts for what seemed like a long time, aimlessly stroking the fur in one direction, then another. When she looked up she said: "Remove the sinew and the second skin and cut each hare into eight pieces." Then she turned back to her work without another word.

Madame Clos was a remarkable cook and for that she could be forgiven her sour manner. She was an artist in the kitchen, precise, but widely inventive, and so had earned Lucia's respect. She was rude, but rude to everyone, to the knife grinder on the boulevard, to vendors in the markets, even to her betters, even to Monsieur Babineaux. Lucia thought it showed integrity and admired her for that too. In the following weeks Lucia saw subtle but important changes in the kitchen. Now she was invited to sit down with Madame Clos for a cup of tea, sometimes with a plate of stale ladyfingers or a dry piece of cake. The cook was never one to waste Madame Babineaux's food. Most of what the servants ate was left over from the meals abovestairs.

Once, while scraping the crumbs on her plate into a neat line, Madame Clos talked about her father, who worked in a bakery and was a Communard. He had been a Socialist in the revolution and had fought to defend the last barricade in the rue Ramponeau in Belleville. When the barricade was overrun he was dragged to a wall and shot. Madame Clos was fourteen at the time and sent to work in a wealthy household where she was a kitchen maid for a family who had fought against the revolutionaries and against her father. She relayed all this in a flat tone that made it sound as if the events had happened to someone else, someone who lived a long time ago in another country.

•   •   •

In the late spring after the trees had leafed out in the Parc Monceau, when the ladies were once again wearing muslin and the lawn chairs appeared in the park, Madame Clos made a startling announcement. She gave Lucia permission to make the sauce Nantua. It didn't sound like much, considering Lucia had been making sauces on Dobra Street since she was ten years old. For this reason she had to explain to Babusia, the next time she wrote home, that kitchen maids never made sauces. They might make an omelet or throw together a green salad. They cut up vegetables, sorted legumes, grated ginger, and chopped garlic, but they never made anything as delicate as a sauce. It was a great honor and one that Lucia did not take lightly.

She was never taught how to make the sauce. Nevertheless, she paid close attention whenever Madame Clos made it, even making notes, recording ingredients and measurements and cooking time, getting it all down, step by step, until she had a recipe of her own making.

She went to work shelling the shrimp and cleaning the fish heads. When the water began to boil she dumped them in along with onions and their skins, parsley, carrots and carrot tops, bay leaves, and any other aromatic vegetable she happened to find in the pantry. Later, in a smaller saucepan, she melted the butter and added a tablespoon of flour, stirring it with a whisk and watching it carefully so it would not burn. When it was time she added the clear stock. In a bowl she blended an egg yolk and cream and added it to the sauce, a little at a time, stirring it slowly, her gaze never wavering, her stomach fluttering, because she was nearly finished.

When the time came to serve, Madame Clos took a taste with the silver tablespoon reserved for just this purpose. She swallowed the spoonful slowly and closed her eyes. She didn't say anything of course, but a soft grunt of satisfaction escaped her lips before she could catch it. She dipped another spoon into the sauce and handed it to Lucia. Lucia blew on it and tipped it into her mouth, swirling it over her tongue.

Madame Clos watched her closely, waiting for a response.

Lucia nodded. "It is good, yes?"

"Good? Is that all you can say?"

Lucia blinked.

The cook gave her a heavy look and took the spoon back. "I want you to feel it. You are the cook, n'est-ce pas? You want to be a good cook? Then you must feel it."

"Feel what?"

The cook looked to the heavens. Then she dipped the spoon into the sauce again and handed it back to her. "This time I want you to feel it inside."

"Inside my mouth?"

"Inside of you. The places you cannot see. Inside your head and heart. I want you to let it wash over you," Madame Clos whispered. "Let it flow to every part of you."

Lucia sipped the sauce slowly this time.

"There, can you feel it now?" the cook asked, keeping a steady eye on her. "The salty wind. The sea. It's like swimming at the shore."

Lucia had never been to the shore and didn't know what it felt like to swim there, but she had been to les Halles, to the great market, to the fish hall that sat under the soaring dome of iron lacework and glass. All around the great expanse were stalls displaying artful tiers of lobsters and crabs, mounds of mussels and oysters, snapper and halibut, and giant groupers laid out side by side still glistening with saltwater and ice.

She took another taste and this time she could smell the brackish air of the hall and the crates full of live prawns and shrimp, their antennae twitching, tails arching in their frantic attempt to get back to the sea. Another taste, and it was all around her, the hectic activity of the market, the bustle of the shoppers, the excitement; the heady surge that always came whenever she was sent to buy fish.

"Yes," she breathed. "It's all there."

Madame Clos gave her a rare smile and handed her the ladle.

•   •   •

In July the family went off to their estate in the Loire Valley, leaving Paris to the factory workers and servants. Without the family around, Lucia, Iris, and Madame Clos settled into a routine of ease. Instead of rising at five they slept until seven. Lunch was early, dinner at six, and everything was put away by eight o'clock. Naturally, the chores still had to be done, but not with the usual zeal. The beds were changed every two weeks, the copper pots and pans polished every ten days, and the meals were simple.

One hot morning, as they were finishing their buns and coffee, Madame Clos announced that there would be no lunch or supper that day. She had been acting strange all morning—not exactly cheerful, but brighter somehow, and once Lucia thought she heard Madame Clos hum a tune, although she may have been just muttering to herself. She put down her cup, dabbed at the foamy milk on her upper lip, and with an uncommon smile gave them the day off.

Iris reached for another bun and, while spooning on a generous helping of jam, announced that she would go see her cousin, the one who worked for the Jews. Lucia didn't know what she would do. She could do anything that didn't cost too much money. She could go anywhere in the city. She knew the omnibuses. Iris had given her a map of the lines and taught her how to use it. The city was still frightening, but also exhilarating with its shops and parks, cafés and electric lights. She had been subsumed by it, but it wasn't alarming or malefic, as she had feared, but intoxicating. The freedom was dizzying.

Subsumed.

After the breakfast dishes were put away Lucia went upstairs to change and came down wearing the only other dress she owned. She met Madame Clos at the door and they both seemed surprised by how well the other was turned out. Madame Clos was wearing a frothy skirt and a shirtwaist for summer. Her hair was piled up under a hat decorated with silk violets and a wide satin band. She looked happy, her eyes glittering, her cheeks ruddy from rouge and anticipation.

"Where are you going, *ma fille*?" the cook asked, putting on her gloves.

"I thought I might visit the shops and then go to vespers." Lucia had been thinking of going to the Polish shops in la Villette, not to buy—she didn't have any money—but to be among her countrymen, to hear Polish and be reminded of home.

"Vespers? On your day off? Surely, God wouldn't mind if you had a bit of fun."

Lucia dropped her gaze. "I like going to Mass," she said uncomfortably. She had never crossed Madame Clos before, at least not to her face, and that, and the cook's changed appearance and her heresy, were making Lucia nervous. She vowed to include the woman in her prayers that night. She had grown fond of the cook over the past few months and didn't want to see her burn in hell for all eternity.

"Listen, you come out with me, my girl. I'll show you a proper Saturday. You like to dance? Ever been to a *guingette*?"

Lucia let her eyes wander out through the open door to freedom. "I don't know," she said quietly. She didn't especially want to *come out* with Madame Clos. It seemed somewhat terrifying, as if they were friends as Lucia and Ania were once friends. She admired the woman, admired her talent and her starchy capability, but they were not friends. Even so, Lucia didn't see how she could refuse.

The *guingette* happened to be on a dance hall boat moored near a bridge on the Marne River not too far from Nogent-Sur-Marne. The deck of the boat was protected from the sun by a blue-and-white-striped canopy decorated with flags and streamers. A boisterous crowd sat at round tables covered with white tablecloths and ate fried fish. Fishermen stood on the bank nearby catching more to keep up with the orders. Men in baggy trousers and straw boaters and women in sudsy lingerie dresses reeled around the floor to dance tunes played on an accordion and a guitar.

Madame Clos led the way up the gangplank and eagerly stepped aboard, where she was greeted by one couple after another. She seemed alive, humming with excitement, kissing cheeks, hugging, calling out and waving to friends across the room. One large man in a sleeveless undershirt clapped his arms around her back and nearly lifted her off the ground. A family across the deck hailed her over.

It wasn't long before the cook was on the floor dancing with a man with a nose like a spatula, a careful dresser in a dark blazer with a stiff collar and tie. Someone had given her several strings of cheap beads and they bounced about her neck as she whirled around the room. With her cheeks flushed, her gaudy beads flying, her skirts lifting halfway up her calves, she looked like a different Madame Clos. This one held little resemblance to the vinegary woman Lucia had been working under all these months. This Madame Clos threw her head back and laughed out loud. She had friends. She had a first name.

"*Isabelle!*"

Lucia stood at the railing and waited for Madame Clos to return. She wished she had gone to the Polish shops in la Villette. She caught the eye of two men sitting at a nearby table. They sat at one end, their wives and children at the other. The little girls were playing with the streamers, draping them in their hair, while their mothers regarded her with suspicion. She was a stranger. She was not wanted there. She did not belong.

Later, Lucia and Madame Clos got a table and were joined by Madame Clos's cousin, who brought a chair over and sat down next to Lucia. His name was Arnaud, and he delivered ice to the cold cupboard on Tuesdays and Fridays. Usually he wore a work shirt and a leather apron, but today he was dressed in an undershirt and baggy trousers and wore a straw boater over his thinning hair. While the sun slipped behind the plane trees and the swallows swept over the glassy surface of the river, they ate a stew of eel and river fish and drank two more bottles of muscadet. Arnaud accused Madame Clos of being a flirt in her day, of breaking hearts and dancing with all the boys. Names were brought up, one in particular.

"You chased him away, remember?" Madame Clos said to her cousin. "You scared him half to death. He told me you threatened to kill him if he came around again. How was I supposed to have a romance with a *moule* like you chasing all the boys away?"

"Not all the boys, Izzy. Just him. He was no good for you, remember? He would've broken your heart. Where would you be now if I hadn't chased him away?"

The cook fingered her glass and let her eyes wander out over the river. Her gaze followed a small boat chugging upstream, trailing a smudge of blue smoke. A muffling fog seemed to descend on her spirits and for a moment Lucia recognized the cook she knew. "Sometimes I ask myself that very question," she said. Then she shrugged, grabbed a waiter by his coattails, and ordered another bottle.

While the waiters lit the paper lanterns and the bats took to the sky, a woman from the audience stepped up to the platform and sang a song about a dead girl. Lucia listened to the song and leaned back in her chair, watching the reflection of the lanterns on the river shimmer and dance, breaking up whenever a fish surfaced to feed. It was late and the families with children left hours ago; now only slow dances were being played.

Madame Clos leaned across the table, dragging her sleeve through a puddle of wine, and took Lucia's arm. Her voice cracked with emotion as she tried to hold back tears. "When I look at you

I see little bits of myself. Little tiny bits. Like when you make a mayonnaise or *vol-au-vents*. You are going to be a wonderful cook someday," she said, her voice fervent and damp. "They will come from all over just to eat your brioche."

Lucia sat there for a moment, watching the cook dab her eyes with a corner of the tablecloth. She wanted to believe her, but she knew the woman was drunk and drunks often said things without thinking. The cook held on to Lucia's arm, her eyes brimming with tears: "You are so young, *ma fille*. You do not know anything. When it is your turn and you are a cook in a grand house with all the responsibilities, just remember you are not part of the family. They will tell you otherwise. Maybe they will even believe it themselves. But you are only a servant and in the end you will mean nothing more to them than the brioche you bake." Her eyes began to droop. She struggled to keep them open for a few moments longer, but soon gave up. Once they closed for good, she dropped her chin until her cheek came to rest on Arnaud's shoulder. When she started to slip off the chair he slid his arm around her back and kept her from falling.

•    •    •

In the fall Madame Babineaux decided to give a dinner party. It wasn't an important event, not in the usual sense. The guests were not clients of Monsieur Babineaux, nor were they influential or powerful in the government. The evening was important to Madame because the guests were her friends from school. It was something of a reunion—a time to show off her family and her home and everything she had achieved since graduating from Lycée Julie-Victoire Daubié. For this reason everything had to be perfect, the house, the food, and the service. The menu was carefully arranged, five footmen were hired for the night, and the house was filled with flowers. For once, the husbands of her schoolmates, successful lawyers, doctors, and men of business, were entirely superfluous.

The timing of the event was troublesome, however, because Lucia had been seeing signs lately: a window that cracked for no reason, a picture frame with a piece of broken glass, a crow on a chimney pot—all these pointed to a dark outcome. Something she did not like to think about. She kept the signs to herself, until that morning when she cracked open an egg and found blood in the yolk. That was a warning, darkly prophetic, and she could not ignore it. She quickly crossed herself and muttered a hasty prayer to Saint Lucyna.

When Lucia told Madame Clos about it, the cook said, "Well, that can't be good. What does it mean?"

"An ending."

"What kind of ending?"

"Not a good one."

When the time came for lunch Madame Clos insisted that they have the lobster bisque left over from the night before. It had been on the hot stove all morning and Lucia wasn't sure it was still safe to eat. Madame Clos insisted that there was nothing wrong with it and to prove it she sat down and ate two hearty bowls, proclaiming it to be "delicious" and "greatly improved" for its time on the heat.

Madame Clos had a strong constitution, so it took her nearly an hour before her stomach began to pitch and roll. She reached for a mixing bowl just in time. Fortunately, it was a large mixing bowl, big enough to accommodate even her second helping of bisque.

Lucia, who had not touched the soup, followed her into her room with a bucket and a wet towel. She helped the cook unbutton her collar and loosen her stays. Madame Clos's face was the color of baking soda and glistened with sweat as she hung her head over the bucket and waited for the next onslaught. "It's up to you, *ma fille*. You have to carry on without me." She said this with some difficulty, like a general breathing his last on the battlefield.

A prick of fear and Lucia could feel herself going as white as Madame Clos. "There is no one else we can send for?" She struggled for breath in a rising tide of dread. "What about Madame Fournier? She is just down the street."

Madame Clos leaned over the bucket and retched again. The smell was rank and biting but with a hint of the sea. "No," she said, catching her breath. "No one comes into my kitchen."

"But how will I manage? I cannot do it alone."

"Iris and the charwoman."

"What do they know?"

"Teach them." She retched again.

Lucia tried talking sense to her. She reminded her of all that still had to be done, how precise the preparations had to be, and how difficult they were even for a seasoned cook.

Madame Clos collapsed back onto the pillow and waved Lucia off, saying that she was wasting time.

When Lucia told Iris what had happened, the parlor maid laughed and said the old cow got exactly what she deserved. When Lucia asked for her help, she declined, saying she had enough on her plate. "And besides I do not take orders from the *bonne de cuisine*." She helped herself to a boiled egg and began to peel it with a complacent dedication.

"I would never presume to give you orders," Lucia said evenly. "I will be very nice to you and request most respectfully."

"Besides I don't know anything about cooking."

"The dishes are simple. And you are so bright and accomplished. You will be able to do them easily. And they will keep you in the kitchen."

"Why would I want to be in the kitchen?"

"You have not heard? The footmen are coming."

Iris lifted her head. "From the Hôtel du Rhin?"

•  •  •

All afternoon the three of them labored over the meal while Madame Clos slept in her bedroom. The charwoman, Almandine, was given simple tasks like chipping ice or scrubbing mussels, anything that didn't require skill or concentration. The girl was from the countryside, newly arrived from Brittany. She was a tall, big-busted girl with a wide, honest face, who tried to appear small by slouching. She spoke with the singsong accent of a Breton farmer with its rolling r's and wet vowels. She often pretended to understand her tasks, rushing through her work so she could ask for more, thinking that was the best way to gain favor. As a result her work was reliably sloppy and, more often than not, had to be done over again.

Iris, on the other hand, was careful in her work and treated every potato, carrot, and leek as if it were a saint's relic. If time hadn't been so short, her precision would have been appreciated. As it was, the effort she lavished on the leeks, chopping them with a somber devotion, made Lucia's jaw ache.

At two o'clock Lucia completed the marinade for the brill, while Iris chopped the potatoes and onions for the *boeuf à la Bourguignon*. By three the brill was marinating and the sauces were finished. At four the *Bourguignon* was bubbling on the stove, while Almandine forced the soup vegetables through the food press. Iris cut out dozens of perfect puff pastry squares and stuffed them with pork forcemeat. By six o'clock, three dozen *petits pâtés garnis* were arranged on a baking sheet awaiting the oven. By six thirty the footmen arrived and everything fell apart.

They came in wearing starched white shirtfronts, pink bow ties, black cutaway coats, and gold-and-pink-striped waistcoats. They filled the kitchen with their easy jocularity and the smell of their pomaded hair. The room rang out with the thump of polished boots and three conversations going on at once: Joël, the maître d'hôtel was stealing tips again; football; and the dancer Adèle.

It was an invasion of sorts, an onslaught of masculinity penetrating the feminine realm of precise scales, flour sifters, and aspic molds. Iris, and to a lesser extent Almandine, met the invading army with a fidgety, pink-faced excitement. Chestnuts were left boiling on the stove. Sesame seeds lay abandoned in the mortar. Iris flitted about, serving them dinner, while Almandine hovered nearby looking eager and apologetic. Only Lucia remained at her station working pieces of lobster, mushrooms, and truffles onto the skewers.

At some point between the soup and the hors d'oeuvre, Madame Clos rose from her bed, shaky and pale, and like a censorious specter floated into the kitchen to have a look. Lucia watched her inspect the brill smothered in mussels and the kidneys trimmed and cleaned and waiting for cognac and then drift back to her room.

By the time Lucia slid the partridges into the oven she was pretty sure that everything would be all right. She closed the oven door, straightened, and looked around at the fresh chicory salads, plated and ready to serve, at the blini, the mussels, and all the rest, and took an easy breath for the first time since that morning. She stood back and marveled at all that she had accomplished. If she were perfectly honest, she would have to say that Madame Clos could not have done a better job.

· · ·

Madame Babineaux was an exceedingly generous person, especially when it came to showing gratitude. After the last guest had gone home, after Monsieur Babineaux had gone up to bed, while the footmen were still putting things right upstairs, she came down to thank Madame Clos, as she usually did after every dinner party. She was lavish in her praise that evening and, since she liked to talk, and did so at every opportunity, particularly to her own servants, who were always an appreciative audience, her speech went on for some time. She gushed over the *attereaux*, which she called cosmic and divinely inspired; the partridges were spirited; and the brill was nothing less than a revelation.

Lucia was filled with a swelling pride that she knew to be a sin. She wanted to run, leap in the air, and swoop down from the rooftops like an eagle soaring over the Carpathians, like the picture in her dictionary. Instead she stood there quietly, quelling any outward signs of the jubilation sparking through her body. She waited, wondering if Madame Clos would say anything. Would there be a suggestion, a hint that her *aide de cuisine* might have helped a little, might have even been valuable in some small way?

Madame Babineaux seemed to be running out of steam. In a moment or two she would be saying good night and then it would be too late. If Madame Clos were going to say something, it would have to be now—a word, a gesture, a small token of gratitude. Lucia would've been happy with almost anything. Instead the cook stood there with her eyes fixed on the food grinder, her face smooth and distant.

After Madame Babineaux went upstairs, Madame Clos gazed at Lucia for what seemed like a long time, her eyes steady and remote. Then she turned and went back to her room. That night Lucia went to bed still loving Madame Clos, but perhaps loving her a little less.

The next morning Lucia was already down in the kitchen when Iris came flying down the stairs waving an envelope like a flag. She was half dressed with her hair in a wild tangle around her sharp little face. Her shirtwaist was fastened one button off.

"It was on the floor by the door." Her round eyes were alight with keen amazement. The envelope had been opened. Lucia lifted her head and frowned at her. "I had to open it," she protested.

At first when Lucia separated the flap and found the money inside she thought it was some kind of gift. "I do not understand."

"It's three months' back wages. She's given you the sack!"

Lucia stared at the money as if she had never seen a French franc before. "I do not believe you. You are having fun with me." Iris tried to argue with her, but Lucia dismissed her with a wave and went back to blacking the stove. She worked all that morning, never stopping, not even when the egg man arrived and wanted to gossip, not even for the dairyman, who came with his butter and cream and told her, as he did every morning, that he loved her.

# CHAPTER 4

# September 1902

Lucia had nowhere to go in exile from rue de Logelbach, so she spent the first night in a hotel that she could ill afford. All night long she went over the events of the previous day: the bad soup, the frantic preparations, Madame Babineaux's appearance in the kitchen. She had done something terribly wrong. She had hurt Madame Clos in an unforgiveable way. She had sinned.

It finally came to her, in the frayed morning light, that all the signs were there. God had been trying to warn her and she had ignored him. She remembered standing in the kitchen that night, looking at all she had accomplished and thinking that she could be the cook there, that she was as good as Madame Clos. It was pride that brought her down, the exhilaration, the heady triumph of the moment, and knowing at the time that it was wrong, that it was a sin, and yet not asking for forgiveness. That's what did her in. Vanity.

She did not wait for the morning to begin. She packed up her things and went to look for a church. She didn't think it was an accident that she found one nearby, an enthusiastic testament to God Almighty, complete with Doric columns topped by angels and saints flanking a large blue clock. She bounded up the steps and crossed to the one door that was propped open. Lying before the threshold was a little coir doormat that was meant for a private home or a flat.

It seemed wholly inadequate to protect the floors of the massive cathedral and yet there it was. Lucia was diligent in her use of it. She wiped her feet again and again, until she was certain her shoes were clean. Then she walked into the vestibule where she dipped the forefingers of her right hand into the stoup and made the sign of the cross. Inside the nave she joined the line of old women, frail and wan sinners in their heavy winter coats, standing in line for confession. She tried to imagine their tender sins, closeted away in some perfumed corner of their conscience. She liked being among these women of unwavering faith, steeping in their resolution, in their implacable certainty, like a sponge cake soaking in rum. She did not mind waiting to receive absolution. Waiting would be part of her penitence, and she was grateful for it.

After confession she stayed for lauds. It was a beautiful service and she left feeling lighter, cleansed, and full of hope. She had planned to find a cheaper room for the night, but now all that seemed unnecessary. The day had turned into a crisp autumnal pageant complete with blazing leaves under a flawless sky. She felt flawless too, confident that God had a plan for her and would soon put things right.

She went to the Tuileries to look for signs. She always had better luck in nature, among God's best creations, and thought that if he had sent her a message, she would find it there. She wandered down the grand alley bordered by horse chestnuts, their leaves flaming and smelling of loamy soil. She could see the donkey rides up ahead next to the booth selling toys, and the girls in their starched caps carrying baskets of pastries and barley sugar in the shape of birds, bears, and soldiers. She had just decided to get a green sugar bear when a boy tumbled out of nowhere and landed on the path right in front of her. An instant later another boy somersaulted over the first and was quickly followed by a third and fourth, and then a whole troupe of little ones, girls and boys, tumbling, backflipping, and pinwheeling up and down the path. They were all dressed alike—in black-and-white-striped leotards and tights. Their faces were painted in black and white stripes and each wore a hat made of a bright red paper flower.

Three of the strongest suddenly stood up straight, feet firmly on the ground, palms up, while the smaller ones leaped onto their outstretched hands, feet gripping palms, backs arched, heads high, their arms waiting for the next layer.

A crowd had formed and the children and their *nounous* laughed and clapped at the antics of the acrobatic team. The next layer climbed the pyramid and took their place on top. When the pyramid was nearly complete a little girl bounced on a spring-board and landed on the shoulders of the highest acrobat, grinning broadly, her hands reaching out to the heavens above.

The crowd erupted into a clamorous show of appreciation. The performers held the pose, their muscles trembling from the effort, while they waited for the applause to die down. Then, layer by layer, the troupe jumped down and flipped and cartwheeled back into the greenery. The last to leave was the strongest of the bunch. He ripped off the paper flower from his head, bowed deeply, and handed it to Lucia. Then he retreated through a series of backflips and melted into the shrubbery, a sprite returning to an enchanted glade.

Lucia held up the flower and sucked in her breath. What stopped her was not the advertisement for the acrobatic team that would be performing at a local theater, but the flower itself. It was a corn poppy, the national flower of Poland. This must be the sign she had been looking for. She felt certain that it meant she was close to home. Not that she was going back to Poland necessarily, but that she was about to find her way. She was about to find a new home, a place of belonging in this very peculiar world.

The next morning Lucia stood in line, shivering with the other girls, while she waited for the doors to open at the employment agency. Ahead of her was a young woman who proved to be a talker. Marta Delaune spoke with the kind of authority that comes from knowing you are right most of the time. She had left her mistress without notice, a foolhardy thing to do, but brave and something to brag about.

"Remember that cold spell we had last winter?" she said to no one in particular, although everyone was listening. "Gave me curtains for blankets. Nothing but curtains to keep me warm. It's a wonder I didn't freeze to death. And you should have seen the portions. We were always hungry. Always going on about how poor she was and how she couldn't afford this and that. Wasn't too poor to hire a carriage, I can tell you that. Parading around like the queen of Arabia. I ask you, how can you be poor and live in the *faubourg*? The building had a lift!"

Everyone in line knew what Marta Delaune was going on about. They all knew about mistresses of this sort.

Most of the girls were drab, compliant, and hopeful. They stood shivering in their coats and dingy shirtwaists that had been washed too many times. Lucia imagined their thin underwear and patched stockings, their breakfast of tea and toast. They stood in the somber morning, under a cloud of defeat, pale faces beneath unfortunate hats, waiting for the fog to lift, for the door to open at Madame Gagnon's Agency for Household Help.

Marta was different, however. She was sturdy and bold, definite in her views, and curious. It was her curiosity that was unsettling to Lucia. She thought the girl was going to ask her how she came to be without a situation. Fortunately, Marta wanted to know only what kind of work Lucia was looking for.

"Kitchen maid," she replied, uncomfortably.

Sooner or later Marta was bound to ask about her last place and she would have to say that she was let go. Everyone would hear her of course and want to know why. She felt a prick of shame at the prospect of trying to explain it. The agency would want to know and so would prospective employers. Everyone would want to know how it was that she was let go without a character, even though she was a good worker, honest and capable.

The agency was considered one of the best in the city. Madame Gagnon charged a high fee because it was known that she listed only the best households and never sent her girls to the brothels, as some agencies did. That morning her assistant was late lifting the shade and opening the door. Marta and Lucia filed in with the others to get a good look at the boards. Since they were both looking for the same work they decided to strike out together, agreeing it would be nice to have company. Marta was unaccountably cheerful, especially for one without a position.

That day they went all over Paris, to the Plaine Monceau, to Faubourg Saint-Germain, to Faubourg Saint-Honoré, to a large flat in the rue de Lille, and even to a grand *hôtel particulier* near the Champs-Elysées. As they stood in line at the back door of a large flat off the rue de Médicis a few blocks from the Sorbonne, Lucia told her new friend about the Babineauxes, and about Madame Clos and how she was let go.

"She was jealous of you."

"Madame Clos? Of me?"

"You were too good. She didn't want you in her kitchen, stealing the credit and maybe her position."

Lucia shook her head. "Madame Clos is a brilliant cook and everyone knows it. Believe me, I am no worry to Madame Clos."

Lucia had to step aside when a young man came out of the kitchen door carrying a camera and a satchel full of photographic plates. She thought it odd because he didn't look like a tradesman. His coat was shabby to be sure; however, he had the air of an educated man. He grinned at her, a row of straight teeth peeking out from beneath a wheat-colored moustache. "Shortcut," he said by way of an explanation.

When Lucia's turn came to go into the kitchen, she found a large woman, fleshy with heavy, mannish features, seated at the table where the staff took their meals. A kitchen maid, wearing a shapeless dress and dirty apron, stood at the sink scrubbing potatoes. Lucia assumed that the new hire would be replacing this girl.

Lucia couldn't help but take a quick look around. The kitchen had the smell of a well-run establishment. The range was even more impressive than at the Babineauxes'. It would take her the better part of an hour just to black it and much longer to polish it. She didn't like to think about the chores that would soon be hers again—all the work that the charwoman had lifted from her shoulders—the sweeping, washing, scrubbing, and polishing.

The cook motioned Lucia to a chair. "And you are?" She regarded Lucia from over her specs. That's when Lucia noticed the cook's brooch pinned to her shirtwaist above her heart. "Beautiful, isn't it," the cook said, following Lucia's gaze. "They gave it to me last week. Twenty-five years of service."

"It's a bluebird."

"Supposed to bring you luck, but I don't put much stock in it." The cook admired it. "Very pretty though." Then she straightened. "So, tell me, mademoiselle, what can you do for me?"

"I make sauces," Lucia said without hesitation. "And soups and aspics. I bake cakes and tarts, breads and pies. I scrub and clean and polish. And I'm no trouble." It was the bluebird. It was giving her confidence.

"That's quite a lot." Lucia could tell the cook was impressed. Then the woman laughed. "Well, well, well," she said, cheerfully. "I believe God has just answered my prayers."

"Oh, yes, he has," Lucia blurted out. "And mine too." She almost asked the cook if she believed in signs but thought better of it.

"I need someone right away."

"I can start anytime."

The cook considered her thoughtfully. "Let me see your reference."

"I have a certificate of employment."

This gave the cook pause. "No character?" Her smile faded.

The kitchen maid, who had showed no interest in them up until now, turned to get a better look.

"Why don't you have a character?" the cook asked. "Didn't you give notice?"

"I did not have to give notice," Lucia said with some difficulty.

"She let you go."

"Yes, but I was a good worker."

"Did you steal?"

"I never stole anything in my life." Then she remembered the grosze from her father's tin and colored ferociously.

"Then why did she let you go?"

Lucia shifted in her chair and dropped her eyes. "Pride, I suppose," she said in a voice that was barely above a whisper.

"She let you go because of *pride*?"

Lucia nodded.

"Who is this cook?"

"Madame Clos."

The woman regarded her closely. "I know Madame Clos. She is somewhat prideful herself, wouldn't you agree? It doesn't seem that she would have anything against a little pride."

Lucia blinked, but said nothing.

The woman sighed heavily. "I am sorry, mademoiselle, I do not see how I can help you. You seem like a respectable girl, even if you are a foreigner, but how can I know that for sure without a character? I would be taking a chance if I hired you and I do not take chances here. Not in my kitchen. Not with Dr. Richet and his family."

Out on the street Marta stopped and gave her a look of inflated astonishment. "Why did you tell her the truth? You only tell them what they want to hear. Don't you know anything? Where are you from anyway?"

"Poland."

Marta's father was a blacksmith from Arcueil. She was the oldest of nine children with a tubercular mother, so she was used to helping others with their deficiencies. She was the kind of girl who liked to give advice.

"Poland? And where is that?" she asked, clearly vexed.

"Far away," Lucia said, regretfully. She knew she wasn't being helpful, coming as she did from a foreign country.

"Doesn't anybody lie in Poland?" They were standing at the omnibus stop. "Do you think anyone will hire you without a character and knowing that you were let go? Don't be a dunce. I know you are not from around here, but show some sense. You have to be more clever if you want to get on."

After that Marta instructed her on what to say and how to say it. She told her to be brief, not to say anything that would trip her up later on. She told her to make up a few details and use them in every interview. "Soon, you'll be believing it yourself."

Lucia knew it was a sin to lie. She couldn't do it even if she wanted to. Yet, Marta had a way about her. She was magnetic with her fierce black eyes set like two buttons deep in their sockets, her patrician's nose and firm chin leading the way into the world. She was certain, direct, and practical, like a locomotive pushing through a snowbank, stopping for nothing, least of all for any objections Lucia may have had.

Overhead, the sky had darkened, sending the first drops of rain falling through the bruise-colored clouds. Once the omnibus appeared the girls paid their fifteen centimes and climbed the narrow metal staircase to the top, to the imperial, to the cheaper seats outside in the rain, huddled under their umbrellas with their skirts tucked under their knees to stay dry.

Marta told her about a friend, a milliner's assistant, who happened to be looking for someone to share her room. She described a garret that was a block or two from the slaughterhouses. "It doesn't smell nice, but it's cheap. And she's a clean girl. That's important, you know. You don't want to catch anything. I'm sure she would be happy for the company. And the extra money. I'll talk to her and if she hasn't found anyone, you can move in." She made this pronouncement without even consulting Lucia or the girl. She made it plain by her impatience, by her bristling efficiency and theatrical amazement at Lucia's ineptitude, that the situation was dire and that it was time, perhaps past time, for her to step in.

•    •    •

The milliner's assistant, Olivie, was grateful for the company. She said as much to Lucia on the first day and then imparted that she didn't like being alone, and that she was about to get married. This last proved to be a bit of an exaggeration. There was a boy who worked at his uncle's seed store. They had met at a *caf'conc* some months ago, but he had never once mentioned marriage. Olivie said she wasn't too worried though, as it was "only a matter of time."

Olivie wasn't like Iris. She shared everything and even moved some of her clothes out of the armoire to make room for Lucia's. It was a small room with a bed, a table, and two chairs. A dressing table decorated with a frilly skirt stood against one wall and held a washstand, comb, and brush. Above it hung a shelf where Olivie kept her cosmetics, neatly lined up in glass jars. Hanging on pegs around the room were twenty or so hats of all kinds, even men's hats: a bowler, a visor cap, and one old top hat.

Lucia laid out the acrobat's red flower on the little stand by the bed and hung her mother's cross on the wall above her pillow. She told herself that the cross would protect her and that the flower was proof that Poland was close by. This last was still a mystery, for she felt very far away from home.

"You know how boys are," Olivie continued. She was propped up on her side of the bed, leaning against the pillows. "He won't say it, but he loves me. Of course he loves me. It is not even a question." The very fact that she mentioned it several times over several days made it a question, at least in Lucia's mind.

"I want you to meet Sevrin," she said one rainy night as she washed up at the basin. "He has friends. You can come out with us, and who knows, maybe you might find a husband too. He is so smart and knows everything about seeds and planting and cream separators. They have one in the shop. He showed it to me once. All chrome and porcelain. It's quite lovely."

Lucia hadn't given marriage much thought, mainly because it didn't seem like a possibility. She was a foreigner with no family and few friends and she was a domestic. Olivie had warned her not to tell anybody that she was a kitchen maid. "They don't like servants. The boys, I mean. They think servants are beneath them." Then she thought for a minute, standing in her corset and chemise with the hairpin box in her hand, and said: "Tell them you work in a shop. Tell them you work in a cheese shop or maybe a charcuterie. That sounds more respectable."

"A kitchen maid is not respectable?"

Olivie's cheeks reddened as she quickly tried to obviate her offense. "Of course it is. My aunt is a kitchen maid. That's not what I meant. I just meant it is not as exciting as working in a shop. Especially to the boys. Most of them work in trade, so naturally they are going to find a shopgirl more interesting."

Despite her views on what constituted interesting employment, Olivie was kind and appreciative. She liked the meals Lucia cooked, mostly soups made with cheap ingredients, and often went on about them, though to Lucia's way of thinking they were nothing special. Once Olivie brought home silk violets from work and decorated Lucia's hat without being asked. Nevertheless, Olivie's friendliness and her willing to share did not make up for her constant chatter. Iris, who had none of her good qualities, was a great deal easier to live with, mainly because she left Lucia alone.

•    •    •

It was November and Lucia had been looking for work for nearly three months. There had been a few hopeful interviews, but they had turned sour once the subject of a reference came up. Every morning she would wait for Olivie to go off to work and then sit by the window and count her savings, calculating how many weeks she had before she wouldn't be able to pay her share of the rent. That morning she sat at the window with the bills spread out in her lap. Below her the abattoir workers were plodding to work, men in thick leather aprons, their heavy wooden clogs clacking on the cobblestones.

She had a month, maybe six weeks, and then it would be a life on the streets. She wondered how long Olivie would let her stay if she couldn't pay her way—perhaps a week, maybe more. Olivie needed the money too. How else could she afford the clothes she needed to lure Sevrin into marriage?

Lucia often sought comfort in the church around the corner. She would go there for lauds or just to sit in the pews and pray. That morning she didn't go to the church. Maybe she started out for it, but she was so caught up in a raft of emotions that she didn't notice where she was going. She turned down several streets at random, until she found herself walking in the boulevard de Magenta, near the Gare du Nord. There, a large cathedral stood resplendent on a shabby stretch of street. She had never seen it before and didn't even know its name. Later she would claim that God had brought her there, but at the time she was confused and wretched and did not have a clue how she found it.

She walked up the steps and into the vestibule, where she dipped her fingers in the stoup, and crossed herself before going on into the nave. There she stopped to take it all in: the soaring arches, the stained-glass windows depicting the stations of the cross, the domed apse, the chancel with its carved altar, and all the saints standing comfortably in their stone niches. She recognized Saint Genevieve, Saint Martin of Tours, Saint George with his dragon, and Saint Hilaire. In the last niche, on the Epistle side of the church, stood another female saint. From where Lucia was standing she could see only a stiff stone skirt and a pure white foot encased in a marble sandal. Then as she came down the aisle, passing the old women praying their rosaries, she saw that the statue was a girl holding a tray. Her heart lurched when she recognized the two objects on the tray. They were the eyes of Saint Lucyna. They had been plucked out when she refused to marry a pagan. She had lost her eyes, but not her sight, and she saw clearly where others more powerful were blind. Here was Lucia's patron saint waiting for her. Here was the maiden who had come to comfort her and take up her burden. She was no longer alone. She raised her hands and gave thanks to Lucyna and then to the Blessed Virgin Mother, who had surely brought her here to find comfort in knowing that her life would soon be sorted out.

That day Lucia found an advertisement in one of the papers for a maid-of-all-work in the rue de la Glacière. It was in a modest neighborhood, and because a salary wasn't mentioned, she assumed the pay would be low. It was odd that applicants were instructed to arrive after 7 PM. She never heard of such a thing. Interviews were conducted during the day, usually in the morning, never at night. Still, she couldn't imagine there would be many applicants for such a strange notice, so she decided to go and have a look.

The rue de la Glacière was a narrow street off the boulevard de Port-Royal in the 13th. While the boulevard was wide, busy, and bright, the street was dark and deserted at night. The only light came from an occasional lamp at a window, a weedy glow that cast a halo into the misty air and was quickly swallowed up in the shadows. Lucia wanted to turn around, but instead she pushed on past the patisserie on the corner, the charcuterie, the butcher shop, and the wine shop, their doors shuttered, their windows blind.

She tried to focus her attention on the numbers over the doors, but she kept hearing rustling in the corners, bursts of furtive activity in the deepest shadows, and flitting movement just out of sight. She was on the verge of giving up when she found the number over a greengrocer, a poor dusty shop at the end of the block. She took a step back and looked up at the iron balconies above it. The first two floors were dark, but the third was aglow with a strange blue light. It might have been a blue curtain over the French door, or perhaps a lampshade, but it shone like a lean ray of light, a star leading the way.

The door was answered by a small woman wearing a dusty black dress. She had an intelligent face, marred by smudges of fatigue under her eyes and a high sloping forehead half hidden by a froth of ash-blond hair. Lucia assumed that this was the maid who had given notice, but then the woman opened her mouth to speak and banished all such thoughts.

"You've come about the advertisement."

A sudden rush of relief. The familiar accent, the rhythm of home. "You are Polish," Lucia exclaimed. *Jesteś Polski*.

"*I jesteś zbyt*." And you are too, I see.

"Yes, from Warsaw. From Powiśle. From Dobra Street near the river."

The woman gave her an indulgent smile. "There are many of us here." She stepped aside. "Come in, Dobra Street. We cannot let a patriot stand out in the cold."

It was a small apartment, shabbily furnished with a few wooden chairs and a white worktable. A man was seated at one end puzzling over a gray notebook while he combed his long fingers through his clipped black beard. He looked up briefly when Lucia walked in, but quickly returned to his work without a word, absently shoving a dirty plate aside to make more room. The only bright spots in the parlor were a gauzy blue curtain hanging over the French door and a bunch of sunflowers listing to one side in a blue vase.

The Polish woman led the way into the kitchen where another man, this one much older, sat reading a journal at a table covered in a blue checkered oilcloth. "Who is this?" the man asked brightly.

"I don't know yet," the woman replied.

"Well then, I'll let you find out," the gentleman said, folding his paper and rising with a sigh.

"Is she asleep yet?" the woman asked.

"I think so, but I'll go in and check."

"Don't wake her."

The old man gave her a withering look and left the room.

The kitchen was humble but well organized. Everything had a place; a colander hung on the wall by the sink, a dish towel was draped over a rack below it. A large stewpot sat on the stove, bubbling away. The flame was too high, but Lucia said nothing. It wasn't her place. A pencil outline drawn on the wall indicated where the stewpot hung when it wasn't in use. All the pots and pans had their outlines traced on the wall, along with other utensils: a large ladle, a spatula, and a rusty sieve.

"When were you last in Warsaw?" the woman asked, motioning to a chair.

"Six months ago."

"Six months ago," the woman repeated wistfully. "That's not very long. Is that confectionary still there? The one on the ground floor of the Church of Visitation?"

"The one next door to Monsieur B. Wosinski's watch shop?"

"Ah, Monsieur B. Wosinski," the woman laughed. She pulled a face and stuck her nose in the air.

Lucia laughed along with her. "Yes, it's still there."

"Do they still have those devil's eyes?"

"The ones that make your eyes water?"

"My favorite was red."

"Mine too."

"They always made my teeth ache. I remember if you wanted them fresh you had to buy them on—" And here they both said *Tuesdays* at the same time.

Lucia grew still when the woman wanted to know why she had come to Paris. Here is where it would all come to nothing. For one brief moment she wished she were more like Marta. She wished she could spin a story and have it turn out right, but that quality was not within her. She couldn't lie no matter how much she needed the position. She would have to tell the truth and accept the consequences.

With some difficulty she described her situation at the Babineauxes', the duties that she performed, emphasizing the sauces she had made and the dshes she had cooked. She told her about the dinner party, about Madame Clos's illness, and finally about getting sacked the next morning. The woman didn't try to interrupt her as the others had done. She sat there listening, her gray eyes fixed on Lucia, her features even and enigmatic.

When Lucia had finished, the woman thought for a moment and then surprised her by saying: "I need someone to help with the child. My father-in-law does what he can, but he needs someone to watch Iréne when he goes out, and I need someone to cook simple meals and keep up with the housekeeping. We can't pay much, but you'll have room and board."

"Are you offering me the position?"

The woman nodded.

"And you don't mind that I was let go?"

The woman peered at her matter-of-factly. "No, should I? I thought it was pretty obvious."

"Obvious?"

"Yes, of course. She did not want another cook in her kitchen."

Lucia started to object, to dismiss the idea as she had done with Marta, but then a detail came back to her, one that she had forgotten or perhaps she didn't think was important at the time. She remembered the way Madame Clos's hands trembled when Madame Babineaux came in to praise the meal. How the cook's eyes were fixed on the food grinder; how her face was smooth and still. It was just possible that this woman was right. Maybe Madame Clos did think highly of her that night, so highly in fact that she wanted to be rid of her. Maybe it wasn't her pride that brought her down, but Madame Clos's envy.

A sudden wave of affection for the cook caught her by surprise. A pang of longing so intense she thought she might cry. This was followed by the profound understanding that she would never see her cook again—that Madame Clos would always remain just a memory.

Her eyes slid back to this strange woman sitting across from her. How was it that this stranger understood so much from so little? She had brought Lucia to an understanding, had lifted her guilt and her spirits, and she didn't even know the woman's name.

A child cried out from the bedroom. The woman jumped up. "Tell me your name," she said, stopping by the door.

"Lucia. Lucia Rutkowska."

"Very well. You will do nicely, Lucia Rutkowska." She said this in Polish. Her hair was lit by the glow from the parlor making a reckless halo about her face. There was something familiar about those gray eyes set under a heavy brow, the high forehead, the firm mouth—a needling memory just out of reach. Then Lucia had it; the portrait of the Holy Mother hanging in the Church of Mary Magdalene near Babusia's house, the same aura of incorporeality, of someone apart and yet very present.

The woman was about to turn away when she stopped and said: "Oh. And I am Madame Curie."

# CHAPTER 5

# November 1902

G abriel knew that if he didn't sit next to the medium, there would be little hope of discovering her tricks, so he made sure he was the first one to arrive at the flat in rue Saint-Jacques. The flat was located in the Latin Quarter over a restaurant that looked crowded even at this late hour. The maid brought him into the front parlor, a thoroughly conventional room, except for a medium's cabinet that took up one corner and a large table covered with a white tablecloth that sat in the center of the room.

He was alone for quite some time until a middle-aged couple arrived, looking intense and dreary, and took their seats across from him. The woman was dressed in black, a cheap fabric that was supposed to look like silk, unadorned and ill fitting, most likely made on her kitchen table. She wore a defeated little hat decorated with a feather, unfashionable but brushed with care. She had moist, protruding eyes that were fixed on the tablecloth. Her cheeks and jowls seemed weighed down, and her mouth was a bleak line of despair.

Her husband was a slight man looking uncomfortable in his shirt and collar. Gabriel respected their kind. They lived in his neighborhood. They were small shopkeepers and artisans, hardworking, defiant, and easily abashed in unfamiliar surroundings. The husband was the protector. He had taken on the role with a

grim resolve. His eyes drifted from the window to a Turkish tapestry on the wall to the little bronze dogs on the mantel, always coming back to his wife to see if she was all right. She was not all right.
The dark splotches under her eyes and her vacant stare attested to
the sleepless nights of her recent bereavement.

Two devotees of the spiritualist movement arrived shortly after
that, within minutes of each other, and took their seats at the table.
They were members of a growing number of adherents mostly from
America and Europe, from every social stratum, the privileged
class and the working class, who joined spirit circles and conducted
séances in their homes and attended larger meetings in rented halls.
The woman was middle-aged, rouged and powdered. She wore an
enormous turquoise cuff around her wrist and several turquoise
rings on her fingers. She took the seat next to the couple, while the
gentleman, smartly dressed, sat next to her. It was obvious from
their familiarity that these two knew each other, perhaps from their
time in the movement or from other spirit circles. Before long the
woman was showing off her cuff to the gentleman, saying that she
had just returned from America where she had purchased it from a
genuine Navaho Indian. "You know Navaho?"

"Of course," the gentleman sniffed, his mouth barely moving
beneath his imperious moustache.

"I've been to the pueblo," the woman said. "They are very spiritual, you know. They regularly speak to the spirits and not just to
the human ones. They speak to all kinds."

"I know," the man said, folding one sharply creased trouser leg
over the other. "I know all about them."

The woman remained unruffled and turned to the couple on
her left. She asked them if they had been to this medium before.
The woman in black made no response. Her husband merely shook
his head.

Fortunately, two university students, a girl and her male companion, had just arrived and had taken their seats next to Gabriel.
The girl stepped in to save the garrulous woman. She said she had

heard that the medium was a brilliant clairvoyant. Both the woman and the girl had heard she was young, a schoolgirl really, and wasn't that unusual for a medium with such strong powers? The girl's companion, a young man with greasy blond hair that kept falling into his eyes, whispered in her ear. She gave him a sour look and fingered her earlobe, feeling for the pearl earring that adorned it.

"You can go if you like," she said, lowering her voice. She wasn't pretty, but her thick dark eyebrows, white square teeth, faint moustache, and dusky complexion gave her a sultry look, and that was enough to keep her companion by her side.

Eventually, an older gentleman came into the room and introduced himself as the medium's father. He was heavyset and jowly; his eyes lay in a pair of crinkled caverns set deep under a fringe of curly eyebrows. His rough features were tempered by a well-tailored suit that gave him the substantial air of a professional, a lawyer, or perhaps a doctor. He informed the intimate group that his daughter was feeling a little tired tonight, but that they should not be concerned. "Noémi has contacted her spirit guide, who has told her to go on with the circle. So, she has been resting all afternoon. She will join us shortly."

Noémi Thibeau didn't look much older than a schoolgirl, but one who had dressed up for the occasion, perhaps borrowing her older sister's clothes. She took her seat at the head of the table and welcomed the sitters to her circle, exhibiting a quiet authority that seemed out of place for one so young. She was at once sympathetic, authentic, and shy. She gave an inspirational talk that incorporated such words as *spiritual forces*, *cosmic magnetism*, and *interconnectedness*. Although there was a hint of her roots in the pronunciation of certain words, for the most part Noémi appeared to be an educated young lady, poised, correct, determined, a solid member of the middle class. Gabriel was impressed.

While her father lowered the gas and lit the candles, she sat there motionless: back erect, hands on the table, eyes closed. Some time passed before she began to hum a strange tune that was made all the more eerie by her clear, high voice. Gabriel thought he recognized it. It may have been a song from his childhood, familiar and unnerving, simple and strange.

Soon Noémi was adding a few words to her tune, chanting them over and over again, words that Gabriel could not make out no matter how closely he listened. They were in another language, one that was strange and decidedly not Indo-European. The woman with the jewelry caught his eye and mouthed *Indian* to indicate that the medium was speaking a Native American dialect. Gabriel made a note of it in his notebook, the one he had managed to smuggle in. *Indian*, he wrote and then, *where is the father?* The father had slipped out sometime after the séance had begun, a fact that Gabriel found worthy of note.

After a few minutes one end of the table began to rise. It was the south end where the medium was sitting and it rose slowly but steadily, until it was about a foot above ground. It stayed there for nearly a minute, swaying back and forth, behaving like a gently rocking cradle. The bereaved wife clutched her husband's sleeve, her face pale and still. Then, without warning, it came crashing down, startling the sitters.

Noémi stopped singing after that, resting her hands on the table, palms up. Slowly her head began to sink, her shoulders slumped, and her hair fell in a cascade about her face. After a few minutes she straightened and opened her eyes. She seemed to be focused on a point above the table.

"Yes," she said vaguely. "Yes. Tell her I am here. Tell her she must come forward or I won't be able to speak to her." Gabriel felt a rush of cold air and noticed that the temperature in the room had dropped suddenly. He chided himself for not bringing a thermometer. His brother would have remembered one.

"Yes, I will tell them."

Then to the assembled she said in a voice that was dreamy and melodic: "It is Mapiya. She is here with us. She welcomes you. She is grateful for your presence and wants you to know that there are many spirits among us to—" She stopped and stared at the point above the table. "Did you hear that?"

The husband sat up, tense, fierce, and wary, but then realized that she wasn't talking to the living. He had taken his wife's hand to comfort her. Hers was small and pale; his was trembling despite his efforts to appear firm and in control.

"Who is that, Mapiya?" the medium went on. "Who is that child with you?"

Gabriel heard muttering, a dim flutter of a conversation. It seemed to be between two people, a child and a woman with a high, quavering inflection. He tried to make out the words, but they were too faint. The child appeared to be crying. The woman was soothing.

"I see a little girl," Noémi said, her eyes fixed on the spot. "Yes, that one, Mapiya. The one in the red coat. What are those on her collar? Daisies?"

A cry from the woman in black. She clamped a hand over her mouth and nose while her husband slipped his arm around her shoulders and held her close.

Noémi muttered, "Daphne?"

"Yes, Daphne," the woman cried eagerly. "It's me, Maman. Can you hear me?"

Gabriel glanced around at the others. They were frozen in their chairs. Only their eyes shifted from the medium to the spot that held her attention and back again. Even the skeptical young man forgot to brush the greasy hair out of his eyes.

Another whoosh of cold air.

"She is worried about her house," Noémi said.

"The doll house."

Several sharp raps on the table, and the sitters jumped. "She does not want Lotte to play with it." Here her voice went up an octave and she whined like a little girl. "Lotte will break it, Maman. She breaks everything."

"*Oh, mon Dieu,*" the woman breathed. "That is Daphne. That is her voice."

"You have to tell her to stop."

"*Bien sûr, ma chérie.* Lotte will not play with it." Then to her husband: "I told your sister to keep that child away."

"You are too excited, Josette. Look at you. You are trembling all over." His hands were shaking so badly that it was difficult for him to take hers.

The conversation went on like that for several minutes. There was some talk about a cat and a favorite doll named Claude. The child said she was happy, that Tante Odette was with her as well as Grand-mère and that everything was beautiful. Soon after that the medium's voice began to trail off; her words grew faint and then finally stopped.

The grieving mother waited, her hand clutching her husband's. "Daphne?"

Her husband began to talk to her quietly, urgently, pleading with her to calm down. "She will come again, Josette. You will see. She's not lost to us."

"Daphne," she cried. "Do you hear me?"

Noémi began to speak to the woman in her own voice. "She is gone now. She can't hear you," she said firmly but with compassion. "But you cannot think that this is the end. It is not over. It will never be over. She will come again and you will speak with her. For now there are others here who wish to speak. It is their turn."

"Yes, we understand," the husband said, rising. "My wife is very tired. I must get her home." He slipped his hand under his wife's arm and helped her up. She leaned into him, sobbing quietly. Without another word he guided her to the door. Gabriel followed their progress: the wife clinging to her husband, his whispered reassurances. They moved as one tragic creature.

For a moment nobody moved. The woman with the jewelry sat with her palm cupped over her mouth. The girl from the university held back tears. Her companion whispered in her ear.

Noémi began to chant again, the same tune, the same strange words. "I have a message for Simone Maslin," she said, in a diaphanous voice. The girl from the university looked up, eyes wide.

Noémi's advice for Gabriel came from his brother Victor. "Don't worry about Papa," Victor said through the medium. "He will come around. You are different from them. He will accept it."

Gabriel's eyes fixed on the table, a knot of irritation growing in his stomach. The others waited for him to either confirm or deny what had just been said, but he would not give the medium the satisfaction.

•   •   •

"You're too sensitive, Gabriel," Noémi complained, after the others had left. "Look at you with your sour face."

"How would you like it if I dropped little tidbits about your life, eh? Pigalle perhaps? The photographs? Sessions?"

"Oh, Gabriel, do not be angry. I didn't mean anything by it. And besides, I cannot control what the spirits say."

"Stop it now, Noémi. It's just the two of us here."

"Stop what?" she said with an innocent smile.

He gave her a withering look. "I'm here to learn the tricks."

"What tricks?" She held up her hand against his, palm to palm, as if to measure the difference in size. His dwarfed hers.

He thought about arguing with her. Instead he felt the heat of his palm against hers. He knew Noémi. He knew she wanted to be wooed and won, so after that he decided to use a different tack. He closed his hand over hers and brought it up to his lips. They rested for a while, side by side at the table, amid the sober detritus of the séance: the flickering candles, dried flowers, and bells, talking about the past, about her growing practice, and her plans for the future.

Noémi had nothing in common with the schoolgirl she pretended to be. Once they were alone the real Noémi made an appearance, the girl Gabriel remembered from the cafés in Pigalle—the little *grisette*, who could stay up until dawn and then go off to a twelve-hour shift on the laundry boats. Noémi was the smartest of her lot, an opportunist who always said she would make her own luck. They continued teasing one another until they finished all the wine. Then she invited him up to her room. At first he was reluctant to go, until she assured him that she no longer charged for it. After that he was happy to follow, knowing later, when she was satisfied, she would give him what he came for.

•   •   •

Rue de Poupées, the Street of Dolls, was a narrow lane lined with two doll factories and little else. Even though it wasn't far off the boulevard de Strasbourg, the street was dark and eerily silent. It lay in a kind of trough and so it made its own loathsome weather. Smoke from the kiln stacks mixed with the heavy winter mist to create a noxious pallor that hung low over the street. It was nearly always night in rue de poupées. There were shadows upon shadows, dark and even darker, that seemed to lurch from corner to corner. Depending on which way the wind was blowing, these toxic phantoms swirled and merged, formed and faded in a dance of industrial waste.

Gabriel found that the man he had come to see lived in a flat over one of the factories. To get to it he had to walk through the showroom of the Bébés Gesland, a manufacturer specializing in baby and fashion dolls. These dolls stared at him from every corner of the room, from the top shelves, from the glass cases, and from shelves behind the counter. They were dressed in silks, satin, and velvets, plumed hats, and tiny dancing shoes; their glassy eyes stared out at him with bland complacency. He made a point of not looking at them as he hurried through to the workshop housed on the factory floor. It was childish, he knew, but he never seemed to shake the feeling that there was something beneath the clay and glass, something unnatural behind the fixed smiles, the tiny white teeth, and the painted rosy cheeks.

The factory was not a big concern. It employed only nine workers, all of whom were engaged in different facets of doll making. In a corner a boy stirred a vat of slip, liquid clay, with a long wooden spatula. Two men stood over a long slotted trough pouring the slip into the molds secured with thick bands of rubber. On the other side, men perched on stools at a long table and cleaned the heads, arms, and legs that had been recently released from the molds. They used delicate dental tools and squinted at their fine work in the meager light of the warehouse. Across the room stood the kilns tended by another boy, who kept feeding wood into their fireboxes. Two men were loading the last kiln with green ware. One of them looked over at Gabriel and nudged the other.

"I'm looking for a Monsieur Baye," Gabriel said, after the man approached him with an inquiring look.

"He is up there." He indicated a second story.

"He lives up there?"

"He is a relation of Monsieur Gesland's. If you want to know where he lives, you can go up there and ask him."

It turned out that Monsieur Baye did not like visitors. When Gabriel knocked on the door and explained that Noémi had sent him, he told him to go away. When Gabriel mentioned he wanted to become a medium and that he was willing to pay for the lessons, there was no answer from the other side.

He waited and knocked again. This time Monsieur Baye asked if he was a believer.

"No, not at all."

"Then why do you want to learn?"

"I'm a journalist, *monsieur*. I'm doing a story." This wasn't entirely true, as he was still waiting for word from his editor.

"You want to expose the mediums?"

"I only want to tell the truth."

"And you always know what that is, do you? You know it when you see it?"

"Not always."

Again silence. Gabriel waited for a few moments and then knocked again.

The bolt slid free and the door swung open. An old man stood in the threshold. "A truthseeker, eh?" He stepped aside to let Gabriel pass. The man's right arm hung limp by his side, his right hip sagged, his gait stiff and crablike as he heaved himself back to the table and collapsed into a chair with welcomed relief. He motioned to the chair opposite.

Gabriel settled himself in and glanced around the room. It was small but neat. A bunch of tulips stood in a jar on the table, a fresh coverlet lay on the bed, and curtains hung over the one window that looked out from the back of the factory across a wintery field. Someone had made an effort to make the room comfortable. A hot stove made the room almost unbearable. Even so Gabriel left his coat and scarf on.

"My daughter likes flowers," Baye said, when he noticed Gabriel looking around. "She wants me to live with them, but I am not that far gone. Not yet anyway. So you want to become a medium?"

"I want to learn how so I can write about it."

Baye regarded Gabriel with a thoughtful smile and said: "What if I told you that there are no tricks? That what you see is real. That the spirits speak through these people because they have a gift."

Gabriel paused for a moment deciding what to do. Then he rose: "I think I have the wrong place."

Baye burst out laughing. "No, sit. I will teach you what you want to know. Believe me there is no love lost between me and my former colleagues. I don't care what happens to them. Nevertheless, I don't want to see Noémi get hurt. You must promise that your article will make no mention of her."

"Of course."

"Good. Then I hope you have money because it will cost you."

·    ·    ·

On Thursday Gabriel returned with money, a hemp rope, and a bottle of good brandy. The money came from his editor, but the liquor he had to pay for himself.

Monsieur Baye sat at the little table sipping the brandy and massaging his bad leg while he talked about his career, how he was once a sought-after manifesting medium, how the scientists had come to study him, and how a stroke had ended it all.

It had been only a few days since Gabriel was at the flat, but in that time he saw a great change in the old man. His hair was whiter now, and he moved with greater difficulty. He face looked older too, but that may have been a trick of the light.

"On the other hand Noémi is a test medium," Baye was saying, pouring himself another glass. "She gives names and dates and details about the sitters that she couldn't possibly know, and in this way they learn to trust her."

"How does she do it?"

"You don't believe the spirits tell her?" He gave Gabriel a short laugh and pointed to a book on the shelf. "Here, hand me that."

Gabriel got up and handed it over. "This is the blue book," Baye said, opening it to a random page. "It contains information gathered by mediums as they travel around the country."

Gabriel thumbed through it and found that the book consisted entirely of names organized by city. Under each name were listed family members living and dead, family tragedies, business setbacks, observations of all kinds. Under Paris he found Comtois, Alain and Josette. Daughter Daphne died January 1902, whooping cough. Dollhouse, red coat, daisies on the collar, doll named Claude. Tante Odette died 1893.

Baye sipped his brandy with pleasure and refilled Gabriel's glass. "Test mediums can be interesting, but what I am going to teach you is something different, something rare and precious. I am going to make you a member of the royalty, the rarified few. You, my friend, will learn the secrets of the materializing medium. You will know how to bring spirits into the circles. They will talk and sing and fly about. If you choose to give a sitting, it will be one they will talk about for a long time to come. Are you ready?"

Gabriel nodded.

"Hand me the rope."

Over the next few minutes Monsieur Baye labored to tie Gabriel to his chair. He secured Gabriel's arms, tying his feet together and then running the rope up to his chest and around the back of the chair several times. He finished off the job with a special knot, one that would have taken any man with two free hands a number of minutes to untie. Gabriel was surprised that he made such short work of it. Monsieur Baye didn't look as if he had the strength. He was thin and insubstantial, almost like an apparition himself.

Once he finished, Baye stood back and admired his handiwork. "Yes, that ought to do it. Now, free your right hand," he said, holding up a pocket watch. "You have one minute."

Gabriel tried to lift his right hand, but it was securely fastened to the arm of the chair. "And exactly how am I supposed to do that?"

Baye gave him a look of mock surprise. "It shouldn't be difficult. Go ahead, try. Even I could do it."

Gabriel strained against the rope, but his arm wouldn't budge. He tried wiggling free, twisting and turning his wrist, all to no good. Monsieur Baye watched him grow frustrated and even a little panicked, grinning at him the whole time, clearly enjoying himself. Gabriel did not share in his fun. "Yes, you made your point. Now get me out of this."

While Monsieur Baye untied the ropes he explained that the success of the entire séance rested on one thing—securing enough slack to be able to free yourself once the time was right. "You will be in the cabinet, and the drapes will be closed. No one will be watching, and that is the time you'll need slack."

This time Baye instructed Gabriel to sit up straight while he tied his hands to his knees. This meant that Baye was forced to tie the rope around the thick part of Gabriel's thighs. When he finished he told Gabriel to lean forward. This caused the rope to slide from his upper thighs to his knees—where the legs were much thinner— giving Gabriel enough slack to free his right hand.

Next he told Gabriel to twist his wrists so the thumbs were up as he tied his hands behind his back. When he was done he told Gabriel to twist his wrists back again, giving him the slack he needed to free himself. While Baye wrapped the rope around Gabriel's chest and around the back of his chair, he told Gabriel to sit forward slightly. Then once he was done, he told Gabriel to sit back. Gabriel was surprised by how much slack he had to work with.

"It's astonishing what you can do with your mouth and teeth and elbow," Baye said as he tied Gabriel up in several ways and in each case had a technique for stealing slack. "But everything starts with slack. Once you have that, you can free a hand. Then anything is possible."

Gabriel came for his second lesson on Monday and found Baye just finishing up his supper. A girl, perhaps his daughter, was cleaning up and waiting to take the tray away. Once she had gone Baye brought over a jar from the counter and set it on the table. It contained the heads of more than a hundred kitchen matches that he had been soaking in water for several days. He poured off the water and added a little linseed oil. Then he told Gabriel to turn the gas down and close the curtains. Once the room was dark he held up the jar so Gabriel could see that it glowed like a blue orb. When Baye attached it to a flexible rod and bounced it around the room, its radiance shone like a distant star trapped in a jar.

"All you need now to make a glowing apparition is a gauze mask with a face painted on it and a handkerchief." He had both. He painted the handkerchief with the phosphorescent solution and then holding the handkerchief behind the mask made the face appear as if it were glowing in the dark.

Over the next few weeks Baye showed Gabriel how to make a spirit gown out of a few meters of tulle, how to hide it along with the mask and other props in a guitar built with a hidden compartment. He showed Gabriel how to make a horn play on its own by using a music box hidden inside. How to make a glowing orb dance around the room on a reaching rod, a telescoping device a little over a meter long, that looked like a fountain pen when not extended and could be carried into the sitting in the medium's pocket.

Proudly he displayed his shoe, which had been constructed with a button on the inside of the heel. With a slight movement of his foot he was able to press the button and release the back, which sprang open on a hinge. He explained that while his control kept a shoe on his boot thinking that his foot was inside, in actuality, his leg and foot were free to perform all manner of "miracles."

During one lesson Baye covered a student's slate in white chalk. Then he took a photograph from a newspaper, licked it all over, and set it down on the chalk. He used a rounded pencil to draw over the lines in the photograph, and because the paper was wet, it picked up the chalk wherever the pencil was applied, leaving a black line in its wake. Once the image was transferred to the slate, Baye lifted up the photograph and showed Gabriel the portrait underneath, black lines on a white chalky background.

"Now, it's only a question of substitution," he said, holding the slate under the table. "When the lights are low you substitute the blank slate for the one containing the portrait that you've been hiding all along." Here Baye got up with some difficulty and showed Gabriel the underside of his chair which had been outfitted with brackets that allowed a slate to effortlessly slide in and out

Baye suggested that Gabriel conduct a séance at Noémi's to see if he could put it all into practice. He lent him a wind-up music box, slates, chalk, all the other props needed for a proper materializing séance. He cautioned Gabriel to practice every day, until he felt comfortable with the equipment, and to remember to steal slack.

On the last night, the lesson ran late, so Gabriel had to see himself out. He had been shown where the keys were hidden in the showroom for just this eventuality and had no trouble finding them even in the dark. He had to sort through them using the small wedge of light that stole in through the transom. He tried to keep his eyes on the locks and his attention on the keys, but he kept thinking about the dolls on the shelves all around him. From the corner of his eye he kept seeing movement, a hand, an arm. Here and there a doll's glassy eye glimmered in the light and it seemed to him, although he knew it was ridiculous, that one or two had turned to face him. It was a childish fancy left over from a story Étienne had told him when he was little. He reminded himself that he was grown up now and it was foolish to be fearful of a hunk of clay and glass. Then he heard—or thought he heard—a childish giggle.

He struggled with the keys, trying one, then another. His fingers were trembling, becoming more desperate with each try. Finally, he found the one that fit, turned the locks, and shoved the door open. Once outside he realized that he had been holding his breath and took in a gulp of the noxious air.

He tried to put the incident out of mind. It was a child's night terror. Still, he couldn't quite dismiss the giggling and there was something else, an impression of a child singing. He couldn't swear he had heard it. Perhaps it was in his head. It sounded like the song Noémi sang that night at the séance, the familiar tune he remembered from his childhood. Of course, it was impossible. His imagination was obviously untethered by Baye's brandy. Still, as he made his way to the corner it nagged at him—the thought that he wasn't alone in that showroom. It settled on him like the curious weather suspended over the Street of Dolls.

He hadn't gotten far when he realized that he still had the keys in his pocket and had neglected to drop them through the slot in the door. He was on his way back when he saw Baye leaving through a side door. Baye didn't see him and for some reason Gabriel didn't call out. Instead, from the shadows he watched the man walk around to the front of the building and on down the street.

It took only a moment to realize what had stopped him from calling out. It was the way Baye was walking. He was no longer dragging his right leg. The leg and the arm, in fact the whole body, moved differently. He tramped along the sidewalk, swinging his arms, his legs unfettered, vigorous, inattentive to the dangers of the slippery pavement. He stepped off the high curb and crossed the street, striding over the cobblestones with an unconscious grace, moving like a young man with an appointment to keep.

# CHAPTER 6

# November 1902

Lucia spent a good part of the first week cleaning, polishing, and scrubbing in an effort to reassure Madame Curie that she had not been wrong in hiring her. Each day when the Curies returned home, she expected some comment on her work but never received more than a hasty greeting. When her mistress came into the kitchen on that first night, she took only a quick look at the chicken stewing in the pot and left without a word.

At first Lucia thought that Madame Curie was displeased and so she worked even harder to please her. She cleaned out the cupboards and organized the dry goods, labeling the jars and stacking them on the shelves in alphabetical order. When Madame Curie came into the kitchen that second night it was only to ask if Iréne ate more than pippins and tapioca for supper. "The child cannot live on apples and pudding, Lucia."

"Yes, *madame.*"

On Wednesday Lucia went down the street to the market and bought an inferior cut of meat. Since her new employers didn't have much money, meals would have to be stretched; catfish had to make do for halibut, carp for sturgeon, and the ropey beef had to be tenderized into submission. That evening she made a marinade of cloves, onions, and a whole head of garlic. She added an herb bouquet of thyme, bay leaves, parsley sprigs, peppercorns, and allspice berries. She marinated the roast all night and in the morning she turned it over and basted it every hour until it was time to cook. She braised it for three hours in a broth made from cracked veal knuckles, split calf's feet, and six cups of beef broth. When it was time for supper she cut the slices thin to give the appearance of filling the platter and served it with braised carrots and new potatoes.

She knew it was time to clear the plates when the Curies shoved them aside and began to work. They were huddled over the gray notebook, their heads together, round-shouldered, Madame Curie making complicated calculations on a separate piece of paper.

Lucia waited for some comment, but they were lost in the work. "How did you like the beef?" she asked finally, her tone edged with impatience.

Madame Curie grunted, her pencil flying over the page. Monsieur Curie looked up perplexed: "Did we have beef?"

Monsieur Curie was not like any man Lucia had ever met. He hardly ever spoke to her, and when he did, he almost never looked at her, preferring instead to look just past her or down at his hands, muttering under his breath in a voice so low that she had to ask him to repeat himself, which she did not like to do. In addition, he had a high-pitched giggle, the laugh of an excited adolescent. Once or twice she happened to glance at one of the gray notebooks that lay open on the table. It was divided into columns like a ledger, like Mademoiselle Wolfowitz's grade book. In the far left column the time was noted. Next to it was a description of a candle blowing out. Further down on the page her eye caught a description of a face floating over a cabinet. All the notations were executed in his schoolboy's scrawl.

"Yes, my son, we had braised beef for supper," the old man said with a patient smile. He had just returned from putting Irène to bed. "The best I ever ate, I might add." He winked at Lucia.

She reddened with pleasure and made herself busy with the dishes.

The next day Lucia spent the morning baking bread and in the afternoon she tackled the flue. It hadn't been cleaned in years. Sometime after Iréne's nap the doctor shuffled into the kitchen in his stocking feet and announced: "Come along, *mademoiselle*. The sun is out and we're going to the park."

Lucia poked her head out of the flue. She was standing on a ladder she had borrowed from the greengrocer's downstairs. Her hands and face were covered in soot. "You want me to come with you?" He nodded and told her he could use the company. What a strange family, inviting the servant out for a stroll.

Dr. Curie was nothing like his son. He was lively, a charmer, who laughed easily and had something to say about most everything. He was never still. Even when he was sitting some part of him was on the move, a tapping foot, a bouncing knee; his legs seemed to have a life of their own. He was a short man, a head or two shorter than his son, with a long face made longer still by a patch of white beard on his chin. He favored loose blouses tucked into his trousers and when it was sunny he wore wide-brimmed straw hats, which were usually torn and dirty.

They placed Iréne in her pushchair and together they walked down to the park where they took turns maneuvering the stroller down a gravel path. It was chilly under the trees, the bare branches crosshatching the sky. The doctor seemed to be enjoying himself as he kept up a steady monologue about the trees and the flowers they were passing. At one point he stooped to pick up a seedpod, a green spiky thing that to Lucia looked dangerous. He held it out for her, but she did not want to touch it. "Go ahead. It won't hurt you," he said, urging her with an outstretched hand. "It's a horse chestnut."

She took it gingerly and held it in her palm, bending and patting the spikes. They were pliable and interesting.

"I have no idea why they call it that," he said, stooping to pick up another. "They're not chestnuts and if you feed them to a horse, it'll convulse and die." He scraped the pod with his thumbnail until he broke through the flesh and tore open the outer casing to reveal a large smooth nut inside. He held it out for her and this time she took it without hesitation.

After that, there was more talk about trees, a linden and a cedar, and several species of birds. When they came to a pond the doctor stopped and studied the surface of the water and the sandy shore that surrounded it. Then he brightened. "Look." He was pointing to an unremarkable toad sunning on a flat stone. It was hiding in a leafy grotto at the marshy end of the lake. A moment later he was in the lake, going after the creature, stepping on stones to keep his shoes dry. He was surprisingly agile for an old man, able to leap from rock to log in pursuit of his prey. When he had caught the slippery thing, he held it out for her to see. "A common midwife toad." He was pleased with his prize.

He asked her if she wanted to hold it. She curled her lip and shook her head. He laughed at this and opened his hand. Instantly the toad hopped back into the water and disappeared beneath the murky surface. Then it surfaced again some distance away and struggled to climb up on a rock. "There, she looks happy."

"How do you know it is a she?"

"She's bigger than her mate. In the spring she will give her eggs over to him and he will carry them on his back until they are ready to hatch."

They sat by the lake looking for more toads and frogs and saw a turtle or two. The doctor told her that he had worked in the museum laboratories in the Jardin des Plantes and that made sense since he seemed to know so much about plants and animals. She liked that he didn't treat her as most people did when they found out she was the hired girl.

"Clever girl," he said, when she correctly identified a male midwife toad. It wasn't difficult. He looked just like his mate, only smaller. Still, his praise made her smile and she remembered it later while cutting up vegetables for the soup. That night before climbing into bed she looked up *toad* in her dictionary and got a picture of a fire-bellied toad common in Poland.

Over the next month or two Lucia accompanied the doctor and Iréne to museums, galleries, and gardens. He was devoted to his granddaughter and took her everywhere. Whenever Lucia could find time to join them she was treated to lectures on the natural world, art, music, and the wonders of science. In this way she acquired an education of sorts that may have lacked depth but enjoyed a breadth that was at once splendid and chaotic.

In January the house was full of excitement, because the Curies had received their shipment of dust. Lucia tried to understand what the fuss was about. All she could gather from their conversation was that a mountain of burlap sacks filled with dirt had arrived, several tons of dust mixed with pine needles and something called pitchblende.

The next day the doctor explained that it was a black ore mined on the German-Czech border, the source of uranium. He described uranium as a gray metallic element used to color ceramic glazes.

They were on their way to the park. It was a boisterous day noisy with the clatter of the wind through the bare branches. "The children have discovered a new element and now they are trying to isolate enough of it to get an atomic weight." He described atomic weight as the mass of one atom of an element. "The atom is the smallest particle in the universe. It makes up the elements. If they can get the atomic weight of this new material, then they'll have proved that they found something new."

"And an element?"

"It's the building block."

"Of what?"

"Of everything."

•    •    •

Lucia woke in the middle of the night and lay in her cot listening. She slept in the parlor, as there was no other place for her, unfolding her bed at night and folding it back up in the morning. Something had awakened her and she was trying to figure out what it was. It was a cold night, heavy from the recent rain, the eaves were still dripping from the storm, but that's not what woke her. It was another sound, something unfamiliar. She lay there in the dark motionless until she heard it again. Someone was shuffling around in the kitchen. She could plainly hear the pad of bare feet on the linoleum, a doleful sigh, and the creak of the floorboards. After a while the sounds faded away and soon all she could hear was the wind playing with the roof tiles. She concentrated on the muffled sounds of the night, listening for anything out of the ordinary, but all was quiet and she began to relax. Her eyes closed and she started to drift off, until she heard it again.

A shuffling in the kitchen. Muffled foot falls. A whispery sigh. Someone or something had just come back in. It was drifting about the kitchen seemingly without purpose or reason. Her breath caught in her throat. She knew without a doubt that this was no intruder. This was an apparition. Babusia had always taught her to watch out for the spirits. They were everywhere, and just like with the living, some were bad and some were good. Sometimes it was hard to tell them apart, so her best advice was to stay away.

Something was standing just on the other side of the open doorway. All she could do was lay there and listen to the tiny creaks and groans, the padded footfalls, the feathery commotion that seemed to be filling the kitchen.

Eventually she willed herself to sit up.

She listened harder but heard nothing. She climbed out of the cot and stood. Her legs had gone rickety. She thought that at any moment she might collapse. She wanted to call out and wake the doctor, but he was on the other side of the kitchen in the pantry and she would have to wake the whole house for him to hear her. She crept into the room, which was black and cold, the fire in the stove having been reduced to its last ashy coal. Peering into the gloom Lucia could see a figure standing at the sink, a shadow dressed in a long nightdress or shroud. Lucia stood there unable to move, unable to even cross herself. She wanted to open her mouth and scream when the figure turned and began walking towards her in a jerky, silent way.

A hand touched her shoulder. She jumped and cried out.

"Hush now. I'll get her."

Monsieur, dressed in a nightshirt, moved past her. He took the spirit's hand and kissed it, and when he turned her around Lucia could see that it wasn't a ghost, but Madame Curie. Her eyes were open and staring, and yet she didn't seem to know that he was there.

"What is it? Is she sick?" Lucia asked.

"She is asleep."

"But she is walking around. Her eyes are open."

"She is walking in her sleep. It's the New Zealander, the Italian, and the German. They have her worried, so she walks at night."

"Worried?"

"She doesn't want them to be the first. She wants it for herself. I keep telling her it doesn't matter. If it gets done, that's what's important. Who cares who finds it, as long as it is found."

Lucia had no idea what he was talking about, but by now she was used to that. She stood in the doorway and watched their slow progress back into the bedroom. He was gentle with his wife, helping her along one step at a time. Once in the bedroom he reached past her and quietly closed the door so as to not wake her. It was touching, the way he took care of her, even a bit sad. It reminded Lucia of the male midwife toad and how he took the eggs from his mate and cared for them on his back, until they were ready to hatch.

The next morning the Curies were up early and after a few bites of breakfast began to gather up their things. No mention was made of the night before. Madame looked tired and seemed anxious to get back to the laboratory. Iréne put up the usual fuss, refusing to eat her breakfast and tearful because her parents were about to leave. She held up her arms, fingers splayed and cried, "Mé. Mé." She called her mother Mé and her father Pé. Since she couldn't pronounce *Lucia*, she called her Lulu and now everyone in the household called her that.

Madame Curie put down her satchel, lifted her daughter up out of her high chair and held her, kissing her face and the top of her head. "Give her a proper breakfast, Lulu," she said, kissing the child's foot and making her laugh. "No more pippins and tapioca."

"Yes, *madame*. I'll try."

"Just do it, please."

"Of course, *madame*," Lucia said, uneasily. She was thinking how difficult it was to get the child to eat. There would be tears and a tantrum and it would all be for nothing, for most likely Iréne would, in the end, have her way.

Iréne cried when her parents left and would not be comforted, even when the doctor scooped her up and walked her around the room, bouncing her and singing the nonsense song that he made up on the spot. Finally, when she had quieted down, Lucia put her back in the high chair and gave her an egg and a piece of cheese, which she tore up into tiny pieces but refused to eat. She shook her head and clamped her lips closed when Lucia tried to get her to take a bite. She wanted her tapioca that sat in its customary bowl on the counter and kept pointing to it with a naked urgency that would not be appeased.

Eventually, Lucia gave up and while she spooned the pudding into the child's mouth she asked the doctor about the New Zealander, the Italian, and the German and what they did to upset Madame Curie.

"It's a race," he said, shaking out his morning paper and folding it back. He glanced over at his granddaughter and laughed because she was holding out an apple slice for him with solemn resolve.

"What kind of a race?"

"To find the radio elements."

"The what?"

"Chemical elements that emit rays. Rays of energy. Radiation, that's what Marie calls it. Uranium was only the first. Marie found other metals that give off energy. How is it that even if you lock this material in a drawer or bury it underground or drop it into boiling acid, it still emits these rays? Remarkable when you consider that it is impossible."

"Impossible?"

"Like rain falling up or birds flying upside down. It cannot happen. And yet it does and no one knows why." After that there was talk about the first law of thermodynamics, how energy could not be created or destroyed within a closed system, only trans-formed. Yet these materials spontaneously create energy. Lucia pictured these rays as the same ones that came out of the head of Mary, the Blessed Mother, depicted in the painting of the Holy Mother and Child that hung in the Church of Mary Magdalene near Babusia's house. She imagined them as blue bands flecked with gold, miraculous, the rays of God's light, the Holiest of Holy. When he told her these rays were invisible she thought them all the more wondrous.

"Are they miraculous?" she asked.

"What else would you call them? Energy out of nothing? They would have to be."

That afternoon the doctor told Lucia to dress Iréne warmly, as they were going to the laboratory to surprise the children. They stepped out into a blustery day under a sky pregnant with snow. Lucia carried Iréne on her hip and walked alongside the doctor up rue de la Glacière past a shop where pairs of shoes hung from a cord, one on top of the other, like strange fruit.

The School of Physics at ESPCI, École supérieure de physique et de chimie industrielles, where Monsieur worked and where the laboratory was located, was only five blocks away in the rue Lho-mond. Lucia was disappointed when she saw the building. She had been expecting a resolute seat of learning with a fancy façade and wide stone steps leading up to heavy brass doors. Instead she found an ancient building, grimy with age, covered with a scaffolding of rough lumber placed there by workers who were hired to replace a bank of broken windows. The workmen didn't seem to be in a hurry to get started. They stood around hunched over their cigarettes, not doing much of anything.

Lucia was surprised and pleased to find a respectable lobby that smelled of learning: of old books, stuffy laboratories, and floor wax. She was further encouraged by a glass case that displayed portraits of men looking grave and brilliant in their old-fashioned suits. She took them to be famous scientists and was relieved by their presence. She thought that if they worked here once, then it must be a promising place for the Curies. Perhaps her employers would be famous one day, and she would be the cook of famous scientists? Babusia would be so proud.

The doctor led the way through the building and out into the courtyard at the back. Across the yard sat a derelict shed, its glass skylight gleaming as the sun made a brief appearance through the fortress of clouds. An odd figure bundled up against the cold stood over a smelting basin that sat on an iron grate over an open fire. The woman toiled to stir the contents of the basin with a heavy iron bar and looked to the world like the washerwomen who boiled their laundry in vats on the washing boats moored on the river. Lucia didn't recognize her, not until the doctor called out. Marie Curie glanced up and looked surprised. Then she gave them a little wave but didn't come over to greet them. Instead, she continued to stir the basin until, almost reluctantly, she heaved the iron bar out of the pot and left it propped up against a barrel. When she came over to them Lucia saw that she wore an acid-stained smock; her wild, wind-blown hair was flecked with snow and matted with rain; her fingers were stained black; and her eyes were red-rimmed and watering.

"Mé! Mé!" Iréne called out, holding out her chubby arms, impatient to be scooped up by her mother. Madame took her daughter and held her close. She kissed her forehead and then her cheek. Over the top of her head she said: "You shouldn't have brought her here, Papa."

"Nonsense. She wants to be with her mother."

"You know I cannot leave my work."

"You can leave it for a few minutes. Have some tea with us. It will do you good to get out of the cold."

Madame brushed her lips across Iréne's forehead and kissed

her fingers. Then she took one last look at her bubbling smelting pot and grudgingly led the way into the shed where Lucia hoped they could get warm.

The shed was even more miserable than the courtyard. There was a fire going in the stove, but something had to be wrong with it. It was nearly red-hot, yet it didn't give off much heat. Battered pine tables held glass beakers; racks of test tubes; a piece of equipment made of wires, cylinders, and metal poles; and several rows of shallow porcelain dishes containing some kind of solution.

Iréne wiggled out of her mother's arms and went for the shelves that held great glass jars filled with liquid. Lucia picked her up before she could get too far and when she began to whine and squirm, Lucia put her down and held her hand while they walked around room. They took in everything: the jars of liquid packed in baskets filled with straw, the scientific instruments, and the mountain of bulging burlap sacks that reached almost to the ceiling. One of the sacks lay open on the ground, spilling brown dust mixed with pine needles out on the broken asphalt floor. Here and there the dust had turned to mud where water had leaked in through the skylight.

Monsieur had been at the chalkboard but left it without complaint. He cleared away a table so they could have their tea. Madame Curie seemed distracted and impatient. She drank her cup absently, her eyes on the iron basin out in the yard as it continued to boil and bubble and give off a confused cloud of smoke and steam. Lucia didn't know much about science, but she did know a thing or two about a bubbling pot.

"Would you like me to tend it for you, *madame*?"

"It is not necessary. You'll be going soon." She said this looking pointedly at her father-in-law.

The doctor was good at ignoring her looks. "Why not let her do it, Marie. She can stir a pot."

"I tend to pots every day, *madame*. It's no bother."

"This is not cooking, Lulu."

"You don't mind do you, Lulu?" the doctor insisted. Lucia shook her head.

Madame Curie sighed. After a moment or two, she reluctantly gave Lucia a nod, sending her out into the cold.

Lucia smelled the muck the moment she stepped out into the courtyard. It smelled like a witches' brew of corruption, something that should have been buried at midnight and sprinkled with salt. She forced herself to cross the courtyard. Scant flakes of snow were already falling as she lowered the iron bar into the boiling slurry. The fumes wafting up from the basin burned her throat and stung her eyes. She choked on the toxic cloud and fought to keep her eyes open, even though they felt as if they were filled with ground glass. She moved to the left and then to the right, trying to stay out of the shifting wind. Sometimes she'd get it wrong and then it was a struggle just to catch a breath. Coughing and gasping, with tears streaming her cheeks, she wondered how Madame Curie had done it all these weeks.

•   •   •

By the time they left Marie was back at the fire stirring the boiling mass in the basin. It was a leaden afternoon, the sun nothing more than a soggy orb in the sky no brighter than the moon. She gripped the heavy iron bar, her hands beginning to cramp, eyeing the clouds with suspicion. She cursed the weather when it began to snow in earnest and hunched her shoulders against the cold. She did not fancy standing out in a snowstorm. She stood in one the week before and did not relish doing it again. Nevertheless, she knew that even if there was a blizzard and even if her hands and feet froze, she would not desert the work. It was small comfort that this fevered loyalty brought on a warming rush of emotion that, for the moment at least, gave her some relief.

Without warning the wind shifted again, sending the smoke in Marie's direction, but this time she was too quick for it. She stepped out of the way and turned her back on it while still continuing to stir the slurry. She could see by its consistency and by the way it was behaving over the flame that it was nearly complete. Pierre had returned to his work as well. She could see him through the glass seated at a table surrounded by the odd assortment of tubes, pipes, coils, and wires that made up the equipment he built himself.

He really was a gifted physicist. The way he stepped into a problem and inhabited it. He could live inside of it as if it were a house, going from room to room, exploring it from the inside and then stepping out to gain a whole new perspective. She never thought of herself as gifted, only that she was a hard worker. Still, it was gratifying the way he relied on her and appreciated all that she brought to their partnership. Whenever there was a problem of mathematics, he would always say: *Ask Marie. She'll know what to do.*

This was the way they worked together in a state of almost complete absorption. This was their home, not a physical space, but a place all the same, just big enough for the two of them. Here, in this miserable shed—their affectionate term for the hangar—they worked in tandem. Marie labored with twenty-five kilos of pitchblende residue at a time, reducing down the chemical makeup, hunting for radium in barium chloride.

The residue was the by-product of uranium extraction, the dust, dirt, and pine needles left after the first reductions. It was thought to be worthless and left in piles on the forest floor not far from the chemical plant. It was not worthless, however, at least not to the Curies. To them it was precious, buried treasure; it was radium, their progeny, a sibling to Iréne.

While Marie labored to isolate radium, Pierre studied the properties of the rays it emitted. Each day the Curies were thrilled, frustrated, and amazed by all the tricks their rays could do. Each night they returned home broken by fatigue but buoyed up by curiosity and a steadfast commitment to isolate the radium salts and hold it in their hands.

Marie was confident that through these reductions and fractional crystallizations she could tease out enough radium to get an atomic weight. Once that happened it would be added to the periodic table and no one could refute their claim to the new element. It would be theirs, their sole achievement, provided of course, they got there first.

When the solution was done, she put on the smelter's gloves, braced her legs, and lifted the iron basin off the fire. She struggled under the weight of it as she lugged it into the hangar, where she and Pierre poured it into a great glass vessel. There it would sit until the solution separated and the less soluble material could be collected and further reduced through chemical washings and fractionations.

Since it was late Marie made them tea and they sat by the stove, their hands warming on the steaming mugs. This was a particularly enjoyable time of the afternoon when most of the work was done and they could take an inventory of the day, speculating on the outcome of their research: on the possibilities, the applications, the implications for physics and the nature of matter and its effect on energy.

Pierre was finding that these rays could penetrate certain materials. Some could penetrate glass or foil, others thicker materials. What's more they could induce radioactivity in other substances. As a result, their hangar had become quite active, which was confusing their research, as it became difficult to pinpoint the exact source of the radiation. It was frustrating but, at the same time, exciting. Pierre had begun to pace, as he often did when he was trying on a new notion. He had just discovered that radiation could color glass.

Marie never sat idle for long. She didn't have a minute to waste. She wondered if Rutherford, Schmidt, or Villari ever took time to drink a cup of tea. Somehow she didn't think so. "Hounds at our heels, Pierre," she often said, referring to her rivals: the New Zealander, German, and Italian—although she knew he did not share her urgency to be the first.

The tea was still hot when she put it down and crossed to the table where a row of porcelain evaporating basins sat out of the way of the leaking roof. She had been watching these fractions because she had somehow managed to keep them free of wood ash and coal dust. One particular basin held an intricate construct of barium crystals that she wanted to collect and measure before she and her husband left for the day. She picked up the bowl and began to carry it across the uneven asphalt floor to Pierre's quadrant electrometer that she had hooked up to an ionization chamber.

The chamber consisted of two metal plates, one higher than the other. On the lower plate she would place the barium crystals now in powder form. The rays emitted by this radioactive powder would cause the air molecules to release electrons, which, in turn, would create a weak electrical current that flowed between the metal plates. This current would continue to flow along a wire that had been connected to the electrometer. There it would move a needle that had been attached to a mirror. By throwing a ray of light on the mirror she could watch the needle move along a graduated dial and in this way begin to take a measurement of the current.

It was a delicate operation that required Marie to sit for hours, rigid, fully engaged, holding a chronometer in one hand and weights in the other. At her side a piezoelectric quartz was stretched and weighted by a series of small weights. When stretched, the quartz emitted an infinitesimal current that could be measured reliably. By comparing the two currents over an exact unit of time, a precise measurement of the radioactivity of the barium could be taken.

It took absolute concentration. The wrist and arm had to remain flexible while adding and removing the weights from the quartz until the current emitted by the quartz matched the current emitted by the barium. Pierre liked to brag that only his wife knew how to take these measurements and challenged their friends to try to match her. None could.

"How can we work like this, Marie? The equipment is active, our clothes are active, everything is active. It's impossible."

"We'll manage, my love."

"We need a new laboratory. Surely, you can see that."

"And how can we do that?"

"We have to do it. It's affecting out calculations. We can't work like this."

"It's just a problem, Pierre. Not a disaster," she said, keeping her eyes on the fragile crystals as she navigated the floor. She was only half listening. He was right, of course, but there was nothing to be done about it. They didn't have the money and that was that.

Her mind drifted back to a dinner they had gone to the other night honoring Henri Becquerel and the work he had done on the rays. During the speeches she had amused herself by calculating the laboratories that could be built from the sale of diamonds worn by the society women that night.

It was just a flick, a momentary stumble. Her toe grazed the edge of a broken slab of asphalt, but she overcompensated and a moment later the contents of the basin, two months of killing work, spilled out on the offending floor.

She stood there holding the empty evaporating bowl, stunned by the enormity of the loss. "Pierre," she choked.

He froze while he took it in, the white solution against the black asphalt. Then he came and put his arms around her. He didn't say anything at first. He let her rail against the floor, against the shed and their deplorable working conditions. He let her cry more from exhaustion than from loss. Finally, when she had spent her misery and frustration, she buried her face against his chest, taking a kind of primordial comfort from his warmth, the beating of his heart, and his familiar smell, wood smoke and kerosene.

"What are we going to do?" she asked.

"We are going to go on."

"But we are running out of time."

"We'll be all right, Marie. Things will come right, if you let them." He looked down at her with an expression that was at once sad, slightly confused, and so authentic it was heartbreaking. She wanted to tell him how much she loved him, but no spoken language could encompass all that she felt.

She tilted her face up to be kissed. "No words," she said gently.

He wiped the soot from her chin and leaned down to kiss her. "No words," he murmured, which was their code for love.

•    •    •

That night Iréne sat in her high chair and played with her food. She threw it on the floor, mashed it into her little fist, and smeared it into her hair. She found a number of uses for it, but none of them included putting it into her mouth. Lucia tried to make a game of it. She made funny faces, imitated a chicken, but nothing would induce the child to eat. Finally, she had to admit defeat and give her tapioca pudding and pippins.

The Curies came home late. Now that Lucia knew more about what Madame Curie did all day, she understood why she came home each night half destroyed by the work.

"She has been calling for you, *madame*," Lucia said, taking their coats at the door. "She won't go to sleep until you go in."

Monsieur was already at the table laying out the laboratory notebooks. As usual, he grumbled about his wife going in to see their child.

"Did she have a proper supper?" Madame Curie asked Lucia.

"I tried, Madame. I really did. But all she wanted was her tapioca and pippins."

"Oh, Lulu," she said, sounding annoyed and disappointed. "The one thing I asked you to do."

The doctor looked up from his medical journal. "She tried, Marie. I saw her. The child is stubborn. She takes after her mother."

Madame Curie gave him a look and went in to see her daughter, while Lucia stood there feeling scorched and flat.

"She's tired, Lulu," the doctor said gently. "You mustn't take it to heart."

"Yes, *monsieur*," she managed to say, before retreating to the kitchen.

She put their supper in the oven to warm and slumped over

the kitchen table, dropping her chin on her hands. Nothing would please them. It did not matter if the flue was clean, if the stove was polished. She could serve thin soup and stale bread and none of it would make a bit of difference. Why did she even bother?

She swept a small pile of breadcrumbs into her palm and threw them into the sink. Then she opened up the oven door and bent down to retrieve their supper. She had had enough of their poverty and their dedication to hard work, enough of washing their threadbare clothes, and looking at their exhausted gray faces. They were wearing her out.

She could hear them at the table going over their computations in the notebook. They were animated and excited, as they usually were whenever they went over the day's work. In the past she liked listening to them as they spun off each other's ideas. *What if?* they would say to each other: *What if the atom isn't immutable?*

Immutable.

"What if there are smaller particles within it? What if these smaller particles are in flux? What if it is this flux that causes the energy?" They spoke a foreign language that Lucia could not understand. Theirs was the language of mathematics. Still, she understood and admired their excitement.

"We have the first two, Marie," Monsieur was saying as Lucia came in to serve their supper. "But it's the third that interests me."

"Villiard's."

"Rutherford's calling it Gamma."

"Gamma. Is it ionizing?"

"Yes, but it's not like the others and it's penetrating, even a few centimeters of lead won't stop it. Not entirely. Here, look at this."

Madame bent over the notebook. Her dinner remained untouched. She looked up briefly. "On the magnetic field?"

"And the electronic too."

She studied the figures again and then lifted her head. "No effect."

He smiled at her. After that came a flurry of calculations that sent Lucia back to the kitchen.

She spent the rest of the evening scrubbing the pans and putting away the dishes. When she was finished she found that the slop bucket was full again, despite emptying it only that afternoon. Since there was no kitchen maid to take it down Lucia threw a shawl around her shoulders and tramped down the three flights of stairs to the courtyard. She muttered to herself the whole way down.

It was a clear, cold night, the leaves crunchy with frost. It smelled like snow, but for now the clouds hovered on the horizon leaving the sky a layered scrim of stars. She was glad for the shawl, but wished she had put on a hat. She crossed the courtyard and dumped the slops into the foul wooden barrel that sat behind the box hedge and was just turning back when she saw a dark figure standing in the shadows. An abrupt memory of her grandmother's warnings about white slavers sent a crackle of fear through her.

"Who is it?" she called out, trying to sound brave.

"Ever look at the constellations, Lulu?" It was Madame, her thin shawl thrown around her shoulders, her head tilted back, her eyes on the sky. She was shivering but seemed unaware of the cold. "It's a good night for it. Look, there's the Great Chariot."

Reluctantly, Lucia glanced up at the sky. "I don't see a chariot."

"See? Right there." Madame Curie came over and pointed up at the stars. "Here, follow my finger."

Lucia did not want to, although despite her effort to stay aloof, she found herself following Madame Curie's pointing finger.

"See? There is the box and there is the shaft. Can you see it now?"

She could see it and said as much, forgetting for the moment that she was supposed to be upset.

"It's part of Ursa Major. You know Ursa Major?"

She shook her head.

"It makes up the tail of the Great Bear and its hindquarters. See there is Merak and Dubhe. See the two stars? They're neighbors. Now, come closer. If you move away from Duhbe and go over there to that bright star"—Lucia leaned in to follow her mistress's finger and got the smell of wood smoke and unwashed hair—"you come to Polaris. It's not the brightest star in the sky, but it's brighter than the others in the constellation. Can you see it?"

Lucia nodded. She loved looking at the stars. Babusia always called them God's quilt. She often imagined the angels in heaven snuggling down beneath them.

After that there was an explanation about Polaris, how it was important to sailors and to celestial navigation. Madame Curie explained that it was also called the North Star and that the entire northern sky rotated around it and that's what made it so important if you wanted to know where you were going.

While Madame went on, Lucia's mind began to drift back to the laboratory, to the pile of pitchblende in the corner, to the noxious fumes, and the boiling mass. "Why do you work so hard? Why do you keep going?"

Madame Curie hesitated before answering. "I'm looking for something, Lulu. Something important. And I think I'm about to find it."

"The miracle rays."

She laughed. "Yes. They are a miracle I suppose. At least they seem that way. But that's because we don't know enough about them. They are breaking the rules, you see."

"Energy out of nothing."

Madame gave her a sidelong glance. "You've been talking to Papa."

"I was curious. Is that wrong?"

Madame Curie stopped and regarded her with a look of sudden interest. "No, that is not wrong," she said. "In fact, that is right. Very right."

She stood there a moment longer and then pulled her shawl up around her shoulders and started for the stairs. "Come along, Lulu. Put on your woolens. We're going out."

"Now? But it's late."

"Dress warmly. The clouds are blowing in. It's going to snow."

A few minutes later they were dressed for the cold and climbing back down the stairs. They stepped out into the frosty night just as it was beginning to snow, flat white paddies drifting through the lamplight. They walked the few blocks to rue Lhomond, to the hangar in the courtyard. It was dark and Madame had to fumble with the key in the lock. When she finally got it open she stepped inside, leaving Lucia to stop at the threshold and gape in amazement.

"What's this?" she whispered, astonished and alarmed by what she could not explain. She looked around at the jars of solutions on the shelves, clear and colorless in the daylight but glowing blue in the dark. It was like nothing she had ever seen before. It was some kind of magic. The entire room was glowing blue. She thought this must be what a fish sees swimming in a lake, looking up through the layers of sunlit water to the surface. The jars shimmered blue like the robes of the Blessed Virgin Mary, blue like the sky in heaven, not of this earth, of another realm, ethereal, and frail. And in that moment Lucia realized it was everything she had been waiting for. The reason Saint Lucyna sent her to be with this odd family. Here was the Blessed Trinity, made visible for human eyes. God was in this room with them. This was his light.

"It is so lovely," she breathed. So lovely, in fact, that it nearly brought tears to her eyes. "Some kind of miracle," she murmured.

"No. Not a miracle."

"What then?"

"Radium."

"What makes it glow like that?"

"Radioactivity."

"And what makes the radioactivity?"

Madame Curie smiled. "Exactly."

II.

# CHAPTER 7

# March 1903

Morris Arlington was not one for the ocean. He hated swimming in it or traveling on it. Even the smell of the briny air or the feel of sand between his toes set his nerves on edge. He was never one to stand on the shore and watch the waves roll in with nauseating regularity, which is why he lived in Cincinnati, about as far away from the sea as anyone could get. Unfortunately, he was often called to Europe and while he could usually put off one or two trips, there inevitably came a time when he had to make the crossing. When that time came he employed various strategies for surviving an ocean voyage, some better than others, although none were as effective as staying home.

On this particular trip, he and his wife arrived in New York City a few days early and checked into their little hotel on the West Side across from the park. It was not a particularly fashionable establishment, but a comfortable one where they were known and where they could count on good service. As soon as they were settled, Arlington laid down for his nap, while Edith went to the shipping office to look over the passenger list.

She wanted to find a suitable cabin mate for Arlington. Since she rarely made the crossing herself, he would be required to share his cabin with a stranger. There were always problems living in such close quarters with someone you didn't know, but he had strategies for that too. For example, he had found over the years that it was best to book a cabin with a fella employed in a conservative occupation, like a minister or a banker. The thought being that a man of the cloth or a bank manager might naturally have healthy habits: one who kept early hours, a moderate drinker, a fresh-air enthusiast.

Unfortunately, occupation alone didn't always guarantee that. On one painful crossing, Arlington shared his cabin with an accountant who had a story for every occasion and liked to tell them well into the night. On another trip, his cabin mate, a recently widowed dentist, refused to keep the porthole open even in calm weather. It was a mystery to Arlington why anyone would pay extra for a deck-cabin and put up with the noise of the promenade deck only to keep the porthole closed. The whole point of a cabin above decks was fresh air.

Edith came to see him off on the day he was to set sail on the S.S. *St. Paul* bound for Southampton. They arrived in a cab and had to wait their turn on the wharf so they could get closer to the stevedores, who were loading the trunks. The wharf was mobbed with passengers and visitors, stewards, longshoremen, and hawkers. The second- and third-class gangway was crowded with passengers, an undulating mass of parasols, hats verdant with vegetation, men in homburgs and straw boaters shuffling up the gangplank with suitcases in hand.

A band played somewhere on the upper decks while stewards and bellboys in crisp uniforms hurried about, seeing to the first-class passengers and their luggage. Edith forged on ahead to the second-class dining room, the first of many stops to see to Arlington's requirements. She was a breathlessly pleasant woman, well mannered, diffident, and agreeable, who liked nothing better than to compliment and thank those who served her. However, when it came to securing her husband's comfort, she could be demanding and even unreasonable on occasion. Once or twice she had lost her temper in public.

It had been a great sorrow to Edith that she could not have children, although Arlington never minded. Nevertheless, one of the consolations of being barren was that she was able to keep her figure well into her thirties. The other, at least as far as Arlington was concerned, was that she seemed to have an endless supply of time and energy to devote to his endeavors, a circumstance they both came to expect.

That morning she strode into the dining room, found the head steward, and told him to reserve a table in the center of the room. She always booked a table there for steadiness. Then she spent an hour meeting passengers on deck and in the lounges, until she found just the right people to fill it. Since Arlington would be sitting at the same table throughout the voyage, Edith knew it was important to people it with an interesting, lively group. After that she booked Arlington's baths with the bath steward and his midmorning and late-afternoon tea with the cabin steward, checked in with the purser to make sure his trunk was accounted for, inspected his cabin, and put out a framed photograph of herself on the nightstand.

By the time the Blue Peter flag was hoisted up the foremast signaling one hour before castoff, Edith was in the lounge having coffee with Arlington. She lingered there until the big horn blew, said her good-bye on the gangway under a hail of bright streamers, and blew him two kisses from the wharf as the tugs got underway. He felt like a fool returning them, so he didn't bother.

Arlington spent the next three mornings in a steamer chair under a heavy blanket with his eyes locked on the horizon because he had read somewhere that it would calm his stomach. He made a point not to look at the choppy waves tipped with white foam—instead focusing on the faint gray line where the sea met the sky. He avoided using words like *rolling waves* and *omelet*, because they tended to bring up what little was left in his stomach. Despite these precautions a good deal of his morning was spent within easy reach of the railing.

On the third morning they were locked into a fog bank that blanketed the sea and left a filmy layer of moisture on the jacket of his unread book. The steward came by at midmorning to bring him the tea his wife had ordered. Arlington liked it with milk, but she specifically left word to leave it out as she knew how he would be feeling on those first few mornings. The clear broth arrived at noon just as the fog was beginning to lift; he didn't have the stomach for it and left it to grow cold on the little table beside his chair.

Arlington was a big man, over six feet tall, with the body of an athlete. He prided himself on his rigorous regime of healthy diet and exercise. Every morning at home he sat in the sauna by the side of the house and then jumped into the nearby pond to invigorate his pores and get his circulation pumping. Each month he fasted for two days, and, believing in the efficacious properties of tobacco, allowed himself a cigar every night. He knew that anyone looking at him would not think that any part of his body could be weak. Yet his stomach let him down during every crossing, laying him low and causing him much embarrassment. So much so, that for the first three days, sometimes even four, he would have little to do with his fellow passengers, shunning any activity that required him to get up from his steamer chair or berth.

"Mr. Arlington, let me introduce myself," the stocky gentleman said, as he held out his hand. "Professor Lilliman. Pleased to meet you."

Arlington had seen the fella approach but assumed he was going for one of the empty chairs down the row. He was sure they had never met before, although his face did look familiar: the bland watery eyes, the moist, eager mouth, the thicket of coarse gray hair combed neatly to one side. A man of his age had no right to so much hair. Arlington's had thinned considerably in the last few years, to the point where he felt more comfortable wearing a hat than not.

After they shared a brief handshake, the trespasser continued: "I'm not actually a professor, mind you. That's only my stage name. My real name is just plain Lilliman. Alfonse Lilliman. I'm telling you this because I want you to know that I'm being honest with you."

Arlington knew that he should invite the fella to sit down, but he didn't want him hanging around. He had no idea who he was and didn't want to find out. Though, it was somewhat gratifying to see how his powers of observation had not dimmed despite his present misery. It was obvious that this poor fella lived on a diet of starches, fats, and salt. He could tell that in a glance by the yellowing whites of the man's eyes, his sweaty palm, and his pasty complexion. This was not a healthy man.

"You all right, Mr. Arlington?"

"Yes, 'course I'm all right," Arlington replied, with as much conviction as he could muster.

The man looked a little dubious but went on. "You may have seen my poster in the lobby—Professor Lilliman, Test Medium? I've been hired by the line to perform in the Regency Lounge on alternate nights. I get a pretty good crowd in there. Can't say it's me who brings them in. We're on a boat in the middle of the ocean. Where else are they going to go?"

Arlington gave him a nod, for any other movement in that moment might have proved disastrous. The Regency Lounge was where they served breakfast. Breakfast brought up eggs, and eggs brought up omelet. "What is it that you want, Mr. Lilliman?"

"Well, when I heard that you were on board, I'll admit it did make me a little nervous. My wife urged me to speak to you. She said you looked like a reasonable man."

"Speak to me about what?"

"About my performance. Of course, I know all about you and your work. I'm a member of the SPR." Arlington was the president and a founding member of the Society for Psychical Research. "I get the newsletter. I read about Mrs. Boyne and the Martin sisters. I'm just a showman, Mr. Arlington. I only wish to entertain. I'm not really a medium. I do tricks, not very good ones, but people go along with them. They are generally nice and forgiving. They like to be entertained, so they make it easy for me."

"And what's it got to do with me?"

"The thing is my wife and I agree that someone of your stature, exposing the best as you've done over the years, well, someone like you is bound to see right through me. So, that's why I've come to you. I don't want you to give me away. It's all for fun, you see. I don't hurt anybody. I just give them a good time."

"Mr. Lilliman, you've got nothing to worry about. I've no desire to expose you. I won't even be attending your performance, so I won't have the opportunity."

"Mighty decent of you, Mr. Arlington. The wife will be much relieved. She was having bad dreams ever since we left port. Afraid they would tar and feather me or some such malarkey." Here he paused as if trying to decide if a handshake was in order. "Yeah, well, I won't trouble you again. Get some rest. And thanks again."

By the time Arlington returned to his cabin he had to admit that he was feeling better. He was even hungry and ate a few slices of dry toast. After that he straightened up and organized his things. Fortunately, his cabin mate was out—a chiropractor from Columbus, a regular sport. The man had thoughtfully left some room in the closet and had lined up his things neatly in the lavatory. Arlington hung up his shirts, put out his shaving kit, threw out the tea that had been ordered for him, and put his wife's photograph back in the trunk.

·　·　·

Four days later the ship docked in Southampton and then it was on to Le Havre by ferry and finally the train to Paris where Edith had booked him and Eusapia Palladino into the Balmoral in the rue de Castiglione. He had braved the Atlantic Ocean, spilled his vitality on the rolling waves, all because Sapia was doing a series of sittings for some of the best scientific minds in Paris and he could not trust her to do it on her own.

On the night of the first sitting Arlington lingered in a corner of the hotel lobby, half hidden by a dusty palm, waiting for the illustrious Eusapia Palladino to make her entrance. After a half hour or so she stepped off the lift like the grande dame she imagined herself to be, a monarch striding forth among her people, shoulders back, head up, chest out, eyes straight ahead. She was a plump woman in her fifties, not elegant or attractive, but substantial, a solid presence, heavily corseted in her full skirts. Her eyes were her best feature; dark and deep set, they gave her the requisite air of mystery. Arlington suspected that without them she would have looked like what she was—a coarse Neapolitan peasant, barely literate, who had somehow stumbled upon an extraordinary gift. For all her faults he knew her to be the most talented medium in Europe, perhaps in the world, which is why he put up with her balderdash.

It was her habit to wear her black hair swept back off her forehead, prominently displaying a swath of white hair growing on the left side of her scalp just above the hairline. It was said that she acquired it after an accident when she was a baby and that it was a sign of her powers. On several occasions, while Sapia was entranced, Arlington and the other sitters felt a breeze coming from that spot. Not a cool breeze, but a definite movement of air.

Arlington could gauge her moods just by looking at her. She didn't speak a word of English and neither of them spoke French well, yet the moment he saw her walk into the lobby with its dark wood paneling, faded chintz, and hoity-toity English tourists, he knew she was in a good mood. That made him happy and a little nervous.

He hesitated just for a moment, a heartbeat really. The phrase *girding one's loins* came to mind as he lifted a hand and walked over to greet her. She seemed calm, and that wasn't like her. Usually, she was self-absorbed and histrionic. Her composure was unnerving and at first he didn't know what to think about it, until he bent down to kiss her cheek and smelled the alcohol on her breath.

"You've been drinking," he muttered, as he escorted her out the door.

She stopped at the top of the steps and turned on him, her lips compressed into a line of wounded indignation. "Are you accusing me?" she said in her bad French. What she really said was, "Are you amusing me?" *Est-ce que vous m'amusez?* But Arlington knew what she meant.

"You know what alcohol does to your powers," he said, while they waited on the curb for the taxi. "These are important men of science. Their opinion matters."

"Cannot I ever be happy? Even for one night?"

"If you had a drink, even a sip—" He clutched her arm and helped her into the taxi. He wanted to say something about Cambridge, but thought better of it. Instead he gave the address to the driver and climbed in beside her.

"Are doubting me, Arlington? Are you accusing me of the sabotage?"

"That's a little theatrical."

"I do not like it," she pouted. "It is not right. You hurt my feelings and now I do not know what about tonight. You know how these uprisings affect my powers. How shall I be tonight with your black energy around my head? You make angry at me and that makes more harm than any drop of wine."

Arlington sighed heavily and kept his eyes on the passing scene outside the window. It had begun to rain and a waiter was dragging a table in from the sidewalk. Of course it was up to him to make it right. It was always up to him. If she hadn't been so remarkable, he would never have put up with her, with her demands and her mercurial temperament, with the hysterical telegrams and the late-night tantrums. Unfortunately, he never met another medium as talented as Eusapia Palladino and probably never would.

Even so, he refused to chalk up his success or the success of the Society for Psychical Research to just one medium. The society sponsored many—and many of them had achieved relative success. It was true that none enjoyed an international reputation, but he certainly wouldn't say that the tenfold increase in funding and the growing membership was due solely to Eusapia Palladino.

"It is just that you are such a marvel, Sapia. You have such a gift. A marvel of nature. *Une merveille de la nature.*" He probably said it wrong, but she wouldn't have noticed. "I want the whole world to see you as I do. I want you to shine." He laid it on thick until she began to relax, her expression softened, and she patted his hand. Fortunately, she was easily managed with a little flattery.

That evening they gathered in Professor Charles Richet's apartment for a light supper in the dining room. Eight of them were seated around the carved oak table, including a journalist, a disagreeable fella, whom Arlington distrusted on sight.

Arlington had a hard and fast rule about journalists. They were never invited to the sittings. In fact, he tried to keep them away from Sapia altogether, although that was not always possible. Experience told him that the press had a deleterious effect on clairvoyants. Journalists tended to weaken and confuse them, ruffling the *Geist* in the room, causing psychic torpor, and generally making it harder for them to contact those on the other side. Unfortunately, there was nothing to be done about this one. He happened to be Professor Richet's younger brother and so he would stay.

At the first opportunity Arlington took Sapia aside to warn her. She was in high spirits, seated at the table surrounded by men, happy to be the center of attention. She waved him off and told him to stop worrying and, moreover, to stop bothering her, she was having fun. She had been flirting with the scientists at the table all evening, seemingly unaware that not one had flirted back, that their interest in her was strictly professional. She told her stories, the ones Arlington had heard many times before: the train breaking down in the snowbank outside of Heidelberg, the séance in Petersburg, her audience with the Danish queen. She laughed too loudly, ate too eagerly, wetly smacking her lips, until he wanted to clamp his hand over her mouth. He tried telling himself as he had done a dozen times before: Her behavior was no reflection on him. They were not related. She was as much a foreigner to him as she was to the others. He had found her and brought her to the attention of the scientific community, but that did not make him responsible for her behavior.

He sat there in a cloud of humiliation waiting for the séance to begin. Once that happened he hoped to be home free. He had little

doubt that when they saw what she could do they would understand why he had brought her here. They would see that there was
more to the great Eusapia Palladino than her table manners.

He wondered if they viewed him as a gentleman and not as
a foreigner, if they recognized that he had a legitimate place
among them. He knew that as president of the Society for Psychical Research he had a claim to their respect. The movement—for it
had become a movement under his leadership—had spread across
the United States and had grown threefold since he took the helm.
At home he was well known, a celebrity in the psychic world, but
here in Europe his standing was less certain. He kept looking for an
opening to insert this information naturally, but none came up. He
didn't want to force it and look bigheaded or worse, like some kind
of boob.

The company moved to the séance room and began to take
their seats. At the sitters' table Arlington directed Charles Richet
to sit on Sapia's right while he took his customary place on her left.
At the last minute, when the photographer called Professor Richet
over to ask him a question, the younger Richet, the journalist, who
had been watching Arlington orchestrate the seating, took advantage of his brother's absence and stole his seat.

Arlington was surprised but decided not to say anything. He
didn't think it was necessary. He assumed that once the elder Richet
returned he would take his rightful place. Instead, the man merely
noted that his brother had taken his seat and found another. Before
Arlington could object, or more precisely had time to think about
the consequences of objecting, Sapia appeared at the door accompanied by the trusted maidservant, who had examined her. After
the maid testified she had found nothing and was dismissed, Sapia
took her place at the head of the table in front of the medium's cabinet. The gas was lowered and the candles were lit. She took young
Richet's hand in hers and reached out for Arlington's. Then she
slipped her foot under Arlington's boot and presumably under the
journalist's, lowered her head, and began.

The stenographer for the evening was Professor Pierre Curie, who was sitting at his own table by the window. Curie lit a candle and by the light of it began writing down the time in the laboratory notebook. He added the temperature in the room, the humidity, and made a note of the rain outside the window. Then he sat back and absently combed his fingers through his beard while he waited for the next entry.

Arlington knew that nothing would happen until Sapia's breathing changed. Her quickening breath was the signal that contact had been made between her and John King, her spirit guide on the other side. He listened to her breathing, waiting for it to grow heavy, for the groans and whimpering to begin. Outside the rain thrummed against the windows. Thunder rumbled off in the distance or perhaps it was just a passing carriage. Sapia's head lowered slowly, until her chin came to rest on the cameo at her throat—still her breathing remained even and regular.

They all heard a faint screech of alarm, but no one reacted to it. Professor Curie made a note of it. "We have mice," Professor Richet remarked somewhat apologetically. Curie wrote *Mice* and added a question mark as an afterthought. Minutes passed and when Professor Curie's candle began to gutter, Arlington thought it was probably a draft from the windows and said as much. Curie noted *draft* in the book.

Nearly an hour passed and the séance remained uneventful, yet Arlington had been fully engaged the whole time, his attention divided between Sapia and the journalist. Young Richet sat with his back to the window, silhouetted by the frail light seeping in through the curtains. Arlington could see that the young man kept a close watch on Sapia. He imagined the journalist's crafty eyes fixed on her every move—suspicious, superior, and remote; his boot on her shoe; his hand clasping hers. He told himself to relax, that this was Paris, not Cambridge, and he had nothing to fear.

Another quarter of an hour and still nothing happened. The rain had stopped, and now and again, the clamor of a passing carriage broke the silence. The house was so quiet Arlington surmised that the family and servants had been given an order to keep it that way. At one point he heard a door close quietly and footsteps retreat down the hall.

"John?" Sapia had lifted her head and appeared to be listening. "John, is that you?" *Giovanni, è che voi?*

Arlington couldn't be sure, but he thought he heard a male voice muttering in the darkness. He didn't know if it was one of the sitters or perhaps something else. "Did you hear that?" he whispered.

"What?" his host wanted to know.

"I thought I—" he broke off to listen. "That. Did you hear that?" It was only a word or two, unintelligible, but it sounded complaining and impatient.

Professor Richet said, "Professor Arlington and I heard a male voice in the room." Curie noted it with the time and temperature.

"John, wait. Wait!" Sapia spoke in Italian. She wasn't shouting, but against the silence in the room her voice boomed loud and demanding. *Giovanni, attendere, prego.* She went on a bit, pleading and cajoling, but apparently it made no difference. "He will not listen," she said in Italian. *Egli non vuole ascoltare.* Then in French she added: "I do not know. I do not know what I do? He says I have been bad. How was I bad?" she asked the air.

Suddenly there was a loud slap and her head jerked to one side. She cried out as if in pain. Her hand flew to her cheek. "Did you see that? How he treats me. He is so cruel. Look what he did." She took her hand away and showed her cheek to the men around the table.

Curie wrote: *Red cheek consistent with a slap* and noted the time and temperature.

After another half hour or so, it was apparent that the sitting was a blank. Sapia was exhausted and dejected. She couldn't understand what had happened. With what little French was available to her she tried to explain about John King.

"He refuses to stay. He will not say why. He is angry with me for something I do. I do not know what. I tried to reason with him, but he would not listen. He flies into these hot angers and there is nothing I can do."

Richet tried to reassure Eusapia. "If you knew how many blanks we've had in this room, you wouldn't think twice about it."

"He only does this to torture me. He is so hard and cruel." Her voice was soggy with self-pity. She eyed a corner of the ceiling. "You are not a nice man, John King. *Tu non sei un uomo gentile.* And I don't care if you are angry with me."

There were more reassurances at the door. No one seemed to be bothered by the blank, only Sapia. Arlington noticed that the reporter watched them get into the cab. He stood there after the others had gone inside. It was probably this fella's fault that the night had been a failure. Arlington knew his kind—the spoilers. How their energy could taint the room.

"You were right, Arlington," Sapia said. She pronounced it *Ar-lean-ton.* "I did take a sip of wine. Perhaps two. I did not think it would matter."

She wanted reassurance from him, to be petted and fussed over. She wanted to hear the words that would once again make her feel safe and calm. Unfortunately, he was too tired for that. It was not the usual fatigue that came from the late hour or from the rigors of a long journey. It was a crushing weariness that came from the steady necessity of holding himself back, of having to become someone else: the patient father, the kindly counselor, the forgiving impresario. There was no room for him in this arrangement. He was the planet orbiting her bright star, subjugating his own health and happiness to her moods, her fears, and her constant needs.

Now, for the first time in their long association, he wondered if it was all worth it. There were American mediums of equal stature, or if not equal, then at least good enough to be developed. They wouldn't be difficult to find. He had a reputation and a steady stream of applicants. All he had to do was look.

He gazed out the window at the tumult on the boulevard. They had just passed the park and were approaching the Odéon where the taxis were already lined up at the curb waiting for the audience to let out. The drivers stood nearby hunkered down in their great coats, the horses shifting their weight from one foot to another, shaking the water from their backs, and marking the air with their patient breath.

Sapia looked miserable huddled under a mound of carriage blankets, watching the café society pageant out on the street. He knew he had to pull himself together. If the séance had any hope of success, he had to give her what strength he had, nourish her, and bring her back from the dark place. Her powers were so fragile, so mercurial. He had to guard them closely. When she faltered, he had to hold her up. He had to keep her away from the shoals, the fearful places that drove her to take desperate measures.

"Don't let this little setback bother you," he said, taking Sapia's hand. "You've had a blank before. It means nothing. You know that. John will be back. He always comes back."

She looked over at him with grateful tears. "Do you really mean that?"

"Of course. I have no doubt you will be miraculous tomorrow. How could you be anything less?"

She smiled at him through her tears and brought his hand up to her lips. He patted her hand before returning it to her lap. Out on the sidewalk several young men in evening clothes emerged from a café. Their leader in a top hat and overcoat waved a glove at their taxi, but then seeing that it was occupied yelled something that Arlington couldn't quite hear. He sat back in his seat, closed his eyes, and smiled at the one happy thought he had held all evening. Tomorrow Sapia would be sleeping until two, which meant he would have the whole morning to himself.

•   •   •

The next evening Arlington took Sapia out for an early supper at Café Tortoni. He knew she would like it because it was only a few blocks from the opera and she enjoyed watching the fancy carriages drive by while she ate. She sat in the chair opposite, not bothering to keep up her end of the conversation, watching the parade of plumed horses trot by with their liveried footmen standing on the footboards or riding in the rumble. Once the food came she ate mechanically and afterward ordered her customary ice.

"I know it will be fine, Arlington. I am not to worry."

"Of course, you'll be wonderful. You're always wonderful."

"Yes. I know that. And John assures me that all will be well. I contacted him last night before I went to bed. Did I tell you?"

He nodded and took a sip of wine. It was the third time she mentioned it.

"He said that he has it all arranged. I will be as usual. Of course, I will be wonderful. When am I not, eh?"

Arlington told her that he was not worried, not one bit, and that everything would be fine. He managed to sound convincing, even though in truth he had a bad case of the jitters and for a good reason. Cambridge started out this way, with a blank, then assurances and denials, and finally the withering fear of another blank. He couldn't go through that again, the mortification, the derisive looks, and later the formal accusations in the journals. He remembered, after the humiliating event, standing by the front door. No one to see them off—only the parlor maid, who handed them their coats and sent them out into the night to find their own way home. No, he was never going through that again.

•    •    •

Arlington didn't know how the professor's brother secured the seat on Sapia's right for a second night. He told Sapia to request that someone else sit there, but when the time came and the brother took the seat, she was distracted and did nothing to stop him. Now the journalist held her hand and was watching her every move, alert, predacious—a danger to everything Arlington held dear in his life: his reputation, the society, his livelihood. Even in the murky light Arlington could see that she had the man's full attention. Once he even peered under the tablecloth, no doubt to verify that her other foot was being properly controlled.

Arlington sat on her left, gripping her hand, keeping a steady pressure on it, and finding some comfort in the fact that he knew for sure he had it all to himself. Her hands had always been slightly repugnant to him. The short, pudgy fingers, pale and moist, reminded him of something he might find under the house. Even so he would not let go, even when her palm grew slippery with sweat. Then he simply moved his grip up to her wrist and held on with his thumb and fingers, giving his palm a good airing out.

It was not Sapia's habit to sit still during a sitting. She often thrust her hands into the air without warning, first one, then the other, writhing right and left as if trying to escape. On this night at first nothing happened. They sat for a while listening to the crowds in the street. At some point she became restless and began shifting about as if she were trying to get comfortable.

A few minutes after that she began to whimper like an animal.

The whimper turned into groaning, her breath quickened, and then, without warning, she arched her back and thrust her breasts out as if she were in the throes of carnal passion. She stabbed the air with her left hand, then her right, then her left again, while Arlington held on.

The table began to rise in minute increments, stopping, hanging there, and then rising again. Magnesium flashes exploded, one, two, three, illuminating Sapia, a corner in the room, and the mantelpiece. The bright flashes blinded Arlington and for a moment he couldn't see anything but spots. He began to panic. He had no idea what she was doing. She could have been up to anything and he wouldn't have been able to stop her. He gripped her wrist and fought down the urge to yell *Cambridge!*

Someone shouted in the room. It was a loud bark and everyone jumped. The door slammed shut and then it sounded as if it were raining, right there in the room, as if there was a downpour inside the very house. Water seemed to be sheeting down from the ceiling, a deluge from every corner, and yet nothing was wet.

The sitters called out their impressions to Professor Curie, who wrote them down with rapid efficiency. At 10:55 Professor Richet shouted that the door had slammed on its own. Arlington added that he had control of the medium's right hand and that his left boot was on top of her right shoe. "Her head is resting on my shoulder and she seems to be asleep." The phantom rain was louder. "It's all around us," Richet shouted out. "Note the temperature, Curie. It could be important."

The rain stopped three minutes later. The room was silent, until a man's voice could be heard coming from somewhere up near the ceiling. Sapia was writhing in her chair, whipping her limbs around in an effort to free them. Arlington kept a firm grasp on her hand and shouted to young Richet to do the same.

Seven minutes later a strong wind blew through the room. Richet called out to Curie, "Make a notation that all the windows are shut and locked. I saw to it myself." The curtains of the cabinet billowed out, and a man's face could be seen in the folds. Arlington recognized the face. "That's John King," he shouted. Curie marked it down.

"John, you are hurting me. Stop it. *Giovanni, mi stai facendo male.* Stop it, John."

More flashes. She was writhing now, punching the air with her fists and groaning. As the table came down Arlington heard the same male voice moving about the room. The words were in Italian, but the tone was unmistakable, impatient and reproachful.

"Don't let go of her hand," Arlington shouted. He was worried that Richet's brother might get distracted. Then he realized he was speaking English. He paused, trying to remember the French for hand. "*La paluche! La paluche!*" he called out in his best French accent. Later, he realized he was shouting *paw, paw* into the gloom.

Sapia seem to deflate after that. Her head slumped forward on her chest, and her breathing became more regular. For a quarter of an hour nothing happened. A distant bell sounded, but it may have been a clock chiming in some other part of the house. Then Arlington glanced up at the ceiling and with a jolt saw two green eyes looking back at him.

"Up there!" Sapia said, pointing to the ceiling. Everyone looked up. The eyes glowed in the dark. They were animal eyes, the pupils vertical slits, unblinking, cold and shrewd. They were set into a square head. It was a glowing green snake undulating around the coving, confidently moving around the room, its tongue flicking in and out, curious and probing.

Sapia bent her head and in a moment or two Arlington saw the convoluted folds of ectoplasm just beginning to form above the crown of her head near the swath of white hair. It was pale and lumpy, tortuous like the intestine of a large mammal, and it seemed to be coalescing into a hand. Arlington's heart beat resolutely in his ears. It had been two years since she manifested ectoplasm. He reached out to touch it.

"No!" she bellowed.

He snatched his hand back. He did not know if that was meant for him or some spirit in the room. The loathsome thing continued to grow and soon two hands appeared with three misshapen fingers on each. It made him a little queasy to look at it, yet he couldn't stop. The fingers were pale and glistened in the candlelight, slithering over her hair like curious slugs, inching forward on her scalp, until they came to rest on her forehead, lying flaccid and white just above the hairline.

Richet and the others continued to call out the events, while Curie wrote it all down. At one point he stopped to make a sketch, even though it was unnecessary. The cameras kept going off all around them, catching the event from every angle. By the next flash the pseudo fingers were on the move. This time they were slithering down her face.

The male spirit was back in the room, belligerent and blaming. Arlington could almost make out the words. Even though they were in Italian, the tone was clear. He was furious at Sapia. She pleaded with him, as she had done on the previous night, begging him not to be angry. "What have I done, John? *Che cosa ho fatto, Giovanni?* Tell me." The fingers were at her throat now, slowly tightening.

She grappled with them and tried to pull them off. "Stop it, John. Stop it." She was choking.

Arlington and Crookes were on their feet, but before they could reach her, the fingers let go. She clutched her throat and gasped for breath. A moment later, the fingers were gone. Her head slumped forward on her chest, her breathing slowed, until she finally lifted her head and looked around. "I am exhausted."

As the sitters filed out of the room their excited chatter filled the hallway. She and Arlington were shown to the door surrounded by the scientists, who were talking among themselves, congratulating Sapia and shaking Arlington's hand. The only exception was Sir William Crookes, who stood apart from the others, looking a little dazed. "I have never seen anything like it," he said breathlessly when he approached Arlington. Arlington noticed the man's hands were still trembling.

Arlington couldn't have been happier. His medium had performed beautifully. She had been brilliant, wondrous, and strange; even Richet's brother had been impressed. As he climbed into a taxi he made a mental note to wire Edith and have her book them into several more cities. Perhaps Milan with Professor Lombardy and Berlin with the German Society. He would leave that up to her.

After tonight the whole psychic world would be talking about the séance. They would publish the photographs. There would be articles about Sapia, but of course he would be mentioned. He would be in the photographs. There might even be articles about the society. He sat back and absently took out a cigar.

It was a cold night and Sapia had taken all the carriage blankets for herself. She had been going on about the evening, hands fluttering, rings glittering, the diamond bracelet cuff biting into her thick wrist. She did not seem upset in the least by John King's behavior. On the contrary, she was proud of his abuse and referred to it as an accomplishment on her part.

Then she noticed Arlington's cigar and stopped in midsentence. Tossing the ostrich-feather boa about her neck she said: "You are not going to smoke that, *Ar*-lean-ton."

He realized he had the cigar in his hand, mumbled an apology, and put it back in his waistcoat. He was content to let her prattle on about her triumphs, her special gifts, and her titled followers. He had developed his own talent for appearing to listen while he was actually planning their next tour. The new staff he would hire, and calculating to the penny the generous raise he would give himself.

# CHAPTER 8

# May 1903

I t was a gray morning, damp and gauzy with mist. The Luxembourg Gardens were a blurred collection of shapes, of spectral branches overarching the Médicis Fountain, hazy topiaries, a garden path veiled in fog. The only bright spot, as far as Henri Becquerel could see, was his new yellow waistcoat. It was satin with pearl buttons, perhaps too showy for someone of his station, but he admired it so.

He hadn't planned on stopping in on the Curies that morning. He was late to a lecture at the academy and didn't think he had the time. But then he found himself in rue Lhomond and there was the School of Chemistry, and behind it the derelict shed that once held cadavers and now housed the Curies' laboratory, such as it was. He knew he was interrupting them the minute he walked through the door. Diebierne was pouring a precipitate through filter paper, Curie's wife was at the electrometer, and Curie himself was studying the effect of radioactive barium on a mason jar full of ice water.

"Have I come at a bad time?" Becquerel asked with the air of someone who never worried about such things. Becquerel liked to think of himself as accepting of those who were his inferiors. He always treated Pierre Curie with courtesy, never alluding to the disparity of their social or professional positions. Becquerel didn't like social hierarchies, believed that he was above them, but what can one say about a man like Pierre Curie, whose highest degree was a licentiate in the physical sciences and who was a teacher at EPCI, an industrial school?

Madame Curie got up from her work and offered him tea, trying to appear as if she were glad to see him. Even at her best, Curie's wife was a severe woman. She rarely smiled and was often in a state of hectic disarray in her dirty lab smock, with her wild hair escaping from the pins, fingertips permanently destroyed by the chemicals. He supposed that she would be considered a modern woman. She was nothing like his beloved Lucille, however, who had been sweet and compliant all her life, a paragon of womanhood, until her death in childbirth all those years ago.

Monsieur Curie made only tepid overtures to Becquerel that day. After a halfhearted attempt to explain his experiment, he returned to it, leaving the social exigencies of the visit up to his wife. Curie was an awkward man, abrupt and inappropriate at times, but he generally wasn't this bad. Becquerel assumed that Curie's reticence had something to do with his unsuccessful bid to become a member of the academy. For some reason the man blamed Becquerel for his disappointment. Becquerel had done what he could for Curie, but what could anyone do really? The man didn't even have a doctorate. The members of the academy were esteemed in their fields. Becquerel himself was the third generation in his family to hold the physics chair at the Muséum National d'Histoire. The gulf was deep and wide, an impossible distance to cross, especially by one so stymied by ordinary social intercourse.

Still Becquerel had done what he could. He had talked up the man and even delivered two of the papers that Curie had written with his wife a few years back to the academy. Both were met with polite indifference. No one was much interested in the findings of an industrial arts instructor and his student wife, a Polish woman who had once been a governess.

When Becquerel declined the tea, a shade lifted from Madame

Curie's face and for a moment she relaxed and became almost pretty. Nevertheless, he observed that her relief was short-lived, for there were still the few uneasy pleasantries to get through before she could show him the door. They talked about his recent work with crystals, their ability to absorb and polarize light. He thought Curie might be enticed to join them, given his own passion for the subject, but he continued to work as if they weren't there.

When the time came for Becquerel to leave she handed him the glass tube containing the radioactive barium that she had thoughtfully wrapped in brown paper. He thanked her and dropped it into the pocket of his new waistcoat. He was grateful to the Curies for giving it to him. Their technique of fractional crystallization yielded a far more active barium than anything he could buy from a factory. Since he was interested in the properties of the rays and their ability to transfer radioactivity to other materials, it was important for him to work with a highly active sample.

He spent the rest of the morning at the lecture and at an impromptu discussion afterward with a few of his colleagues. In the afternoon he met Poincaré for lunch at a little restaurant near the academy. They settled into a corner by the window and ordered a bottle of wine. It began to rain and for a while they sat in companionable silence watching the passersby huddled under their umbrellas hurrying to get out of the weather.

Being with Poincaré was a little like being with a sibling. They had met during their student days at the Polytechnic and had been close friends ever since. The two Henris shared a similar background in physics, although Poincaré was mainly a mathematician. Both came from prominent scientific families, both were currently teaching at the École Polytechnic, both were members of the Academy of Sciences. Poincaré was a citizen of Becquerel's world, a notable member of his community. Curie, on the other hand, resided in a poor neighboring village.

When they were well into their coffee and cigars Professor Charles Richet stopped by their table on his way out the door.

Pleasantries were exchanged and promises for future meetings were made. When he left, Becquerel sat back and puffed on his cigar to get it going. "Is he still working with his mediums?" Becquerel asked, not bothering to hide his derision.

"He's not a fool."

"I didn't say he was."

"The Curies are working with him and Crookes as well. Richet found an Italian, and she's supposed to be the real article. They say she manifests ectoplasm."

"Ectoplasm?"

"That's what Richet calls it. It's a substance of some sort. The spirits are supposed to drape themselves in it when they're in the physical world. They say it's viscous like mucus and comes out of the orifices of the medium." Poincaré took a puff on his cigar and smiled at the look of incredulity on Becquerel's face. "Yes, I know," he said wearily. "But he has photographs."

"You are acting like you are interested."

"Curious perhaps."

Becquerel shook his head and gave him a little laugh.

"What?"

"Sometimes you are curious about the strangest things."

Poincaré puffed on his cigar and the smoke swirled over the espressos in their polite little cups. "But isn't that what we do?" he asked, without rancor. "As men of science. Aren't we supposed to be curious about the strangest things?"

Becquerel eyed the contents of his cup, took a sip, and replaced it in its saucer. Then he looked up brightly. "Did you see Rutherford is in town? He's going to deliver that paper on thorium X."

"Transmutation?" Poincaré laughed.

Becquerel smiled. "Maybe we should start calling him an alchemist. I think he's on to something, though. Makes sense when you think about it."

"You're backing away from the aether?"

"Doubts. That's all. Nothing firm, but I'm interested in reading his paper. Might clear things up. Better than this muddle we have." Becquerel looked up to find a half smile of satisfaction playing on his friend's lips. "Yes, I know. You are for the atomists."

"I didn't say anything," Poincaré said innocently. "It's just a bit of a surprise to see you jumping sides."

That afternoon Becquerel returned to his laboratory to finish up some paperwork and answer a stack of correspondence he had been meaning to get to. He worked into the early evening until he realized that he would be late for supper. He had one last note to send off and that was to his friend Richet. He sent a *bleu* expressing interest in the Italian medium and asked to be included in the next sitting.

When Becquerel reached home he found he had just enough time to change before supper. As he relayed it later to the Curies, to Poincaré, and to the others, he was standing in his room, in front of the armoire to be exact, just reaching for a fresh shirt, when he remembered the test tube of barium that he had been carrying around all day in the pocket of his waistcoat. He took it out and laid it on the nightstand next to his bed, thinking that he would bring it to the laboratory the next day. Then he unbuttoned his waistcoat and his shirt, and when he took them off he found a burn on his skin in the shape of the glass tube right on the spot where his waistcoat pocket had been resting on his ribcage. It was an angry burn and yet it didn't hurt.

Curious.

•   •   •

The Curies had rented a proper house on boulevard Kellermann located on the southern edge of the city. It was a square building with a flat façade broken up by tall shuttered windows that opened out onto a garden. The house was set back from the street and protected by a high hedge, which offered privacy and comfort from the carriages and the few passersby.

That spring Paul Langevin, a colleague of the Curies, came to the house to ask Lucia if she would put together a little party for

Madame Curie at his expense. Madame was defending her doctoral thesis at the Sorbonne on Wednesday and he and a few friends wanted to plan a little celebration afterward. When Lucia asked him what he wanted her to serve, he thought for a moment, shrugged, and said: "Meat and cheese, I suppose." She nodded agreeably, but had no intention of serving meat and cheese. In the five months she had been working for the Curies, she had learned that physicists, mathematicians, and chemists knew a lot about how things worked—still there was a lot they did not know.

On Wednesday she rose early before the first light when the kitchen was still dark and still smelled of fried onions and fish from the night before. She slept in a little cupboard off the kitchen that was just big enough for a bed. A curtain across the doorway gave her the privacy she had been longing for and there was even a little shelf for her red flower and a candle to read by. Every night she slept beneath her mother's cross, comfortable in her new routine, still missing Poland, but less so.

She sat on a wooden chair in the kitchen and pulled on her boots, glancing up through the window at the tentative predawn light. In a few minutes Iréne would be up, then Madame and the doctor. For now the house was quiet except for the ticking of the grandmother clock in the parlor and the swish of Monsieur's stocking feet as he shuffled through the rooms. They met in the pantry by the back door as she was putting on her hat. He didn't look at her, not directly, but he gave her a quick nod as he limped through the kitchen, his legs stiff with pain, his face a grimace of bleak resolve.

Monsieur Curie spent a good deal of his nights wandering the house because of the pains in his legs. In the last few months his rheumatism, or whatever it was, had gotten worse and this despite the special diet Lucia prepared for him. The pains had come on so gradually that for a while she supposed he had just ignored them. He never complained about them, not until they got so bad he couldn't sleep. Then there were visits to the doctors, bottles of medicine, diets, hot baths, and electric-magnetic treatments, and still no one knew for certain what was causing them. For a while it was thought he had neurasthenia, and cyanide was prescribed. But when that didn't help they decided it was rheumatism, although Babusia had the rheumatism and it never looked like that.

All morning long Lucia cooked and baked a Polish feast that she thought would please her mistress. She made stuffed cabbage, stuffed eggs and pickled mushrooms, boiled crayfish and Kielbasa, almond babas, and pierogies filled with meat and cheese. The baker had been given strict instructions to bring the ice cream at four o'clock. By midmorning she asked a neighbor, Agnès, the Perrins' maid, to lend a hand and together they set up the tables and chairs outside in the garden.

That afternoon the crowd from the Sorbonne came traipsing in from the road and Lucia could see right away that it had gone well for Madame Curie. They were a noisy bunch, a convivial pack of scientists and mathematicians either from the Sorbonne or from the ESPCI, many of them neighbors like the Perrins. Although many were members of the academy, they belonged to the younger set and did not share Becquerel's view on richer or poorer villages. Legitimacy based on diplomas, and the importance of family connections, did not interest them. To them all scientists were members of the same community, a great family of scientific minds, to which the Curies were an integral part.

They bantered back and forth as they made their way through the house to the yard. Even Monsieur Curie moved with greater purpose that afternoon. He was caught up in an animated conversation with Émile Borel, the mathematician. They both agreed that radioactivity was linked to the atomic proprieties of the elements, but *how* was the question. Borel was for changes within the atom. Curie was for energy from the outside acting upon it. Lucia was familiar with both these arguments because the doctor had explained them to her only the night before.

Despite the fact that it was a celebration, the rest of the afternoon looked very much like any Sunday at the Curies', with several conversations going on at once, usually about radium or radiation, departmental gossip, or politics. The guests were seated on blankets or wicker chairs in the shade of the sycamores. A line of lilac bushes followed the fence, the mounds of purple flowers pitted with rust. Here and there clumps of irises and lilies offered tilting wands of color. Beyond the fence was a ragged field of purple and green grasses dotted with red poppies, where the ground rose and fell into hillocks and gullies draped with thickets of yellow broom and gorse.

There were a few new guests that day, notably Ernest Rutherford, a physicist, a New Zealander, who had been working in England under J. J. Thomson at Cavendish and then in Canada at McGill. He arrived with his wife and sauntered out to the yard, eventually settling down with Monsieur and Langevin next to Iréne's tiny kitchen garden. He was a big man with a red moustache and a heavy jaw that was never still: talking, laughing, making sardonic comments embroidered with sly looks of amusement. His full lips barely covered his protruding teeth and even though he had large ears that stuck out on either side of his head he was still an attractive man: vigorous, buoyant, and impishly argumentative. When Lucia heard his name she remembered the New Zealander who tried to rob Madame Curie of her discoveries and had set her to sleepwalking. Now that she had won the race and isolated enough radium to determine the atomic weight, these two had become friends.

Later on, while Madame Curie sat in a lawn chair with her mending, pushing and pulling the needle through with her ruined fingertips, Rutherford came over and stretched out beside her on a blanket. At first they chatted about the source of this mysterious energy and then about the possible medical uses for it. They both shared the same intensity of purpose, the same exhilaration, and dedication to detail. They both had a natural ability to push all extraneous concerns aside and focus on the one question at hand. It was obvious that despite his disregard for formalities, convention, and even manners, the New Zealander had a deep and abiding respect for Lucia's mistress.

The afternoon stretched on in a series of quiet calamities—Didi the cat ran out into the field chased by the Perrins' dog. The children ran out after them scratching their bare legs on the broom and tripping over clods of grass. Four-year-old Aline caught her new dress on a thorn and pulled it free before she had time to think about the damage she was doing. She stood there in disbelief when she saw what she had done and ran to her mother, Henriette Perrin, who fussed and cooed over her, rubbed her scratched shins and kissed them. Henriette whisked the dress off over her daughter's head and sent her out to play in her shift, while she brought the dress over to her best friend, Marie, who was already darning a muffler.

Out in the road Borel was teaching his young wife, Marguerite, how to ride a bicycle. He was not a young man and had to struggle to keep up with her. He held on to the seat and ran beside her, shouting instructions at her, which only confused and frustrated her, until he slipped on the cobblestones and went down hard, gashing his knee on a sharp rock.

He came into the yard looking stunned and helpless, his trouser leg rolled up to reveal his pale and bloody shin. Marguerite followed him out of the house with iodine and bandages and took care of the wound, prompting Rutherford to remark that even with a house full of doctors there was no one qualified to bandage him up. Monsieur Curie found this especially funny and let loose one of his braying laughs that rang out over the gathering.

By four the ice cream arrived and the children were given as much as they wanted. Afterward, they gathered around Henriette to hear her stories, while her husband, having grown tired of arguing with Georges Sagnac about the nature of matter, burst into an aria from *Das Meistersinger*. Lucia went around gathering up the bowls and shooing away the flies. When she came over to Madame Curie and Rutherford, he handed her his bowl and then with a devilish grin asked her what she thought about the burning question at hand.

"What question is that, *monsieur*?"

"What makes the radium glow, my girl. Any idea?" He spoke

French with an English accent that made it difficult to understand. Nevertheless, his intention was clear enough. He meant to have a little fun at her expense.

Lucia stood there with three dirty bowls in her hand and frowned at the question. Madame Curie started to protest, but Lucia cut her off. "I'll answer this, *madame*, if you don't mind." She pulled herself up, wishing there were some place to set the bowls down.

"While the evidence is still inconclusive," she said, peering down at her adversary with a look of studied indifference, "my opinion is that the energy is coming from some process of disintegration within the atom. I believe that is your theory as well, *monsieur*. Madame, on the other hand, is working on the continuous aether theory, a sort of glue that holds everything together. She imagines rays of energy filling the space around us and being absorbed only by certain heavier elements. Either way, Monsieur, atomist or aetherist, the question isn't so much why does it glow, but rather what is the structure of everything."

Rutherford stared at her for a moment and then burst out laughing. "Well done, my girl. You've stuck it to me that time." Then to Madame Curie he added: "Where did you find such a talent?"

Madame Curie smiled briefly. "She's been talking to Papa. Lucynka," she said affectionately in Polish, *"Jeste? mój genialny dziewczyna."* You are my genius girl.

Lucia's cheeks reddened with pleasure. It had been a long time since anyone had called her Lucynka. A moment later Madame Curie held out her hand and in Lucia's confusion she thought her mistress was offering her hand to hold. Actually, she was directing Lucia's attention to a stack of dirty bowls on a nearby chair.

That evening Lucia served a light supper and afterward the party gathered out in the back to look at the stars. It was a dark night and the black expanse of sky was flecked with twinkling pinpricks. By now Lucia had learned many of the constellations and would have gladly called them out had anyone asked. Instead the company wanted to talk about radium: radon gas, the proprieties of radium, the industrial uses, the medical uses—radium, always radium. Monsieur Curie held up a vial of radium bromide that he had been carrying around all day in his pocket. "I give you radium," he said momentously, the air seeming to quiver around him. Its blue glow lighted his face, which was animated with something akin to religious ardor. It also lit up his ruined fingers, raw and burned, irretrievably damaged, looking painful and even grotesque in the celestial light.

•    •    •

In August the Curies took a house for the month near the shore in a little village called St. Trojan les Bains on Île d'Oléron, a small island located off the southwest coast of France in the Charente-Maritime. It was an idyllic spot, fringed with sandy beaches, dotted with coarse bent grass, and surrounded by wide swaths of oyster beds.

The odd little cottage had a red tile roof and a blue door that had been freshly painted over peeling paint, so that now the surface was lumpy and already beginning to flake. It sat back from the dirt track amid piles of windswept pine needles and broken roof tiles, standing courageously with the other cottages on the road against the wind and the brackish sea air. A crudely lettered sign at the corner designated the lane as rue Docteur Geay. Lucia kept expecting to meet this doctor, but he never appeared, nor did anyone speak of him. It occurred to her that he was probably dead.

What made the cottage strange was that they were not alone. The owner, an old fisherman, was still living in it. He had moved his things down to the cellar at the beginning of the summer so he could rent out the rest of the house for extra money. He said he would be quiet and they would never know he was here, yet Lucia could hear him rattling around down there, coughing and swearing, and banging the cellar door whenever he went out.

Although he made an effort to make his house comfortable for the paying guests, Lucia kept finding peculiar objects about the place that gave her pause. Hanging on the wall in the parlor was a framed label from a fishing crate showing a flying shrimp against a dead blue sky. The shrimp was grinning with a mouthful of white teeth. Fortunately, no one minded when she took it down and put it in the closet.

In the kitchen an old bicycle wheel outfitted with fishing hooks hung from the ceiling, meant to hold pots and pans. Once she caught a finger on one of the hooks taking down a saucepan and never used the contraption again. There were other inventions too: A fishing bucket suspended over the sink delivered water through a rubber hose; a cane turned into a butterfly net, a flute, and an umbrella; a wooden box attached to a crank peeled potatoes, although she never figured out how it worked. Otherwise, the house displayed a certain crude domesticity; lace doilies sat on the backs of the chairs, shells decorated a lamp base.

On most days Lucia helped the Curies down a series of footpaths to the water where they set up a camp on the beach. The bay was smooth and behaved like a well-mannered lake. Tiny wavelets lapped up on the shore and slapped against the fishing boats anchored nearby. On this particular morning Monsieur was voicing his usual complaint that he had on every vacation. "It seems to me a very long time since we have accomplished anything, Marie. Isn't it time we got back to work?" They had been on the island for exactly five days.

"Not yet, *mon amour*," she murmured. "Let's give it a while longer."

The Curies needed a long rest, that much was certain. Madame was pregnant and not well. Lucia could hear her being sick and not just in the mornings. The other day she found her mistress lying on a hooded lawn chair in the back under the pines with a colander of peas in her lap. She had a glazed look in her eyes, and a vague expression of exhaustion wilted her features.

"She should be gaining weight, not losing it," the doctor fretted to Lucia on the way down to the beach that day. "It's been five months and the sickness should be gone by now. Her appetite is not what it should be and she sleeps badly. Her coloring is not good. I do not want to worry her, but these signs are not encouraging."

On most mornings Lucia stayed on the beach only long enough to set up the little encampment before returning to the house to begin her work. On that day she left the Curies under the umbrella and stopped off at the marina on her way home to pick up a bucket of oysters and a couple of whiting from the returning fishermen. Here at last was fresh fish they could afford, cod and whiting, bream and shellfish. Fish that was out of reach in Paris could be obtained for a few sou. She used the old recipes from the Babineauxes, exuberant, luxurious, a triumph every night. It felt good to be free in the kitchen with real ingredients, fresh herbs, vegetables, legumes, an array of choices.

Still, she had to put up with the house. It was too small and there was a lot of work to do. The rest of the morning was spent making the beds, dusting, sweeping, and emptying the chamber pots, which had to be washed out and sprinkled with talc. She had gotten spoiled on boulevard Kellermann after Madame had won another chemistry prize and installed an indoor toilet.

When it came time to start lunch she dragged a chair out to the porch, brought out a short knife and a little towel, and began to shuck the oysters. She was just about to pry open the second one when she happened to see a young man sauntering down the road carrying a tripod and a camera. He stopped at their gate and leaned over to speak to her. She thought he might be selling portraits or perhaps someone who had lost his way. He was handsome, a few years older than she, romantic looking, or so she thought. He had closely cropped light brown hair, a long narrow face, and a tawny moustache, taut and decisive, that gave him an air of authority.

He introduced himself as Gabriel Richet. When he reached over to take her hand, she caught the faintest whiff of sweat, wild grass, and sea breeze, as if he had been lying in a field near the shore. He explained that he was a journalist from *Le Matin* and asked her if she was Madame Curie. She laughed at this and told him Madame Curie was her mistress and that she wasn't at home.

"You're the maid then?"

"The cook, *monsieur*," she said curtly. That was how she referred to herself when speaking to tradesmen or other domestics in the neighborhood—although, in all honesty, she couldn't name one cook who emptied chamber pots.

When he found out that Madame Curie was out, he said: "Maybe you can help me?"

"With what?"

"I'm doing a general interest article on Madame Curie. Well, on both of them really, but mostly on her."

"In *Le Matin*?" Lucia looked surprised. The doctor was always reading that paper. She kept a stack of them by the stove in the parlor to light the fire.

"Yes, and I'd like to take some photographs if she'll let me."

Lucia laughed. She thought he was having fun with her. She noticed how blue his eyes were and how, for the moment, they stayed on her. She particularly liked the offhand way he leaned on the gate with an air of confidence, almost impertinence. Even though his eyes were still on her she got the idea that his attention was fleeting and that in a moment or two he would move on to something more interesting. He was careless and changeable—she could see that at a glance. Yet, instead of being cautious, as she should have been, she was drawn in. "My mistress in your newspaper? Why?"

"She is a *lady* scientist. That's something you don't see very often. A Polish governess who marries a Frenchman, discovers radium, and receives a doctorate from the Sorbonne. You don't think that will sell papers?"

Lucia sat there with the oyster still in her hand too amazed and fluttery to open it. First there was this attractive man bristling with passion for his subject and then there was what he was saying. She recalled sitting in the parlor with Madame Curie sewing dresses for Iréne and talking about her mistress's time as a governess for the Zorawskis in Szcuki. She was called Manya Sklodowska then, and she fell in love with the eldest son, who refused to marry her because she came from a poor family. There were other stories too of young Marie's student days living on watery soup and sleeping in freezing garrets, fainting from hunger, and working until dawn. Lucia had seen the punishing work in the shed in rue Lhomond—the freezing cold, the snow and rain, the boiling mass, and the noxious fumes. There were prizes and acknowledgments along the way too. Lucia had known for quite some time that her mistress was extraordinary, but it hadn't occurred to her that others would see her in the same way.

"My mistress might like being in your newspaper, but my master"—she shook her head—"he won't much like being famous."

When the Curies returned that afternoon and she told them about the journalist Madame Curie sat down, her face blank while she took it in. Monsieur Curie began to pace the room. "Well, I'm not going to be put in a paper," he announced stubbornly. He strode off to the bedroom and came back with his laboratory notebook, slamming it down on the table. He pulled up a chair and hunkered down over the pages like an old war veteran perusing his dusty relics.

After some time had passed Madame Curie seemed more amenable to the proposition. She appeared even eager to meet this journalist, asking twice when he said he'd be back. When he returned that afternoon Madame showed him out to the backyard where they sat for some time in the shade under the pines, discussing her work, or so it seemed to Lucia the few times she came out first with the tea and then the brioche and jam that she had made just for this occasion.

When they finished Madame came in to coax Monsieur out to the yard so they could have their picture taken. Monsieur Richet asked that Iréne be included, so she was awakened from her nap, grumpy, wrinkled, the marks of her pillow still on her cheeks, and made presentable for the photograph. He also wanted to interview Monsieur Curie, but he refused, saying he had work to do, even though they were on vacation and there was no laboratory to be had anywhere.

It was a small house with thin walls, so Lucia could be forgiven for overhearing Monsieur complaining bitterly that night to his

wife that he didn't want to be famous, that he didn't want the attention, the bother, and all that came with it. "It seems to me a very
long time since we have accomplished anything," he said, reverting
to his old lament. "Isn't it time we got back to work?"

Over breakfast the next morning Madame Curie announced
that she and Monsieur were going on a cycling excursion for three
weeks and would be leaving in a few days. She said it as if it were a
normal, everyday occurrence and needn't be of concern to anyone.

The doctor put down his cup and regarded her with a look
of dismay. "How could you think about going on such a trip?" he
asked incredulously. "What about your condition? What about
Pierre? What about the pain in his joints?"

"We've been getting stronger every day. And we won't go far."

"This is madness."

"I think the cycling will do us good, Papa." Pierre said.

"Well, you are wrong, *mon fils*. You don't need exercise. I
thought that much was quite plain. You need rest and lots of it."

"I know you are worried, but we will rest often. We are aware of
our limitations," Madame Curie said gently, tapping his hand with
her fingertip.

The doctor pushed his chair away from the table and stood. He
went to the window and looked out on the deserted road. "Complete idiocy."

Lucia knew that despite the doctor's best arguments they would
do exactly as they liked. Indeed, three days later they left for their
excursion, waving gaily from the seats of their bicycles as they ped-
aled off down the road and disappeared around the corner.

That morning Lucia went down to the greengrocer's to pick up
a few things and ran into the daughter of the proprietor, who was
working on a display of early pears. The girl had a mobile mouth
and a square face that wasn't especially pretty, but she always wore a
red jewel, a garnet perhaps, on a velvet ribbon that somehow transferred its luster to her. Lucia asked her about the young man—the
one who had checked into the hotel across the way.

Lucia described the stranger as handsome with a blond moustache. She did not mention the color of his eyes or the way he smelled, she didn't have to. The girl knew exactly whom Lucia was talking about. She said that he had come in yesterday at this time for a bag of oranges. She said he arrived a few days before and that he booked one of the front rooms with a view of the sea.

"They say his clothes are shabby, particularly his coat, but that he has a fine pair of new boots and two shirts."

Lucia knew that the girl's information was coming by way of the hotel maids.

The greengrocer's daughter didn't have to ask why Lucia was interested. Every girl on the island wanted to know about the stranger staying at the Calais. The appearance of an attractive bachelor on Île d'Oléron was something to talk about, particularly since so many of the boys on the island had left to find work on the mainland. Lucia loaded up her basket with potatoes, onions, and garlic. The girl was just ringing them up when Monsieur Richet walked in the door.

"*Mademoiselle*, what luck to see you here. I was just coming up to see your mistress."

"They are not here, *monsieur*."

"Where are they?"

"Off on a cycling excursion." She put down the few francs and lifted the basket. It was heavier than she would've liked.

"Madame Curie is a cyclist?"

"Oh, yes, *monsieur*. She rides often."

"But she is pregnant."

"Yes, *monsieur*," she said, dropping her voice to a near whisper. He surprised her with his blunt assessment of the situation.

"A cyclist, that's a nice piece of color. I'll need a picture of her on her bicycle. When are they getting back?"

"In a few weeks. I cannot say for sure."

"I don't know if I can stay that long. When will they be back in Paris?"

"In a month."

"Well, that is a problem. Maybe I'll have to turn in the article without the photograph." He was muttering to himself. Then he noticed her struggling with the basket. "Here, let me walk that up for you."

Lucia reddened. "I wouldn't want to trouble you, *monsieur*."

"I was going up anyway. It's no trouble."

She offered a weak protest for the sake of appearance but gave in quickly when it seemed that he was going to take her at her word. A few minutes later they were on the path that led back to the rue Docteur Geay and she asked him how his article was coming along.

"I have a few technical questions; otherwise it's going well." Then he asked about her life with the Curies. He wanted to know about their daily schedule: when the Curies went to work and when they came home, when they saw Iréne and what they did on Sundays when they weren't working. She told him about the doctor, about the garden in the back, and even about Didi the cat.

They stopped on the main road to let an omnibus full of English tourists go by. It was an open-air affair and almost every seat was taken by a couple or single women in pairs clutching red Baedeker's guides to France in their gloved hands. Without taking her eyes off them she said: "They work hard, Monsieur. Their life is not easy, and yet they are very happy. Have you ever seen radium at night?" He shook his head. "It is God's glow in a jar. His light made manifest. Quite a miracle."

They stepped aside to let a group of bathers go by, three young men and a girl. One of the young men had an extravagant moustache coated with a thick layer of wax. It curved out from his upper lip like the horns of a mythical beast. Once they were alone Lucia and Gabriel Richet stood there for a moment watching the fishing boats come in with the morning's catch.

"The sea has been good to them," she said. "Cod, I'm guessing."

"How can you tell?"

"See how the hulls are riding low in the water? The cod are migrating, but they will have stopped here to fatten up on shellfish and sea cucumbers. There should be plenty, if the sharks don't get them."

He paused to look at her. "You know about fishing?"

"I know about whiting and cod. I know how to dress them up in sauces and make them look pretty."

He smiled at this and together they walked up the path to the house. She stopped once or twice to point out a rare flower or grass that only grew on this particular island. He appeared to be interested and maybe even a little impressed.

"Tell them I came by, will you?" he said, holding the gate open for her. "In case they get back early."

She promised that she would, and this seemed to reassure him. Then a strange thing happened as he was handing over the basket. He paused in midair and regarded her for a moment. It wasn't anything she had said, for she hadn't said anything.

"Maybe we'll meet again soon," he murmured, giving her one of his smiles. His manner was easy and familiar, as if they had known each other for a long time. She had already reached for the handle of the basket, but instead of letting go he held on to it, so their fingers met briefly.

She met his gaze and her heart took a step

Then it was over and he was turning back to the road. "Tell them I'll need that photograph. It won't take long."

That night she lay in her cot in the kitchen listening to the brief summer rain drumming on the roof tiles and sweeping through the pines. She recalled the ladies on the omnibus clutching their Baedeker's guide as a talisman against the hazards of foreign travel. She remembered the bathers on the path, his sudden interest at the gate, the brush of his fingers against hers, the weight of him over her and how in one moment he was so thoroughly there with her, studying her, admiring her, and in the next gone, back with his work, beyond her reach. How thrilling this dance was, the choreography of near misses, unintended caresses, and vague possibilities, and how impatient she was for the next one to begin.

•   •   •

The Curies arrived home from their cycling excursion one evening right after supper and went straight to bed saying they were too tired for food and just wanted to sleep. Madame Curie looked exhausted, drained, hollowed out, and Monsieur was in terrible pain. They had cut their trip short by two weeks and had ridden home in the back of a cart.

The next morning Lucia made them eggs and croissants. They had steaming bowls of café au lait and a pot of strawberry jam that she had made from the island's berries. They were supposed to be sweeter than the ones on the mainland, but Lucia couldn't taste the difference. After breakfast they all went down to the beach, to swim and rest in the sun, all except Lucia, who stayed behind to do her work. At one point in the morning she went down to the Calais to tell Gabriel Richet that the Curies had returned but found he had checked out the previous day.

In the middle of the afternoon Madame Curie came back alone saying that she was not feeling well and would go in for a nap. Lucia offered to make her a cup of tea, but all Madame Curie wanted was to rest.

Later, when Lucia was out on the porch plucking a bird, she heard Madame cry out from the bedroom, her voice sounding choked and startled. Lucia hurried inside where she found her mistress lying on her side, her knees up to her chest, her face contorted in pain. "Go for the doctor and Monsieur," she panted. "Tell them to be quick."

Lucia ran down to the beach where she found them on a blanket under the umbrella. When she told them that Madame was in trouble, the doctor ran back up the path with Monsieur hobbling behind. They crowded into the tiny bedroom where Madame Curie lay on the bed curled up in pain. She was just as Lucia had left her, only now there was blood on the sheets. The doctor went to work palpitating her stomach, putting an ear to her belly, listening for a heartbeat.

Finally, he looked up, sorrow creasing his brow. "I'm sorry, Marie."

Her only reaction was a shuddery intake of breath.

Monsieur Curie was ordered out of the room and told to watch Iréne. Lucia rushed to the kitchen for towels. "She won't die, will she?" she whispered urgently.

"Unlikely," the doctor replied. "It's just that she's so weak. If she bleeds . . ." Here he broke off, his face pale and still.

Lucia massaged Madame's back and that seemed to help a little. Sometimes she would help her stand or squat over the bedpan; sometimes she would rub her neck and shoulders or go for more towels and clean rags. She prayed for her mistress and for little Iréne out in the yard oblivious to the danger her mother was in. She prayed to the Blessed Mother and to Saint Lucyna, but mostly she prayed to her own mother, who was surely in heaven. She begged her mother to intercede on her mistress's behalf.

*Unlikely.*

The pains got worse and still Madame Curie did not utter a sound. Her face was flushed, her hair plastered to her forehead. Lucia tried to keep Madame cool with a damp cloth, but sweat rolled off her forehead and pooled on the bedsheets.

"Lulu?" she panted.

Lucia took her hand. "I'm here."

"Lulu?"

With a stab she remembered Babusia telling her how her mother kept calling out for her, even though Babusia was there the whole time. Lucia could not sit still. Her stomach filled with ice water. She forgot how to pray in French. "Do not die," she whispered in Polish. "Please, Matka, keep her alive."

*Unlikely.*

It took nearly three hours before the ordeal was over. Through it all Madame Curie bore it without complaint. She asked to see the child. It was a girl with dark hair and eyebrows. Her skin was strangely wrinkled and translucent, her hands and feet not fully formed and yet thoroughly recognizable as human. Lucia washed the little thing and wrapped her in a linen cloth. Then she gave her to Madame Curie, who held the tiny creature in her palm and traced the child's delicate hand with her finger. "Give her to Monsieur," she whispered, handing the frail bundle back. "He will know what to do."

Monsieur Curie did not seem like he knew what to do. He looked confused and uncomfortable as he held the sad little package in his hand. He stared at it for a while and then handed it back to Lucia. Lucia lay the baby in her room for the time being and went to help her mistress bathe. She brought the tub in and heated water for her bath. She changed the sheets and brought in fresh rosemary from the garden. She wanted to comfort Madame Curie, to ease her way. She was grateful to her for not dying. When she was done she helped her into a clean nightgown and got her into bed.

As soon as she was able, Lucia took the little bundle to the undertaker and then went off to find a priest. She wanted reassurance. She wanted to know that she had done everything right, that the poor mite was in heaven. When the old priest assured her that the child was indeed with God, she felt a great burden lift. That evening Lucia tiptoed into the bedroom. "The child is with the angels now, Madame," she whispered. "She is with God." More than anything she wanted to bring her mistress a little peace.

Madame Curie looked at her, said nothing, and turned her face to the wall.

Two days later they gave the little girl a proper burial. Monsieur was there and the doctor and the girl from the greengrocer. It was a simple ceremony. Lucia placed a bunch of wildflowers on the tiny coffin before it was lowered into the grave. After the funeral they packed up their belongings and went home to Paris.

# CHAPTER 9

# Paris, August 1903

I t was early morning, still hot from the day before. The night had brought little relief from the devastating heat, which is why Lucia decided at first light to tramp through the Gentilly gate and head out to the woods of Clamart to find fresh sorrel. She was making Madame Curie's favorite soup, *zupa szczawiowa*, in an effort to get her to eat. She could have gone to the market in rue Mouffetard or rue d'Alésia, but the sorrel would not have been fresh. She had to pick it herself and wrap it in a wet cloth if she hoped to keep it crisp until she was ready to chop it, sauté it in butter, and add it to the rich beef broth.

She found the sorrel growing under a grove of elms. She picked a bunch, dipped the cloth in a stream, and wrapped it up. The sorrel took longer than expected to find, so by the time she walked back, the sun was up in earnest, wilting the flowers on the balconies, baking the sidewalks, and spoiling the produce in the markets.

Even in such heat she took the time to look for signs, hoping for respite, maybe even a miracle, anything that might signal Madame Curie's recovery. Nothing stood out, except a bunch of perfect yellow roses standing in a bucket of water in front of a flower shop. There was nothing remarkable about them, except that they were there, in the middle of the summer heat, looking fresh and plump and hopeful. She wanted them to be a signal of happier days to come, some marker of divine providence. She thought of yellow as the color of the sun, of life and health, the brightest color of the rainbow saturated with hope and promise. She couldn't say they were a sign for sure, but she would tuck them away as a possibility, grateful for the small measure of comfort they brought her.

Later as she walked down boulevard Kellermann toward the house she felt that familiar stitch of hope. Maybe this time she would find the Curies' window open, the drapes pulled back to let in air and light. Maybe her mistress would be at the window, shouting down to her, to hurry up, she needed help dressing, she was going back to work. Instead when she pushed the gate open and glanced up she found the window dark, the drapes drawn, the house silent and murky in the sticky heat.

The doctor and Monsieur were waiting for her when she walked into the parlor. Monsieur was pacing the room as usual, because he said it helped his pain. "We want you to go up there, Lulu," the doctor said. "It's time to bring your mistress down."

Lucia remembered last year when her mistress's father died. They waited too long then. They believed by giving her time to grieve she would find her own way back. Eventually, she did, but it took months. This time they would not wait.

Lucia forced herself to climb the stairs, steeling herself for a confrontation. She looked back once before she reached the landing and saw Monsieur Curie and the doctor standing at the foot of the stairs, Monsieur Curie smelling the back of his hand, a nervous habit, the doctor keeping his eyes squarely on her. She knocked once and, without waiting for a reply, opened the door.

"What are you doing in here?" Madame Curie asked, her voice sounding hoarse and alarmed. She was merely a lump under the bedcovers.

Lucia threw back the drapes and opened the window. "You need air, *madame*." The room was dark and it smelled like a sick-room, like Ania's room that time she had the croup. It was only eight in the morning and already the air was close.

"No. It's too bright in here. Go away," Madame Curie said, burrowing deeper into the bedclothes.

"Come now. It's time to get you up."

"I don't want you here, Lulu."

"I'm making *zupa szczawiowa* and your daughter is waiting for you in the garden. She is asking for you."

"I don't care. I'm not going anywhere."

"Yes, *madame*, you are. The doctor has sent me to get you up."

"I want to speak to Pierre. Where is Pierre?"

"Monsieur agrees with him. He thinks getting out into the sunshine will do you good. Now, I'm just going to help you sit up." Lucia slipped an arm under Madame Curie's back and began to lift her.

"Lulu, I am *tired*. Can't you understand that? I am exhausted. I want to rest. *Jestem zmęczony*." She shoved Lucia away and because Lucia was already off balance she stumbled against the nightstand, spilling a plate of congealed venison stew all over the rug and wall.

They were both startled. Madame Curie bolted upright and shouted at Lucia, ordering her out of the room. Then she burst into tears. Lucia ran for the door and flew down the stairs. When she told the doctor and Monsieur what had happened, the doctor said he would go. But he didn't get far before Monsieur Curie laid a hand on his arm.

"She is my wife," Monsieur Curie said quietly.

Monsieur struggled to climb the stairs, using the banister to pull himself up, his face a map of pain. He remained in their room for quite a while. But when he eventually came out, he had his wife on his arm, supporting her as he led her down the stairs and out into the garden.

A week later Lucia opened the door and found Gabriel Richet standing on the stoop. He looked fresh and well dressed, his beard neatly trimmed. She greeted him shyly, unconsciously smoothing her hair and then swiftly taking off her dirty apron.

"*Mademoiselle*, you're looking well," he said with a teasing half smile that was confident and careless.

She wanted to say something clever, but she was too rattled at his unexpected presence to think. She noticed that he was carrying a tripod and camera and then knew that he had come for the photograph. "If you are here to see Madame Curie, she is not well, *monsieur*."

His smile faltered. "She is sick?"

"She cannot see you."

"Is it serious?"

"She is not seeing anyone."

"Shall I come back tomorrow?"

"Tomorrow will be no better. I'm sorry."

"Then it is serious," he said quietly. He looked past her as if he could see for himself.

When she saw the worry on his face, she paused. "She will recover, *monsieur*. But it will take some time."

He nodded slowly while he took it in. "Yes, I understand. I'll tell my editor he won't be getting that photograph. Let her know I came by, if you think it would help. That I wish her well. I know I can't offer much, but if there is anything . . ." He left it at that.

She thanked him, and he turned to leave. But before he could reach the gate she called out to him. "I might be able to help you."

•   •   •

Three days later Lucia walked into a little café in rue de la Glacière, a few blocks from the École Normale Supérieure. It was crowded with university students, young men mostly, but a few girls in starched white shirtwaists and straight dark skirts. They sat at the tables alone or in groups with their books open or deep in conversation about politics, philosophy, or economics. Many of the young men eyed her when she walked in. It thrilled her to think that they might mistake her for a university student. Maybe they thought her market basket held books.

She didn't see Gabriel at first and it wasn't until she went into the next room that she found him seated at a little table in an alcove by the front window. He jumped up when he saw her and held out a chair for her. Then he took the one opposite.

"How is Madame Curie?"

"Better. She has been going out to the garden."

He gave her a brief smile and looked relieved. "Did you bring it?" he asked.

She pulled out the photograph from her market basket and handed it over. It was still in its simple wood frame. It was a picture of Monsieur and Madame Curie on their bicycles. Madame Curie's basket was decorated with flowers.

"It's their wedding photograph. Doctor Curie says you may have it for a day, but then you must bring it right back."

Gabriel nodded while he studied it. He held it as if it were a piece of the True Cross, then he looked up at her. "It's perfect. It'll make the article." He let her know how grateful he was and how much this meant to him. He was in high spirits, not only because of the photograph, but because he had just come from his office where he learned that the article would run on page four.

"Even my editor liked it," he said, beaming. "And he rarely likes anything."

After that he ordered coffee that arrived in stained cups with a plate of indifferent biscuits and store-bought jam, but none of that mattered, because she was sitting there with Gabriel Richet, in a students' café with pictures of famous writers on the wall and a bust of Hugo in the corner under a moose head. She wished Gabriel had brought his camera and tripod. She would've asked him to take a picture of her so she could send it to Babusia. How excited she would be when it arrived. *Look at my granddaughter*, she would say to the women on the road. *Look how far she has come.* She would remind everyone in the village how she predicted it, how it was God's will, and how she had seen the signs.

A few students had gathered around an upright piano in the corner. One of them began to play a song that Lucia knew well from the café-concerts. It was popular all over Paris, on the street and in the markets. A couple of students hung over the piano and sang along. The pianist wasn't very good and kept stumbling over the keys. The singers grew impatient and taunted him, which he gave back with relish, saying he would play better if they knew how to sing. Finally, the taller of the two with a thatch of black hair that kept falling into his eyes dragged his comrade off the bench and called out to Gabriel.

"Help us out here, Richet. Bourbeau is hopeless." When Gabriel waved them off, the student whined: "Don't be like that. Be a sport. We want a song."

Gabriel dropped his chin on his hand. "They won't leave me alone. I used to come here all the time when I was a student."

"Why don't you play for them?" Lucia replied.

"You like Ravel?"

"Of course."

"Then I'll play for you."

Gabriel took his place at the piano. He played entirely without effort, as if he had been doing so all his life. The students were right. He was good. He played one of Ravel's new songs, one that she hadn't heard before. The students joined in and soon their singing filled the café.

When it was over they prodded him to play another. He tried to put them off, but they wouldn't let him go. They badgered him until he finally agreed to play one more, but only if his friend consented to join in.

Lucia was grateful for the many gifts that God had given her. She was an exceptional cook, she had beautiful hair, and an extensive vocabulary even in French, but singing was not one of her talents. In fact, she was so bad that it became a joke at school. Even Mademoiselle Wolfowitz, who admired her abilities in arithmetic, writing, and history, always put her in the back row during concerts. There she would stand behind Marysia Malinowska, the best singer in the class, with strict instructions to mouth the words but never sing.

Lucia shook her head and waved off the crowd who was urging her to sing with them. They became adamant when Gabriel refused to play another note until she joined them. She got up determined to mouth the words silently, but when he started to play and the new Ravel song moved through her like a gorgeous wind, it came to her that she was in a Paris café, among a group of student singing under a moose head, next to the bust of Victor Hugo, not five blocks from the Sorbonne. She got caught up in the moment and forgot herself in degrees. She began to sing softly at first, but then with more enthusiasm, not quite with abandon, but certainly loud enough to be heard.

At first Gabriel cocked his head and gave her a quizzical look. Then he looked down at the keys and suppressed a smile. He seemed to be thoroughly enjoying her performance. His playing became more animated and she thought she saw him laugh. He was laughing at her, but she didn't mind. She was laughing too.

Afterward, he walked her to the omnibus stop.

"You have an extraordinary voice," he said with a grin.

"It's bad, isn't it?" she said with mock gravity.

"Remarkably so." They looked at each other and laughed. He took her hand and they crossed the street. He stayed with her until the omnibus arrived. Then he gave the driver a coin and helped her up. "I'll bring it by, tomorrow," he said with that careless, confident smile. He held up the photograph and mouthed *thank you* as the omnibus dipped back into traffic.

•　　•　　•

All through the fall there were good days and bad. Sometimes Lucia would come up and find Madame Curie dressed and ready to go. On other days she would have to drag her out of bed. They called it putting her together. "Come put me together, Lulu," Madame Curie would say. On bad days she would say nothing, except for the usual complaints when Lucia insisted she get up and face the morning. Even on good days Lucia walked Madame Curie to the station so she could catch her train to Sèvres. Sometimes she would take Lucia's hand, other times she would be lost in thought. "I'm having a think, Lulu," Madame would say. This meant that Lucia had to be quiet, so Madame could puzzle out questions about physics or chemistry or the classes she was teaching, and that was a good sign.

Often in the afternoons when Madame Curie wasn't teaching, they would sit over a cup of tea at the little table in the kitchen and Madame would share stories about her childhood in Warsaw. They spoke Polish, and both seemed to take comfort in that. Lucia would try to steer the conversation away from the history of death in Madame's family, her mother and her older sister, but invariably they would come around to the recent loss of her father and of course her baby girl. Lucia believed that all this brooding wasn't healthy. It always seemed to lead Madame back to her chief concern, her husband's health. She fretted about his pain and the fact that he wasn't getting any better despite the doctors and their cures.

Lucia wanted to be more reassuring, but she knew her mistress and knew that Madame Curie would rather have the truth, no matter how difficult, than attempts to placate her with easy reassurances and hollow optimism. The truth was Monsieur was not getting better. He was growing weaker and the pain was getting worse. So, rather than pretend, Lucia would say nothing. Inevitably, they would lapse into silence and then it was up to her to fill the void with neighborhood gossip, news of Iréne, or the daily business of running the household.

She often accompanied the doctor and Iréne to the park even when the weather changed and the air took on a chill and the last leaves of autumn clung to the bare branches with a fierce resolve. It was late in the afternoon and they were sitting on a bench by the lake. Iréne was perched on a boulder at their feet poking at a dead beetle being devoured by ants.

Lucia glanced up and saw a woman across the lake racing along the path, hatless, without a coat, her black dress billowing out behind her, creating a stir among the visitors in the park.

"Who is that, Lucia?" asked the doctor.

It was Madame Curie running toward them as if chased by all the demons in hell.

"You have to stop him, Papa. He's going to give it all away." She was out of breath, her face flushed, her voice catching on the tears.

"First you must sit down, Marie. You are overwrought."

She started to argue with him but thought better of it and did as she was told.

"Now, tell me. What is this about?"

"He got a letter from Mittag-Leffler."

"About the prize?"

"They only want to give it to Pierre and Becquerel. They're saying that he and Becquerel isolated radium together."

"That's a lie."

"Of course it's a lie. Pierre thinks this is Becquerel's doing. He wants to refuse it, Papa. You have to speak to him."

"He should refuse it. They are not including you."

"Papa, we're talking about the Nobel Prize."

"It's just a prize, Marie. You get them all the time."

"It's not the prize, Papa. It's the money. It is seventy thousand gold francs. Do you know what we could do with seventy thousand francs? A laboratory. A real laboratory."

"But they are not acknowledging your work."

"I do not care. I want the laboratory. It's the work that matters, not all this pompous drivel."

Lucia took her hand and began to talk to her in a quiet, soothing manner. "It will be all right, Madame. They cannot do you such an injustice, not with the whole world watching. There will be an outcry, you'll see. The scientists won't stand for it. Monsieur won't have to turn it down." This seemed to calm Madame Curie, at least for the moment. Lucia brushed a leaf out of her hair. "Come now we must get Iréne home."

In November a letter came for Monsieur Curie by way of a special post. Lucia saw that it was from the Royal Swedish Academy of Sciences. She showed it to the doctor, who weighed it in his hand.

"Shall we open it?" he said with an impish smile. Lucia shook her head. He sighed. "No, you're right, *ma bonne fille.* I guess we'll just have to wait until they come home."

Marie came home first from Sevrès. Teaching was taking its toll on her health. She walked in looking gray and exhausted, until she saw the letter waiting on the hall table. She stood there staring at the name on the envelope.

"Well, aren't you going to open it?" the doctor asked, impatiently.

"It's addressed to Pierre."

"Do you really think he would mind?"

She hesitated, but only for a moment, and then tore it open. She read it quickly and handed it to the doctor. When he read it he yelped in jubilation. Then he hugged her, nearly lifting her off the floor.

At first she seemed too excited to speak. Her color was back and her eyes were blazing. "All that money," she whispered.

The doctor kissed her on both cheeks. "Well done, my girl. They're doing the right thing. Not the idiots I thought."

But soon her grin faded and her brow furrowed. "They want us to go Sweden to meet the king. Do we have to go?"

"Not now. Tell them you'll come next year. Tell them you are not well."

"Yes, of course," she breathed. Then she hugged Lucia. "You were right, my clever girl. I'll have to listen to you from now on." She clapped her hands once. "Where is Pierre?" She grabbed her coat off the rack. "I must find him. I cannot sit still."

That evening the Curies stayed up late drawing plans for a new laboratory and making lists of equipment they would buy to fill it. Lucia found these lists in the morning and made a neat pile of them before going off to the market. There she bought ready-made croissants, because no one would notice.

When she saw the crowd that had gathered outside the front gate she assumed something horrible had happened. Her first thought was for her mistress. These men weren't scientists. They spoke too loudly, too quickly, and without thought. Some were carrying tripods with cameras affixed to them. They asked her questions, a mob of eager, hungry faces: *Who was she? Did she live with the Curies? Were the Curies at home? Would they come out soon?* They were reporters and they wanted to know about the Curies and how it felt to win the Nobel Prize.

In the beginning neither Monsieur nor Madame nor the doctor understood the enormity of the event. They thought it would be like it was after Gabriel's article came out in *Le Matin*, a bright flash of recognition and then a return to normalcy. But this was something else. Monsieur bought a new pair of shoes, but only because Madame insisted. Madame Curie made plans to wallpaper the back bedroom and brought home a book of samples. Even during those first few days when reporters and photographers began to show up at the gate, the Curies assumed they could be sent away. Then more arrived and bags of mail began to pile up in the front hall. Soon the parlor and laboratory were filled with foreign visitors and their comfortable life began to unravel.

One morning as Madame and Lucia were walking to the railway station a small woman with a pert green umbrella stopped them at the park's entrance. She made no apologies. She just stood there gazing into Madame's face with interest. "Aren't you that lady scientist I read about in the papers?"

"No," Madame Curie said, politely, exchanging a look with Lucia. "I've never heard of her."

•   •   •

Madame Curie was not much interested in spiritualism. She went to the séances now and then, but never often and never with much enthusiasm. Lucia was glad for this, because it always worried her when Monsieur went off to speak with the spirits. She never rested on those nights, not until he was safely back home and she heard him shuffling through the kitchen on his nightly rambles.

It came as no surprise that Madame Curie declined to go to the séance that evening in late November. She said she had work to do and that she wanted a think and that Monsieur should go on without her. She said she might go another time, but that she couldn't make any promises.

Monsieur Curie was not pleased with this development. Especially since it came at the last minute, suddenly, without warning, a jarring reminder that the world could be chaotic and unpredictable, a condition he found hard to accept. "They want a woman there, Marie," he complained. "They made that abundantly clear. And I already told them you were coming. You said you were coming."

"I am tired. I want to stay home and get my work done. Take Lulu."

Lucia looked up from the chessboard.

"You'll go, won't you, Lulu?"

"I don't know. I suppose," she said with great difficulty. She could not imagine going to one of those things. Babusia had always warned her to stay away from the spirits. To invite them in wasn't natural, and moreover it was dangerous. The living weren't meant to visit with the dead. It was against God's will. And who knew what mischief could be stirred up by it?

Monsieur shut his notebook and regarded his wife with a look of distress. "But they want you, Marie. They specifically asked for you."

"I'm afraid they would be very disappointed with me, *madame*," Lucia added quickly. "They asked for Madame Curie."

Madame Curie remained unmoved and continued to look over her notes. "Well, they will have you instead, Lulu. I'm sure you will suit them. You are a very clever girl. And besides, you will enjoy yourself. Professor Richet invites only the best mediums to his séances."

A spark at the mention of Richet. "Does he have a brother, this Professor Richet?"

"Yes, of course. That journalist. The one who wrote the article."

•    •    •

The séance started late that night, so it was nearly half past nine by the time they boarded the omnibus. Lucia placed a hand under Monsieur's arm to help him up the steps. Of course, he said he didn't need assistance, but she ignored him, as she always did, and gave him a lift up. He didn't like being helped, because it drew attention to his infirmity.

It was fortunate that his attention was on the steps and not on the side of the omnibus where he would have seen an advertisement for La Crème Activa, a beauty cream containing radium that guaranteed a more youthful appearance. If he had seen it, he would have said something, most likely a prickly comment too loud for the omnibus. Monsieur couldn't help but say exactly what was on his mind. He practiced no artifice. For that she grew to respect him, and certainly she wanted to protect him. He seemed too tender for the world, like the inside of a mouth or some delicate creature from beneath the sea.

The yellow line took them up to the rue de Médicis, where they had to walk a few blocks to the flat. All the way along she thought about the dark room and the spirits that would appear in it and the terrible unknown that waited for them. As she followed Monsieur Curie up the steps she realized that she had forgotten her Saint Christopher's medal. Now she had no protection.

The parlor proved to be a welcome distraction. It had been a long time since she had been in such a room, not since that summer at the Babineauxes' when they were on vacation. It was designed to give the visitor the impression of a secret glade. The fringed sofas were covered in green velvet. The drapery was also velvet in a deeper shade of green. Great Chinese jars full of chrysanthemums, white peacock feathers spilling out of a vase shaped like a mushroom, and cloche bell jars displaying fairyland scenes of miniature fern forests completed the effect.

Lucia saw at a glance that there were only men in the room and that they were all scientists of one sort or another. She recognized them as colleagues and friends of the Curies. There was Perrin and Paul Langevin, Georges Gouy and Sir William Crookes.

She stood a few steps behind Monsieur and watched as their host came over to greet him. Here was Gabriel's brother. She recognized him at once, the same agate-flecked eyes, same closely cropped hair, and tawny moustache, only his was carefully groomed, a badge of pride. He lacked his brother's reckless smile. There was nothing playful about him, nothing exciting. She scanned the room looking for Gabriel and was disappointed when she found he wasn't there.

Since Lucia was mostly ignored, it gave her a chance to observe the others. It struck her how well respected Monsieur was in this circle and how proud she was to be a member of his household. Men exchanged a few words and remarked on this bit of news or that. The talk was mostly about the electricity that their host had recently put in. Richet showed off the light switches and plugged an electric fan into a wall socket. The fan was a little marvel.

Sometime later an older woman swept into the room accompanied by a tall balding man, who tried to appear comfortable, though he was too rigid for a man at ease. He was easily the tallest man in the room, and he occasionally wiped sweat from his brow with a fine handkerchief. The woman glided here and there greeting the guests with a proprietary air, as if this was her room in her house and these were her guests. Lucia assumed that this spirited woman must be Madame Palladino. She was an interesting-looking woman, not pretty, but imposing with her armored bosom stuffed into a satin shirtwaist and her thick middle cinched by a cloth belt. She wore a voluminous skirt of the same material decorated with lace medallions and flounces.

The room seemed to have been made for her. With her flashing diamond rings, her confidence and power, her dark eyes outlined in black pencil and the odd streak of white in her black hair, she looked like a fairy queen, a being from another realm, mysterious and magical.

At some point the medium came over to Lucia and said: "Come along, *chérie*, we mustn't keep these big heads waiting." She reached out and took Lucia's hand and in that instant Lucia felt a thrill, a jolt as though she had just grabbed a hot pan.

The woman led the way out the door, turning back once to make sure Lucia was following. Lucia had no idea where they were going and finally asked when it was clear they were about to climb the stairs.

"To the bedroom, of course," the woman said, a little impatiently. "Where else would we be going?"

Lucia wanted to ask more questions, but wasn't sure she was up to it. There was something so imperial and imposing about this woman. She felt small and insufficient next to her.

"So, tell me, *chérie*, how do you know the Curies?" Madame Palladino asked, leading the way past several closed doors. Their way was lit by electric sconces, mischievous cupids holding glowing alabaster bowls. There was a stained-glass window at the end of the hall that portrayed a fairy queen sitting atop a lily throne.

"I am their cook."

"Their cook. That is good. They are very famous."

Lucia smiled shyly.

"So, what is your best dish?" she asked.

"I have many best dishes."

"Tell me one."

Lucia thought about it and shrugged. "*Canard à l'orange*, I suppose."

"And what is the secret of this dish. There is always a secret, *n'est-ce pas*?"

"The oranges. They must be brightly colored and very sweet. I cut that sweetness with red wine vinegar. That way you get a complicated flavor. Dainty and layered."

"You really are a cook."

Lucia nodded proudly.

"I was a laundress once. A servant like you."

Lucia's eyebrows flared. She couldn't imagine this woman serving anyone.

The medium led the way into a little bedroom lit by an electric lamp. It was simply furnished, except for the leopard skin rug on the floor and the vase of glass flowers on the overmantel. While

Madame Palladino struggled with the tiny buttons on her blouse she chattered on about how she was orphaned at twelve and taken in by a family who put her to work doing laundry. She paused and looked at Lucia. "What is it, *chérie*? You look a little lost."

"I don't know why I am here."

"Did not Monsieur Curie tell you why they wanted a woman?"

Lucia shook her head and Madame Palladino burst out laughing. It was a hearty, inviting laugh, deep and full of vitality and appreciation for the situation. For a moment Lucia saw a flash of the peasant in the medium. Despite her diamonds and eccentricities, there was an informality, an intimacy about her that Lucia found familiar and comforting. At heart Madame Palladino was a woman of Lucia's class and no amount of silks, gold, and precious gems would change that. Lucia had known her kind all her life. They belonged to the same world. Fellow travelers.

"You must think I escaped from the madhouse." Her plump white arms jiggled as she struggled to remove her corset. "You are my control, *dolcezza*. You have to make sure I have nothing hidden in my skirts. No rope, masks, that kind of thing. They have to know that the experiment is upright. Upright, yes? You must search my clothing and say that I hide nothing."

When Lucia understood what was being asked of her she relaxed and even laughed a little. She searched Madame Palladino's clothing and found nothing in her skirts but a little velvet box containing a crucifix, a Saint Benedict's medal, a pinch of dried monkshood, and a pinch of basil.

"They keep me safe from the bad spirits."

"My grandmother talks about them," Lucia said, lowering her voice in case they were listening. "She told me to stay away from them."

"She is very wise, your grandmother. The spirits are just like the living peoples. Some are good and others are bad. How do you tell them apart? Very difficult. Very confusing. You think one is good and, no, he is bad. They do all sorts of harm. They can be most unpleasant."

Palladino noticed that Lucia's eyes were wide and fixed on her.

She picked up the box. "No, you must not worry. I keep everyone safe with this. You understand? I never let on. They are scientists. They know nothing about such matters." She dropped it into her pocket.

"I won't say anything."

Madame Palladino squeezed her hand. "Have you ever been to a sitting?"

"No," Lucia said quickly. "Nor do I want to. It is wrong in God's eyes. And anything can happen."

Palladino dismissed her concerns with a wave of her hand, the rings catching the weak light of the room. "You have something," she said. "Inside you. Do you know that?"

Lucia shook her head.

"Ah, but it is true. You felt it earlier, when I took your hand. Do not deny it. You have a power, and for that, I will keep you safe."

Palladino took her downstairs to the séance room and announced to the assembled that her little friend would be in attendance. Her companion, the nervous balding man, took her aside to whisper his objection. There was some urgency in his words, but they seemed to have little effect on the medium, who ignored him and showed Lucia to a chair. After that Palladino took her place at the head of the table, sitting down in front of a smaller table where a toy bugle, an accordion, and a guitar sat next to a tray of wet clay.

Richet had already taken his seat on Madame Palladino's right, Monsieur Curie on her left. The others settled around the table wherever they could find a place. Crookes installed himself over by the window at another little table and acted as stenographer.

Then turning to Lucia, Richet asked: "Is the control complete, *mademoiselle*?"

"Excuse me?"

"Was everything in order? Did you find anything on the medium?"

"No, *monsieur*." Lucia flushed at the small lie. It was wrong, but necessary. Saint Lucyna would understand.

"Have the record state that the medium was searched thoroughly and nothing was found on her person." Crookes wrote this down in the battered laboratory notebook and then looked up waiting for more.

Lucia recognized the other Englishman seated next to her at the table, a physicist named Lodge. He was an older gentleman whose mouth was completely hidden in the dense thicket between his gray beard and moustache. She remembered him as a quiet presence at the Sunday gatherings who had, nevertheless, earned the respect of others, for what, she could not say.

When it came time to begin Richet took up Madame Palladino's hand and directed his remarks to Crookes. "I have Madame Palladino's left hand in my right. My right foot is directly on top of her left boot and I can feel her left leg against my right knee."

Monsieur Curie added: "I am holding Madame Palladino's right hand in my left. My left shoe is on top of her right and I can feel her leg under the table."

Richet continued. "The door is locked and I have placed the key on the table in plain sight. The control is complete. We are starting out at number one lighting. The light is good enough to read small print. The medium has requested that we not use photography."

"It is John, not me. He does not like the bright light."

"Flash," said her companion.

"Yes, exactly. He does not like the flashes. I do not mind them. I am used to them. But once he settles on something—" Here she shrugged helplessly.

After that she lapsed into silence. Her eyes gradually closed and her head sank slowly to her chest. Next her shoulders slumped and her limbs went limp and as far as Lucia could see she had slipped into some kind of trance. The silence in the room was broken only by Richet's frequent observations to Crookes. He called out any unusual sounds or impressions, any drop in the barometric pressure or temperature change.

Throughout, Lucia stayed alert to every sound, bracing herself for something dreadful and terrifying, anticipating the worst, but also a little impatient for its arrival. Down the hall she heard a door click shut and bits of a conversation. Below in the street a motorcar rumbled by. Then came something she could not have imagined. It was nothing like the séances Babusia described. There were no spirits or floating heads, no fluttering shrouds or shimmery apparitions. Instead, Madame Palladino began moaning, quietly at first, but then with a growing intensity, until she was writhing in her chair and making suggestive motions with her pelvis and breasts. Richet and Monsieur had to move quickly to keep a grip on her wrists. She began to call out for someone named John, pleading with him to make himself known to her, all the time breathing hard and fast and behaving like a woman of the lowest character.

Lucia tried not to appear shocked by this display, even though she could feel her cheeks blazing. She was too uncomfortable to do anything but keep her eyes on her hands that lay folded on the table. Not one of the gentlemen seated there registered anything but a dispassionate interest in the woman's behavior. If they were shaken by what they saw, they didn't show it. They acted as if her conduct was customary and to be expected. Through it all Richet continued to dictate his observations. Monsieur added remarks of his own; commenting on the proceedings without judgment, impassively, methodically, in what Lucia supposed was the scientific way.

A few minutes later the table began to rise and there were several sharp raps.

"He wants the lights lowered," Palladino said.

Richet lit a lantern made of red glass and turned off one of the lamps. "Medium states her guide has requested that the lights be lowered. We are now at two and unable to read small print."

More raps on the table and several on the wall directly behind Lucia, startling her, her heart juddering, her hands trembling. She wanted out of the room and away from this place.

"He wants them lowered again," Palladino sighed regretfully. "He wants the electric off. He does not like the electric. He says it hums."

Richet turned off the last lamp and dictated to Crookes that they were now at three. The only light in the room was Crookes's candle and the red lantern.

A moment later Palladino gasped, thrust her arm into the air, and struggled to get up from her chair. "The door! The door!" she called out in alarm. They all turned to the door just as something began pounding on it. Richet continued his dictation, raising his voice to be heard over the hammering. Monsieur Curie shouted that he continued to have complete control of the medium's feet and hands.

Lucia held fast to her chair. The pounding was so loud it seemed to come from inside her. The drumming of her heart matched its rhythm, while her breath came in shallow bursts.

The pounding stopped.

"He is coming," whispered Palladino. "Quick, the key!"

Lodge observed that the key was gone. Even in the gloom of the half-light Lucia could see that it was missing. Before she had time to react, the locked door flew open and a rush of cold air swept over them.

Lucia screamed, a strangled yelp, and crossed herself.

"The cabinet!" cried Palladino.

An accordion hung in midair over the top of the cabinet. A moment later faint sobbing could be heard coming from somewhere in the room.

Lodge suddenly lurched forward and fell off his chair. "Something just pushed me. I felt a hand on my back."

Lucia reached down to help him up and when she straightened she saw an object floating nearby, possibly a quilled pen; she couldn't make it out in the gloom. Whatever it was kept a steady progress toward her, creeping closer and closer at eye level. She knew it was something dreadful and alive. Finally, she saw that it was a single long-stemmed rose, a yellow rose, plump and fresh, inching toward her through the darkness. She wanted to leap up, to get away somehow. But she couldn't. Her limbs would not move. Never before had she felt such fear—not in the slums of Powiśle, or that snowy night on the bridge on her way to Babusia's house, nor that day Madame Clos threw her out on street. She leaned back in her chair to get away from it, but the rose kept coming, until it stopped right in front of her face.

"Go away," she whimpered. "Make it go away."

It caressed her cheek. The petals felt like velvet against her skin. Impulsively, she shoved it away and it disappeared into the darkness.

For a while nothing happened and Lucia thought the worst was over. Then Eusapia Palladino began to writhe again, muttering the same phrase in Italian over and over. In the next instant the door slammed shut. Lucia jumped.

"The key," exclaimed Crookes. It was back on the table. A fine mist floated up to the ceiling and drifted over to the door where it seemed to dissolve into the wood. After a few moments Madame Palladino lifted her head, opened her eyes, and announced that nothing more would happen that night.

The lights came on and the sitters talked over each other, excited by what they had just seen. They got up in ones and twos and began to file out of the room. Lucia wanted to go with them, but she worried that her legs wouldn't hold her up. She wanted to call out to Monsieur to wait for her, but he was engaged in an animated conversation with Professor Langevan. Madame Palladino rose from her chair with a look of triumph on her face, her eyes lit with something Lucia could not name. She bent down to Lucia, close, hot breath in her ear.

"He likes you," she said.

Lucia leaped to her feet and hurried to catch up with Monsieur. She would not be left alone in that room. She glanced down the hall at the fairy queen in the stained-glass window. Her gracious smile had turned into a smirk. The cupids holding up the globes seemed to follow her with their sly, smiling eyes. In the parlor she noticed that one of the fairy glens under the bell jar had withered and died. She tried to remember if it was like that when she first arrived. Fortunately, Monsieur was too tired to stay long and soon they were at the door gathering up their things. Their host went on ahead and waved down a taxi in the street. Lucia was grateful to be outside again as she took in a gulp of the cool night air.

The next afternoon Monsieur announced that Madame Palladino had put in a request for her little friend to come back that night. Lucia shook her head. She would not return to Professor Richet's house on any account. Monsieur did not argue with her. Instead he went to have a talk with his wife. Madame Curie came into the kitchen a while later to ask Lucia why she did not want to go. She listened to Lucia's objections, her fears of stirring up the dead, how it was unnatural and against God.

"I don't want you doing anything you're not comfortable with, but if you could find a way to go I would be grateful. Think of the séances as experiments. And you would be a part of them, a valuable part, adding to our knowledge about the aether and its functions and properties. We are attempting to understand the nature of radioactivity, where this energy comes from and why it's independent, self-generating. Maybe it comes from the same source that these so-called spirits come from. We don't know. Will you help us?"

Lucia could not answer at first. She wanted to say, yes, of course, anything to aid madame's work, to be a part of it, to make a contribution. But the truth was she did not think she had the strength to go back.

"You will be safe, I promise," Madame Curie said. "My brave girl." *Moja dzielna dziewczyna.*

That night Lucia lit a fire in the woodstove with an old newspaper of the doctor's. She noticed that the headline of the front page made mention of Madame Palladino. As the nascent fire curled the edges of the paper she recognized a picture of the medium sitting at a table that seemed to be floating above the floor.

•   •   •

Lucia returned to Professor's Richet house and to the little bedroom on the second floor to search Madame Palladino before the séance. This time Lucia brought her rosary.

"Do you know why I wanted you to come?" Palladino asked.

Lucia shook her head. She unbuttoned the medium's dress and helped her step out of it. She wanted to hurry her along because the scientists were waiting for them.

"I will show you. Give me your hand." Lucia hesitated, but Madame Palladino would not be put off. "Do not worry about them. They can wait." She took Lucia's hand in hers. "Now, concentrate."

The medium stood there with her eyes shut until Lucia grew restless.

After a moment, her eyes opened. "There. Did you feel that?"

"What?"

"It is like a humming. A vibration. You know vibration?"

Lucia shook her head.

"It is power. You have it, *dolcezza*. That is why John gave you the rose. That is why he likes you."

"Me? No. I'm just an ordinary cook."

"Very strong. I knew it when I first walked into the parlor last night. True, it is undeveloped, but it is there."

"I do not think so."

"It does not matter what you think. You have it." Palladino took up her hand again. "Now, be quiet. Listen. You will see that I am right."

Lucia stood in the little bedroom, her hand in Madame Palladino's, her eyes closed.

Nothing.

All she felt was an urgent need to get the medium to the séance room and to get this night over with. It crossed her mind to lie, to say that she felt whatever it was that Madame Palladino wanted her to feel, but she did not wish to lie and, besides, she thought Madame Palladino might know if she did.

"You do not need to lie to me. Pay attention. It is there, a little something. A twinge perhaps."

Lucia did feel something, or at least she thought she did.

"It is so little you cannot be sure if it is there. Let it take you. Let it live inside of you."

Lucia felt her hand vibrate, not much, a moment. Then it was gone. She looked up.

"You felt that." Madame Palladino kissed her hand and then released it. "It is a start."

"Was it real?"

"Of course, my child. It is more real than anything in this world."

Lucia nodded, unconvinced.

"Ah, I see that you still do not trust. Sometimes it takes a little longer. Soon you will understand."

Lucia delivered Madame Palladino to the sitters, but she would not stay inside the room. Instead she went down to the kitchen where she was bound to find a stove, a sink, cupboards, pots and pans—a safe haven comprised of the ordinary and predicable ingredients of her world.

She recognized the kitchen at once, the enormous black range, the impressive cold cupboard. She recognized the cook too with the glittery bluebird pinned over her heart. Fortunately, the cook didn't recognize her. There was no mention of the girl who had been turned away for want of a character reference. Instead the woman welcomed her as the cook of Monsieur and Madame Curie. She was invited to sit down and was offered a cup of tea and fresh croissants with homemade strawberry jam. They spent the next hour or so comparing recipes, complaining about the quality of local seafood, and commending the few vendors they both agreed had exceptional produce. For a time Lucia was able to forget the madness Palladino was summoning upstairs.

•    •    •

A few days later Lucia received word from Madame Palladino requesting she come to her rooms at the Hôtel Balmoral. Lucia had all but decided not to go when a delivery boy arrived at the front door with a bunch of perfect yellow roses. They came with a note that just said: *Please.*

She took a taxi that evening driven by an odd little man who had to stretch to see over the steering wheel. She noticed by the lamps along the boulevard that the man's hair at the nape of his neck seemed to extend down his back inside his blouse. She told him where she was going and without a word he put the motorcar into gear. The boulevards were busy and the café-concerts were still doing a brisk business even at that late hour, but the smaller streets were deserted and even the ones she knew well seemed unfamiliar, melancholy, and even a little peculiar at this late hour.

"It is just the two of us. I hope you will not feel awkward," Madame Palladino said, showing Lucia into the private sitting room. "I had them set up a little table for us. I thought it might be more useful if we were alone."

"Useful?"

"Sit here."

Lucia took her seat across the table.

"Now, are we not comfortable? And was I not right to order the table?"

A stack of blank newsprint sat on the table alongside a vase full of pencils. At first there was no mention of it. Madame Palladino talked about small, unimportant things: a visit to a friend's house in the 8th arrondissement, a new kind of water for her health, complaints about the hotel staff. Then, indicating the stack of paper, she said: "By the way, this is for you."

Lucia could not imagine why this strange woman was giving her a stack of blank paper, but she thanked her all the same.

"Have you ever heard of automatic writing?" the medium asked, looking up at her with a quiet intensity.

Lucia shook her head.

"It is when the spirits speak through the medium and she writes down what they say. They guide her hand. It is very popular. I thought you might want to try?"

It was proving to be such an odd night: the late hour, the sitting room with its flickering candles, Madame Palladino with her probing black eyes and that strange streak of white in her hair. Lucia wondered why Monsieur Arlington was not with them. She had not said two words to the man over the course of the sittings, and yet, she liked him. There was something comforting in his large frame and forthright manner. She found herself trusting him, even though she had no reason to.

"I don't think so. But thank you for the offer."

"Please, you try."

"No, I am sorry. I follow the word of God. I have no wish to contact the spirits."

"Nonsense. What has God to do with it? I go to Mass. I go to confession. It is not a sin. Here, I will show you how it is done."

Lucia felt hot and prickly. "I cannot. Please . . ."

Eusapia Palladino held out the pencil. "Just once for me."

Lucia eyed the pencil as if it were a dangerous animal. Then she shook her head.

Palladino regarded her with a thoughtful expression. She smiled faintly, the corners of her mouth lifting, and nodded as if to say she understood. A platinum snake curled around her wrist. She twisted it around so the cool emerald eyes were facing Lucia.

For a while there was an uncomfortable silence between them. At least, it was uncomfortable for Lucia, who at that moment felt obstinate and difficult. Palladino didn't seem to mind though. In the half-light Lucia could see the medium gazing at her, studying her with those penetrating black eyes. She felt self-conscious under the woman's scrutiny, until she realized that Madame Palladino wasn't really looking at her. Her body was present; her eyes were on Lucia; but she was far away.

Then Palladino's eyes began to close and for a moment Lucia thought that she was falling asleep. Lucia would have welcomed this lapse in manners. If the medium had fallen asleep, then she would have slipped out the door and gone home. She longed for her little cupboard in the kitchen, to be back in boulevard Kellermann, back in her own bed with the one candle and her book of mystery stories. Safe near the red flower and her mother's cross.

"I see a river," Palladino said, her voice dreamy and vague. Her eyes didn't close all the way but remained glittery slits in the candle-light. "It is a wide river and cold. You know this river?"

"I know lots of rivers."

"It is summer and it is hot, but the river is cold. There are many boats on it. Brightly colored row boats bobbing on the water."

Lucia began to feel uneasy. "That could be any river."

"I see a little girl and a fat woman. They wade into the water. They are washing clothes. They have their skirts tucked up into their waistbands. Their legs are bare and brown from the sun." Here Madame Palladino paused: "No, I am wrong. The woman, she is not fat. She is with child."

Lucia's heart leaped. She looked up, breathless for the moment and unable to speak.

"Soon she will have a baby. Any time now. She has golden hair like the child. The child tries to climb up over her belly. The woman laughs. She lifts up the child and kisses her. The child wraps her legs around the belly. They are very good together, this mother and child. So much love. Very touching."

Lucia's eyes filled with tears. She could feel them sliding down her cheeks.

"She is your *matka*, yes?"

Lucia nodded.

"She has a message for you."

"A message? What kind of message?"

Here, Eusapia Palladino hesitated. She sat there for some time and then slowly opened her eyes. She rubbed her face and stretched. "I must have dozed off."

"What is the message?" Lucia wanted to know.

"The message?"

"The pregnant lady."

"Oh. I do not know. It is gone, my child. Did I say something about a pregnant lady?"

"She has a message for me."

"She does? Oh, I am sorry. I don't know no message. Sometimes I cannot remember when it is over. It is like I wake up and cannot remember a dream."

Lucia's face went still as she brushed away her tears.

"Oh, do not look so sad, *mia cara*," Palladino sighed. "If you really want to hear this message, all you have to do is ask."

"Ask? Ask who?"

Palladino picked up a few pieces of newsprint and laid them down in front of Lucia. "Ask *her*."

"And how do I do that?"

She handed her a pencil. "You draw circles on the paper. That is all. You draw these circles and they will help empty your mind. The circles will free you, and the message will come through."

Lucia gave her a sidelong glance but took up the pencil with a sigh and began to draw a circle. She knew that nothing would come of it, it was a waste of precious paper, and worse, it would make her look ridiculous in the eyes of Madame Palladino.

She stopped and looked up.

"Go on." Palladino urged. "Draw another."

She drew another and then another. The circles were easy, but her mind kept going. She thought about that day at the river and that night when her mother's screams would not stop. Then they did and she remembered the anguish on Babusia's face when she came to tell her that her mother was in a better place.

The pencil went over and over the same lines; the circles got darker and soon the whole page was covered with them. As soon as she filled up one page, Madame Palladino replaced it with a clean one. In this way Lucia went through three, four, five sheets of paper, covering them with scribbled circles. She found that the faster her hand moved, the easier it was to stop the thoughts. For the next few minutes her hand flew over the sheets of paper, filling every inch with circles, wearing down the pencil points or breaking them, forcing her to reach for another.

Then, without warning, she wrote: *Listen to her*. She looked up in alarm.

"What does that mean?"

Eusapia Palladino gave her a little laugh and took her hand. She stretched out Lucia's arm and using the tip of her finger like a pencil pretended to write something on the inside of her arm. "It is time for you to go, *mia cara*. It is late."

"But I don't understand."

"Go home. Get some rest." Palladino rose and got Lucia's coat. "I am exhausted. I do not know why I am so tired lately."

That night Lucia let herself into the house and hung up her coat and hat on the rack by the door. She found her way to the kitchen in the dark and lit the candle that she kept on a shelf above her bed. She unbuttoned her blouse and slipped out of it. She was about to take off her corset when something on her arm caught her eye. She held up the candle to get a better look and was surprised to see blue writing on the inside of her arm just above the wrist. She held the candle closer so she could see what was there.

It said: *Listen to me*.

# CHAPTER 10

# January 1904

Lucia woke the next morning to find that the writing on her arm was gone. A slight tightness on her skin confirmed that it had not been a dream. She didn't know if it was an invitation, a signpost, a divine message, or perhaps something darker without a name. She wished she could write to Babusia. Her grandmother would know what it meant. That was impossible, however, because then she would have to admit to Babusia that she had attended séances, that she had a private meeting with a medium, where she had somehow acquired the strange writing on her arm.

She spent the early hours of the morning scrubbing the kitchen floor, polishing the chrome in the new bathroom, and cleaning out the woodstove and its flue in the parlor. It was the first time in weeks that she had a chance to clean the house properly. It had been full of visitors since the prize was announced, so many comings and goings that she couldn't keep up. That day the house was empty. The doctor had taken Iréne to the opera house to a children's matinee and the Curies were off with their plans for the new laboratory to meet with the builders.

By late morning she finished her work, put on her hat and coat, plucked her market basket and umbrella off the hook, and, after skirting the mailbags that kept arriving every day, stepped out into the steel-gray morning. It had been raining for two days. The front yard had turned into a small pond. Fortunately the walkway was still above the water, so she was able to keep her shoes dry. Out on the street she saw Monsieur Arlington striding toward the house. He recognized her at once and lifted a hand.

"I'm sorry you've come all this way," she said. "The Curies are not at home."

"It's not them I came to see," he replied, smiling down at her.

He seemed eager and that made her nervous. "You came to see me? Why? Did Madame Palladino send you?"

"Not exactly. Can we go inside? I think it's about to rain again."

"I'm on my way to the market and if I don't get there soon, the produce will be picked over."

"Never been to a French market. Mind if I tag along?"

"It's just a market, *monsieur*. I'm sure it's no different from what you have in America." She didn't especially want his company, but when it appeared that he would not be put off, she led the way down to the avenue d'Italie where they waited at the stop for the omnibus. They had to stand well away from the curb or run the risk of getting drenched by the passing traffic. The avenue was busy at this hour, even this far down in the 13th. The wide street was crowded with delivery carts packed with merchandise, barrels of dry goods, lumber, bolts of fabric, heading up to the prosperous neighborhoods, to the fancy shops and the building sites.

"Do you know very much about Madame Palladino?" he asked her.

"She talks to the spirits."

"Yes, and she's quite good at it. But she does more than that." He took her arm at the curb and helped her over the flooded gutter. "She helps people. They come to her when they've lost a loved one. She gives them comfort. She helps them see that death is not necessarily the end. She's a good person, Lulu."

Lucia wondered why he was telling her this.

"Yes, I know she's eccentric. And believe me I know she can be difficult, but she has a fine gift. And she truly cares. Do you know anything about her early life?" It began to rain and they opened their umbrellas. His was beautiful with a carved ivory handle. Hers had a bent rib.

"She was a laundress, I believe."

"She was an orphan. Did you know that?"

Lucia nodded.

"She was orphaned at twelve and sent to live with a family who put her to work. It was a terrible life. They worked her hard; she didn't get enough to eat. You never get over something like that. Then she married her first husband, not a nice fella from what I gather. Then came number two, and he was worse."

The omnibus arrived and they climbed aboard. Arlington dropped a few coins in the box, while Lucia found them seats inside. They settled across the aisle from a man in a dusty overcoat and top hat. He had a bulky sack at his feet full of plaster statues. Seated next to him was a student with a heavy book satchel, and further down the bench, a matron dressed in furs held a little dog wearing a yellow rain cape. The dog was trembling all over, so she wrapped it in her fur to keep it warm.

Lucia looked out over the heads of the passengers to the street, to the factories, poor shops, and empty fields strewn with trash.

Arlington went on: "Sapia looks strong on the outside, but in many ways she is like a little girl. She's scared. She's needs comfort and reassurance. She needs people around her, who look after her. Otherwise, you don't know what she'll do."

Lucia turned to him. "What do you mean?"

Glancing out the window, he stood. "Isn't this our stop?"

They clambered off the omnibus and ran to catch another just as it was pulling away. The neighborhood had changed in just a few blocks. Here the street held respectable shops and restaurants and was crowded with carriages and even the occasional motorcar. When they got off at the market on rue d'Alésia they found it so thronged with people that it was hard to navigate the aisles of stalls and carts. She scolded herself for not coming earlier. She might have avoided the crowds and the weather, and perhaps even Arlington.

They passed stalls selling winter vegetables: beets and turnips, carrots and squash. There was one selling country cheeses and another just for honey and candles made from beeswax. Arlington picked up a chunk of creamy white cheese and smelled it. "You don't get this in Cincinnati." He took Lucia's market basket and held it for her while she filled it with eggs and butter. "She likes you, Lucia. And what's more, John likes you."

She stiffened at the mention of his name.

"I know, he's no sport, but you don't have to be scared of him. He's harmless. And she trusts him. They've been together for a long time."

Lucia moved on to the butcher stall and waited her turn. "How can she trust something like that? He is not even human. I do not know what he is."

"She trusts you too."

"Then she is very trusting, *monsieur*. She doesn't even know me."

"That's the thing with her. She knows right off. She knows if you got a game going or if you're the genuine article. She's pretty sharp."

Lucia didn't know Arlington but had observed him at the séances and knew him to be a quiet man. Yet, here he was talking and talking about Eusapia Palladino and that brute of hers, John King, and she didn't understand why. "What is it that you want from me, Monsieur Arlington?"

"I want you to help me."

The rain fell harder. The sidewalks were packed with waves of black umbrellas, looking like a flock of birds at sea. A trolley rumbled by on its tracks, the two poles sparking blue fire at the juncture. The occasional motorcar swerved around the slower traffic, belching black smoke and causing the carriage horses to shy and nicker. It was then she saw them.

On the corner, under the awning, well out of the rain, a bucket filled with plump yellow roses, fresh and perfect, their petals catching the few stray water drops left by the passing umbrellas. She drifted toward them.

"I want you to come with us to Italy," he said. "I want you to be a companion to her."

"With you? Why?"

"Sapia is sitting for a bunch of scientists there. Important men. It would help a lot if you were there."

"I do not understand." She admired the roses at her feet. "How would it help?"

"She feels more relaxed around you. I don't pretend to understand her feelings. She can be downright confounding or worse—most talented people are. But with you she's calmer. And it's important she stay focused if we want our work to be successful."

"I cannot just leave. What would Madame Curie do?"

"I thought of that. I'm sure they wouldn't mind. It might even help their research. We're going to Tuscany. Beautiful country, ever been?"

She shook her head.

"She has three sittings there. It'll only be two, maybe three weeks at the most."

"I do not know, *monsieur*."

He leaned over and drew a single, long-stemmed rose from the bunch and held it out to her. "You're a servant here, *mademoiselle*," his voice changing to a tone she hadn't heard before, sharp and with purpose. "Think about what I'm offering you. You'll travel with us as an equal. You'll be invited into fine homes as a guest. It's an opportunity to see more of the world. Beautiful villages, old churches. Frankly, I'm surprised you're not more excited."

She held the rose and smelled it, clean and delicious. Her mind was whirring: Italy, the sights, a whole new world. She was just wondering how she was ever going to turn him down when there was a loud boom in the street, it sounded like cannon fire, a motorcar backfiring.

She didn't see the horses spook, the jolt of the runaway cart, the driver wrestling with the reins as cart, wheels, and horses pitched toward her. In the next instant Arlington dropped the market basket and shoved her across the pavement. She landed on her back in a nest of scattered petals just as the cart careened across the curb and grazed the tall man, knocking him to the ground. The horses galloped off, their eyes wide with terror, the driver fighting to regain control.

Lucia recovered herself and crawled to Arlington's side. He was white, his lips drained of color, his right leg twisted at an odd angle. He looked up at her, his eyes glazed with shock. "I think they broke my leg."

A crowd had formed around them. A doctor was called. Two men lifted him up from the wet pavement as gently as they could. He shrieked and nearly lost consciousness; the pain was almost too much for him. They brought him into the flower shop and laid him out on a long table. Lucia took off her coat and tucked it under his head.

When the doctor arrived he took one look at Arlington's leg and sent his assistant off for a stretcher. "We must get you to my surgery, *monsieur*," he said, laying a hand on Arlington's forehead.

When Arlington protested, the doctor assured him that he would soon be out of pain. Lucia held his hand as the doctor prepared a syringe and rolled up Arlington's sleeve. Whatever was in it had an immediate effect on him. He relaxed; his features went slack. As he started to drift off he fought to keep his eyes open. Gripping her arm, he said: "She won't be able to make it alone. She won't have me to look out for her."

Lucia squeezed his hand. "You can't worry about that now."

"Promise me you won't let her go alone."

She hesitated, and then: "Yes. I promise."

He laid back and closed his eyes. A moment later he dropped into oblivion.

•    •    •

The train to Lucca was nothing like the one that had brought Lucia to Paris three years ago. This train had private compartments with plush horsehair seats, beds that pulled down from the ceiling, and tables that folded out from the walls. Heat came through a vent over the door and shades could be pulled down for privacy. There was a dining car where they were seated at a private table decorated with a rose-colored glass vase filled with flowers. Everything about the train was brilliant, even if Madame Palladino complained that the wine was boring and the chicken cold.

That first day on the train Madame Palladino taught Lucia how to gamble. The medium had a passion for it, for faro, lansquenet, and monte bank, and showed Lucia how to play all three. Lucia had to admit it was fun, even though she was sure Babusia would not have approved. Madame Palladino gave her handfuls of Italian coins to play with and then won them back over the course of the day.

"Call me Sapia," she said after only a few hours of playing. "We will be good friends, eh?"

They spent the time gambling and gossiping and making frequent trips to the dining car. Lucia had to divide her attention between the game and the passing landscape. Mostly they were traveling through tracts of forests and past wide swaths of fields and farms. There were many small villages and towns and a few larger cities. Then she saw the two soaring towers of Notre-Dame de Reims and nearly dropped her cards.

While they played, Madame Palladino told her about her second husband, the magician. "We traveled to all the best cities in Europe. The audiences—they loved him. They did not know about his tempers. They knew only his magic. Once he made a snake appear out of nothing. It crawled along the stage. A woman fainted. Then they knew him for his snakes. Big and small, appearing and disappearing. All they wanted was the snakes. They called him brilliant. I called him hard to live with." Again the infectious laugh.

"What happen to him?"

"Fever."

"Do you ever contact him?"

"What for? When he was alive, I had nothing to say to him. And that has not changed. A small man with a big pride."

In the afternoon they turned up the lamps and Lucia read to her from the latest *roman-feuilleton*. She liked the ones set in the English countryside, with governesses and accidents of birth. Later that evening, Sapia ordered coffee with Amaretto and sat back with a sigh, saying that if Lucia liked it, then they would order it every night. Lucia liked it just fine and said as much, which seemed to please her employer. She sipped her coffee while looking out the window, trying to catch a glimpse of the passing landscape. All she could see by the sliver of a moon were a few distant twinkling lights and the occasional farmhouse or outbuilding.

Lucia wasn't sure what it took to be a paid companion. No one she knew had ever taken such a position. When she was a cook she knew what she was about; she cooked and cleaned and went to the markets. She knew her place, which was among the tradesmen and the servants, where she felt most comfortable. But on the train it was all turned around. She was called *mademoiselle*. Chairs were pulled out for her, and her luggage was carried. The porters and waiters made assumptions about her station. They thought she belonged there, but she knew otherwise. She felt she was only playing the mistress and it was awkward, like wearing someone else's shoes.

When Madame Curie heard about the trip, she seemed genuinely happy for Lucia, proclaiming it an adventure. She didn't seem at all put out that Lucia was leaving her without a cook or maid. That may have been because she was too preoccupied with the new laboratory to give it much thought. When Lucia asked her about the duties of a paid companion, Madame Curie said she thought it didn't entail much beyond being agreeable and mending the odd button or two. Arlington, who was still laid up in his hotel room, sent her a *bleu* that merely said *bon voyage, have fun, and don't take any wooden nickels.*

On the second day of the journey a small, brittle woman knocked at the door of the compartment. When Lucia opened it the woman apologized in a quavering voice and asked to speak to Madame Palladino. Lucia was just about to put her off when she heard Sapia's voice behind her.

"Let her in, Lulu."

"I do not wish to disturb you," the woman said.

"That is quite all right. Please come, sit down."

The compartment was taken up by a low table cluttered with teacups and dirty plates. Despite the cramped space the woman was able to slip into a chair next to Lucia and opposite Madame Palladino. She perched there on the edge, her eyes already glistening with tears. "I am Madame Descoteaux. They said you were on the train."

"Would you like some water or perhaps tea?" asked Palladino softly.

She shook her head. "I have come—"

"No. No need to tell me why you have come. Please, give me your hand."

The woman offered a pale hand with pink half-moon cuticles, unadorned, except for a simple gold band on the ring finger. Palladino took it and held it and closed her eyes.

After a moment or two she groaned: "Poor lady."

Madame Descoteaux burst into tears.

"I am so sorry," the medium said gently. "You loved him, yes?"

She nodded. She was too overcome to speak.

"A beautiful family. He is with you, you know that."

The woman stopped crying. "He is here?"

"He is wherever you go. He is always with you. He says 'mouse.' *La souris.* You understand?"

The woman nodded and laughed through her tears. "That was his name for me."

"He says Madame Mouse is not to worry. He will always watch over you and the children."

"Is he all right?"

"He is no longer in pain. He is at peace. And he misses you. But he is right by your side. Always."

The woman wiped away her tears and took a big breath. Then she brought Madame Palladino's hand up to her lips and kissed it. "Thank you."

"Of course. Now, would you like that tea?"

She shook her head and rose. "I have taken too much of your

time already. And I must get back to the children. You are everything they say you are. And so kind."

The woman repeated the words to herself—*so kind, so kind*—as she slipped from the compartment. Lucia shut the door gently behind her. When Lucia returned to her chair, Madame Palladino picked up the cards. "So where were we?" She began to shuffle, her rings flashing in the late-afternoon sun.

Lucia watched her for a bit and then leaned over and kissed her on the cheek. Madame Palladino looked up briefly, patted her hand, and began to deal.

•    •    •

Porters were scarce when Lucia and Madame Palladino arrived in Lucca three days later. The terminal had fallen into chaos as English and American tourists rushed to employ the few workers who were left after a flu had ravaged their city. Most of the tourists, including Lucia and Madame Palladino, needed help in getting their luggage transferred to a local train that would take them up the valley to Bagni di Lucca.

The veneer of social intercourse quickly fell away as the situation got ugly and the passengers fought to make the train. Madame Palladino entered the fray with a calm air of authority, which proved to be justified. She was recognized at once by the captain of the porters, graciously welcomed by name, and instantly assigned to one of his men.

"He knows you," Lucia said, impressed, looking at the crowd around them still fighting for their luggage.

"This is Italy. They all know me."

Their final destination was Ponte a Serraglio, an ancient resort town, one of many in the valley of the Lima River. As their train made the steep climb into the mountains, Madame Palladino, a frequent visitor to the town, described all the delights that awaited them. "Ah, the casino, *dolcezza*. So beautiful. And the vapor baths in Bagni Caldi. We will soak all day. You will love it there. Paradise on earth."

The train climbed out of the Serchio Valley and up into the hills covered in fir, mossy oaks, and bare beeches, their limbs woven into skeletal baskets by the wind and weather.

They arrived in the village an hour later. Madame Palladino had sent word to the villa and they were met at the station by a dour-looking fellow in a horse-pulled cart, who greeted them with a little bow and silently loaded up their luggage in the back.

The fellow joined them on the bench, flicked the reins, and the horse plodded across a stone bridge and up a dirt cart track that led past a villa draped in bare wisteria branches.

"Villa Fiori," Madame Palladino said. "He is nice. From an ancient family. She, not so much. Married up. You know what I mean?" Here Sapia crossed her arms and pursed her lips in disapproval.

Along the way they passed several hotels and quite a few villas, all showing signs of age. It was easy to imagine restless specters floating up the mossy steps or stalking the gloomy corridors of those faded glories that hung from the hillsides like rocky outcroppings. Sapia had something to say about most of them—bits of gossip, scandal, and speculation about the owners or the caretakers. This was the real story of the town, one never found in the guidebooks.

The view of the town from this higher vantage showed a line of ancient stone and stucco houses, three and four stories high, rising straight and sturdy from the shore of the churning river. Their red tile roofs were complemented by the green slopes of the hillsides. Maybe it was just the fog, but to Lucia there appeared to be an atmosphere of melancholy about the place; the lines were hazy, the streets seemed to melt away, a spectacle of plunging torrents and limestone. But the town had an unreal quality, like a stage set, dramatic and unsettling.

When Lucia first saw the Villa Ridotta she thought it was a grand house with its blue shutters and carved entryway, firmly planted on the side of a gorge overlooking the river. Yet the inside was shabby, its terrazzo floors worn smooth over the centuries, the rooms furnished with moth-eaten tapestries, and fusty furniture smelling of age and polish. Still, Lucia could imagine a romance about the place. Standing on the wide balcony outside the main room, she was reminded of the weeklies that she and Ania used to read. There was something ethereal and dreadful about the villa and the town below, with the heavy mist hovering over the roiling water and the occasional screech of eagles soaring above the ragged chasms.

Their rooms were large, comfortable suites on the second floor with four-poster beds and heavy carved oak bureaus and tables. Lucia unpacked for Sapia, hanging her gowns in the armoire and tucking her linens and beautifully embroidered shifts in the bureau. At first she had a hard time calling her Sapia. It did not seem right. But the medium was so warm and winning—and effusive with her compliments—that it didn't take long for it to become second nature.

They spent those first few days walking in the town or taking a carriage up to Bagni Caldi, a few kilometers upriver, where they sat in the hot mud bath at the Grand Hôtel or lounged in the grotto for a vapor bath. In the evening Sapia liked to visit the casino where she spent a great deal of her time and money playing baccarat or roulette. Lucia traveled confidently in her wake, soaking in the pageant of the nightlife, noting with pleasure just how far she had come since Dobra Street.

When they walked up the narrow streets of Ponte a Serraglio, shopkeepers and workers from the spas and hotels came out to greet them. Lucia was surprised to see pictures of Sapia in the gift stores alongside gilded miniatures of the Blessed Mother and the other saints. Apparently, Eusapia Palladino was a celebrity in Italy, a homegrown miracle, recognized in even small villages like this one.

Everywhere they went she was invited in with offers of espresso, a glass of wine, a pastry, or in one case, a bunch of flowers. Lucia missed much of what was said because she didn't speak the language. She tried to glean what she could from expressions, large gestures, and pantomime and often pretended to understand when she didn't. Sapia, on the other hand, seemed right at home, introducing Lucia to the townspeople as *mia nipote*. Lucia was moved when she later learned that *mia nipote* means my niece.

One afternoon Sapia stopped to gossip with the eye doctor's wife and the baker's wife translating for Lucia as they went along. "They say he keeps a woman in Lucca and his wife is beside herself." They were talking about the mayor, whose wife had a temper and threw plates. "They say she does not do herself any good by throwing fits. She would do better to look the other way, but she is too proud." This was a rough translation. A sour smile from the eye doctor's wife, a sarcastic comment, and Sapia burst out laughing. "She says she has gotten good at looking the other way. She had to. Her husband is an eye doctor and there is an epidemic of near-sighted women in the village." Lucia laughed at this and they were pleased by her reaction. The baker's wife hugged her and said something in Italian that Sapia didn't bother to translate. Later, as they followed the footpath along the river, Sapia slipped an arm through Lucia's and sighed, *mia nipote*. At that moment Lucia did not feel like a mill worker's daughter from Powiśle or even like the cook of famous scientists. She felt like something else, something new, a person she was just discovering.

They walked on across the bridge and stopped in the middle to watch the rapids below. The recent rains had turned the usually compliant river into a churning torrent. Sapia was leaning on the stone parapet, laughing and making fun of the scientists that were due to arrive that afternoon, when she stopped in midsentence and stared, transfixed by something in the water. Her body grew rigid and she released Lucia's arm, her black eyes locked on a spot beneath the rushing river.

"What is it?" Lucia asked. She followed Sapia's intense gaze to the froth below. There was nothing unusual there, rocks and a pile of tree limbs caught up on the boulders. Beyond it in the shallows, long strands of river reeds waved like hair in the current.

"Is something there?"

Silence.

Then a moment later Sapia's head dipped and she was back. "Take me home," she said with a quaver in her voice. "Get me away from here."

Lucia helped her off the bridge to the footpath and up to the villa. Once they arrived, Sapia went directly to her room. Lucia followed her up, helped her out of her corset, and got her into bed.

"We are not going to the casinos this afternoon. And tell them I won't be at supper. Tell them I am not well." Then she rolled over, faced the wall, and closed her eyes.

•    •    •

Professor Lombroso arrived in the afternoon and met his guests in the large salon on the first floor to give them a formal welcome. It was easy to see why he chose to rent a villa in a valley celebrated for its thermal baths. He was a bent man with a twisted back that made walking painful. He supported himself on a cane as he hobbled over the tile floor, inviting his guests to take a seat and waiting until everyone had before taking his.

That evening Sapia came out of her room and joined the others, having recovered after her long nap. They all gathered in the dining room under the massive carved beams where they were served by a middle-aged couple, the Abruzzeses, who kept the villa for the guests. The husband, who acted as caretaker, was the bleak man who had brought them up in his cart. His wife, the housekeeper, made up for his reticence with her easy laugh and friendly manner, prone to providing long explanations when shorter ones would do.

Sapia had already told Signora Abruzzese privately that her mother was happy and with her Aunt Adelina in heaven, so she got special treatment that night and the best cut of beef. After supper Professor Lombroso laid out his plans for the week. He spoke with a quiet formality, first in halting French, then in cascades of Italian. Sapia had requested several nights off to recuperate between sittings and he had worked them into the schedule. Lucia knew by *recuperate* Sapia meant playing baccarat at the casinos.

Early the next morning before the sun was up, when the sky was still a drowsy midnight blue, Lucia woke to a woman's scream coming up from the valley below. This was followed by shouts, frantic orders back and forth across the river, and a throng of people all talking at once. Though she could not understand the words, Lucia could sense the panic and urgency around them.

She stepped out to the balcony and looked down on the river's edge. A crowd had gathered near the bridge where she and Sapia had stood the day before. They were watching a man buckle a climbing harness around his waist. Lucia saw that he meant to attach the harness to a rope that had been stretched across the river and was being held in place by several men at each end. They had wrapped the rope around sturdy saplings and were using them as pulleys. The man on the beach clipped himself to the rope and began to wade into the swift current. First it came up to his knees and then to his waist. He fought it all the way, until it became too much for him and knocked him off his feet. He shouted to the men and they pulled the rope taut so that he could slide along it.

It was then that Lucia noticed an odd bundle of sticks and water reeds snagged on a tree branch that had gotten wedged between two boulders in the middle of the river. It seemed that this was where the man was heading as he struggled with the rope and the current. All along the journey his compatriots shouted to each other and fought to hold the rope steady, while the saplings threatened to break under the man's weight.

After the man reached the boulders he tried several times to climb up on one but slid down with every attempt. Finally he was able to gain purchase despite the slimy surface and, after one gigantic effort, hoisted himself up on the rock and lay there panting from his exertions. When he got his breath back he crawled over to the odd bundle of sticks and worked to free it. Once free, he got a tight grip on it and slipped back into the river.

When the bundle unfurled in the water Lucia saw that it wasn't a confusion of sticks and reeds, but a body with two arms and legs and long tresses of black hair. The man shouted to his compatriots and they began to pull him back to shore hand over hand through the rushing, muddy froth. A distraught woman broke free from the crowd and ran out into the water to meet him as he stumbled back to the beach. She took one look at the body and began to scream. After the man laid his burden down, she fell onto the body, scooping it into her arms and rocking back and forth, sobbing. The men stood silent and helpless, watching as the priest took charge trying to comfort the frantic woman, talking to her, praying for her, but she would not be consoled. The dead girl lay in her arms, pale as a specter, her eyes open and staring, her hair plastered to her face, draped over her shoulders like a clump of water reeds, so black it was almost blue.

Lucia stood there trembling, pulling the shawl around her shoulders, a cold lump in her stomach. She turned and found Sapia standing behind her, solemn and resigned, her mouth set, her eyes fixed on the scene below.

•    •    •

Later that day Sapia sent Lucia to the village to find out what had happened. "I would go myself, but the walk is too much and I need to rest for tonight's sitting." So Lucia set off alone with instructions to gather information and bring back the best apples she could find.

The woman at the greengrocer's was only too happy to tell her what she knew. She described in great detail the events that transpired that morning, only it was in Italian and Lucia could not understand a word.

Lucia walked down to the town square where the local farmers had set up carts displaying winter produce. One by one the shopkeepers came out to greet her and soon they were joined by the maids and washerwomen from the hotels. They spoke over each other in Italian, which did nothing to clear up the mystery, that is, until the milliner, a tall, serious-looking woman, carefully coiffed and in a starched shirtwaist and simple skirt, elbowed her way through the crowd and greeted her in French, explaining that she had apprenticed in Lyons.

Signorina Albrici explained that the girl who had drowned that morning was the daughter of Signora Porchella, the patroness of a little pensione on the river side of the main street. Signora Porchella had sent her daughter down the valley to Lucca to pick up supplies and check on a clock that had been ordered for the parlor. She had left early that morning with letters to the suppliers and enough money for a comfortable journey. She was scheduled to return on the two fifteen so she could help her mother with the tea service. When she didn't arrive, her mother assumed she had stayed in Lucca to visit her Aunt Bianca and would arrive by a later train. When she didn't arrive by the five o'clock and then by the seven, her mother began to worry.

"Some say the girl was shy and never gave her mother a moment's trouble. Some say she kept secrets, held to the shadows, and was a loner."

Here, Signora Secondo, whose husband was the *poliziotto,* chimed in with a splattering of Italian. The milliner explained: "She says the girl was standoffish and thought she was better than everyone else. Everyone has their opinion, as you can see, but whatever you choose to believe, the mystery remains the same: How did Rosalia Porchella end up in the Lima River?"

•   •   •

Professor Lombroso had chosen the music room for the séances and had the caretaker and his helper bring in a large inlaid card table from the front parlor along with six upholstered chairs. Once the chairs were placed around the table, the maid poured glasses of fresh water, which were set out for each of the sitters. The room had massive windows that stretched almost to the ceiling, covered with heavy velvet drapes. A fire had been burning all afternoon in the grand fireplace that now held glowing coals under its fresh logs. The massive chandelier hanging in the center of the room remained dark, its candles unlit. The only light came from the fire and the few oil lamps about the room casting energetic shadows on the walls and ceiling. One corner was curtained off by thin black drapes, the medium's cabinet. A chair had been placed inside for the convenience of the medium.

That night Lucia took her seat at the table next to the courtly Professor Lombroso. The other professors were there too: Professor Barzini, a jowly man with a pudding face, who apologized too often and laughed too readily, and the intense Professor Imoda with his watchful eyes. Included in the circle was a woman dressed in black. She had been beautiful once, but now her puffy face was scoured by grief. She kept her eyes fixed on her hands in front of her, looking up only briefly to answer the few questions that came her way. When it became apparent that she wanted to be left alone, the others stopped addressing her altogether.

Sapia arrived a few minutes later, after having been searched by Signora Abruzzese, who was thought to be impartial. After the housekeeper testified that she had found nothing, Sapia took her seat in front of the medium's cabinet with Professor Lombroso on her left and Lucia on her right. They took up hands, Lucia placing her foot on Sapia's, Professor Lombroso presumably doing the same. Professor Barzini, who was sitting on the other side of Lucia, patted her hand and said: "There is no need to be afraid, child. They are just like us, only without a corporal body."

Lucia was afraid, however. She had been dreading these séances ever since they arrived in Ponte a Serraglio. Most of the time, she was able to push her fears aside, especially when they were at the baths, shopping in town, or gambling at the casinos. Now she was part of the circle. The lights had just been lowered. Professor Imoda was acting as stenographer as Sapia dropped her head to her chest and called upon John King, that abomination, to guide her into the spiritual world.

At first nothing happened, which gave Lucia hope that the night might be a blank. The fire flared and then died down as a log crumbled into red-hot coals, sending a veil of burning embers up the chimney. The room smelled of smoke, ordinary and snug. The sound of the crackling fire was lulling, and for a time Lucia began to relax.

Then Sapia's breath came harder and faster and Lucia knew something was coming. She braced herself and held on to Sapia's hand as the room began to change, not all at once, but slowly, in degrees. The smell came first. The woodsmoke was replaced by an odor of damp, of foggy river bottoms, and reeds waving in marshy shoals. Professor Imoda called out something in Italian as he wrote furiously in the notebook.

Next came the distant sound of a rushing river. Sapia was on her feet now, writhing about, her arms thrusting into the air, as she called to John. In Italian she begged him to bring the girl to her. "Bring her here, John. *Portarla qui.*" Professor Barzini translated for Lucia. She was grateful to him, not because she cared to know Sapia's words, but because he was close to her, a solid presence, his voice an anchor to the known world.

The woman in black cried out, a shrill yelp, when Sapia began to speak in a high, plaintive voice like that of a girl poised on the edge of womanhood. She spoke first in Italian, then in French, sometimes from a distance, sometimes up close, as if she were moving about the room, even though it was plain that she never left her chair. "He said he loved me and he would marry me. I believed him. I loved him."

Lucia held Sapia's hand, letting go only once when her glass toppled over, spilling not water but a black, viscous material on the tabletop. It reeked of a swamp, of corruption, of spongy layers of rot.

"Then I was with child. He kept putting me off, saying he needed more time. His father wanted him to marry a rich girl from Lucca. How could he deny his father?"

The spilled liquid moved as if it were alive with a mind of its own, slithering down the table like a snake, coiling around the next water glass and knocking it over. The snake grew, doubling in size, as its black, viscous body toppled the next glass and the next, absorbing the noisome contents sometimes with a faint gurgling sound that Lucia found particularly loathsome. When the snake reached the end of the table it slipped to the floor and glided across the tiles until it disappeared behind the curtains of the cabinet.

It helped that Lucia was Sapia's control and that she had to remember to keep a tight grip on her hand. It gave her something to do—this was her responsibility now—so she wasn't so afraid. It helped that no one else in the room seemed fearful, only the woman in black who sat stiff and still in her chair.

The scent of the river grew stronger.

A gust of wind ruffled the curtains of the medium's cabinet. The professors kept calling out observations to Professor Imoda. Professor Barzini had long since given up translating them. The wind blew harder even though all the windows in the room were shut. The curtains billowed out, and when the wind stopped suddenly, they fell limp against the outline of a figure that could now be seen in the folds. The voice of a girl was heard hovering above the table, desperate and tragic, cascades of Italian, breathy without pause. Finally the voice began to move off until gradually it faded away.

Shortly after that the curtains lay flat, and the air cleared, smelling fresh again, the fetid odor of the swamp retreating. Now the only sound in the room was the sobbing woman in black and the distant roar of the river. After a time Sapia lifted her head and announced that no more would happen that night.

Sapia went to Signora Porchella and held her while the woman cried. She told her that justice would be done. "This boy, he will be unhappy with his bride. You have my word on it. His life will be short and miserable. He will suffer a horrible illness, lose all his hair, and die screaming in pain." All this was translated by Professor Barzini.

Signora Porchella leaned back and dried her eyes. "When?" she asked.

"By the time he is thirty."

She thought about it, nodded, and kissed Sapia on both cheeks. Professor Barzini helped her to her feet. Then, taking her arm, he led her out of the room and closed the door behind them.

"I thought you said you couldn't see the future," Lucia said, once they were alone in Sapia's suite.

"I had to give the poor woman something. I could not leave it as it was—the boy gets everything and the girl dies. That is no ending."

"Did the girl really throw herself into the river?"

"Of course. I told the story just as it was told to me. I made nothing up."

Later that night, while the house slept, Lucia lit the lamp and went downstairs to the séance room. She stood in the middle of the room by the dying fire, trying to ignore her pounding heart.

"Rosalia," she said softly, and listened.

Silence.

She went to the medium's cabinet and fingered the curtains that had once formed the body of the drowned girl. She stooped and touched the floor with her fingertips. They came away wet.

"Rosalia, are you here?" she whispered.

# CHAPTER 11

# February 1904

Lucia stayed with Sapia at the Balmoral when they first returned to Paris. Neither of them mentioned the Curies, although Lucia knew she would have to go see them sooner or later. Sapia wanted her to stay on as her assistant and companion. Her plan was to rent a flat in Paris where they both could live. When it came time to travel, Lucia would accompany her and attend all the sittings. Sapia found it comforting to have Lucia on her right.

Edith Arlington had arrived shortly after the accident to see to the care of her husband. She made sure that he was seen by the best doctors, that the kitchen made his favorite dishes, and that he was as comfortable as possible given that his leg was imprisoned in a heavy plaster cast.

By the time Lucia and Sapia returned they found Arlington fit and even mobile in the special wheelchair that Edith had procured for him. That first day they gave Mrs. Arlington time to herself while they wheeled Arlington into the lift and down to the sunroom to watch the snow falling on the glass roof. After that Lucia made a point of visiting him every day, wheeling him around the hotel so he could get a bit of fresh air and didn't have to stay cooped up in his room. In this way she was able to justify putting off the Curies.

She didn't know how Madame Curie would react when she told her that she was leaving her employ. She hoped that she would take it well. She was prepared to stay if Madame needed her, at least until a replacement could be found. She thought about asking Marta if she knew of a girl looking for a position. She would have to be a special person, someone well suited to the household, someone who could cook and clean and wouldn't mind the Curies' eccentricities.

When she couldn't put if off any longer she set off for the laboratory, preferring to walk rather than take an omnibus, so she could go over what it was she wanted to say. It was a snowy afternoon. The cart and carriage horses plodded through the slushy tracks in the street, while the street sweepers shoveled the dirty snow and steaming horse manure into the gutters, forcing the pedestrians to jump over it or suffer the consequences. Lucia picked her way down the street, avoiding the icy patches on the sidewalk, until she reached the drive that led to the hangar. There she shook out her umbrella at the door and peered through the glass. She spotted Madame Curie bent over a laboratory notebook, too preoccupied with her work to notice Lucia. Seeing her there in a new starched white smock, looking tense and focused, determined and fragile, Lucia knew she could not leave her mistress without notice. She would stay for at least a month. Sapia would have to understand.

She stood there for some time not wanting to interrupt. It was unthinkable to disturb Madame Curie when she was working, a rule etched in her mind from two years of service in the household. She decided to come back another time and was about to leave when Madame Curie looked up, brightened, and waved her in.

"Lulu. You're back." She seemed glad to see her, although she did not get up to greet her. "Did you have a good time?"

"Oh yes. It was lovely."

"Well, good for you. We missed you. But we knew you were in good hands. Was it fascinating? Did you learn a lot?"

Lucia told her about the town and described the séances, particularly the one involving the girl in the river. It was cold in the shed even though the stove was red-hot. She wrapped her arms around her chest and shivered. "I've been thinking," she said, searching for the right words. "Well, what I mean to say is, I thought I might stay with Madame Palladino."

"Yes, I know."

"You know?"

"Yes, of course. I spoke with Monsieur Arlington. He told me you wouldn't be returning. It's all right. We understand. It's a good opportunity for you."

"Arlington told you."

Madame Curie's attention was already back on her calculations. "A few weeks ago," she said absently. Lucia knew she would soon be lost in them.

"But I didn't know a few weeks ago."

Reluctantly, Madame Curie lifted her eyes from the page and frowned. "Well, you do now. Anyway what difference does it make? It is done." Then she made an effort to smile. She got up to hug Lucia, kissing her on both cheeks. "Be happy, Lulu," she said gently. "You're starting a new life."

Lucia should have felt a surge of relief. She told herself it couldn't have gone better. She was free now to follow her own path. Yet, relief wasn't exactly what she feeling when she walked out the door and down the drive. She thought she ought to say something to Arlington. It wasn't right what he did. She was beginning to think that maybe Sapia wasn't the difficult one, that maybe some of her complaints were justified. It was just possible that Arlington wasn't the man she thought he was.

She had brought back some gifts from Italy for Iréne, a stuffed bear and a little box with a ballerina on top. She had to go to the house in any case to retrieve the few things she had left there, nothing of importance, a few books and woolen stockings.

When she arrived at the house she heard voices coming from the garden and went around through the garden gate. She thought to surprise them, so she peered around the corner while staying hidden behind the tangle of bare vines growing up the side of the house. She saw Iréne's sleigh in the snow and heard her voice begging her grandfather for another push. She was just about to call out when she saw the doctor talking to a girl about her own age. He was showing her a horse chestnut.

"I have no idea why they call it that. They're not chestnuts, and if you feed them to a horse, they'll convulse and die." He scraped the pod with his thumbnail until he broke through the flesh and tore open the outer casing to reveal the nut inside. He held it out for the girl, who took it and ran her thumb over the smooth surface.

"Can you eat it?" she asked. Her Polish accent was thick, her French awkward.

"No, you'd end up like the horse. You can boil it and use the solution for laundry, but I'd be careful. It's toxic. You know *toxic*?"

Lucia had seen enough. She left the packages on the stoop and went out through the gate. She walked down to the omnibus stop and waited for one to arrive. No longer concerned about money, she climbed aboard, bought a ticket for the inside, and chose a seat next to a gentleman wearing a fine overcoat and gray kid gloves. As the omnibus rattled past the cemetery buried in snow, Lucia remembered what Madame Clos had told her that night at the *guingette*—about never forgetting that she was just a servant, no matter what anybody said.

•    •    •

People grew accustomed to seeing Sapia and Lucia together. Their picture often appeared in the newspapers, usually in connection with someone well-known in the scientific community. Lucia was careful to cut out the clippings and paste them into a scrapbook that Sapia had bought for her when they were in Genoa. Sapia often bought little presents for Lucia, a tortoiseshell comb, a bit of old lace. She was generous but also jealous of Lucia's time. She did not like being left alone and expected Lucia to be available whenever she wanted to go out. Once when Sapia was out at the *salon de coiffeur,* Lucia used this little slice of freedom to send a *bleu* to Gabriel. She waited for a reply, but it never came.

When Sapia wasn't doing private sittings or being investigated by various researchers, she took a flat in the 1st, on a little side street between the Louvre and the Banque de France. It wasn't a fashionable neighborhood, but it was an easy walk to the cafés in rue de Rivoli where they ate almost every meal. Mostly, they went visiting, shopping, or took carriage rides in the park. The medium wasn't one for walking. At night they got dressed up and went out to the dance halls or to the café-concerts to listen to the singers and watch the silhouette shows. Sapia favored the lower establishments where she was nearly always overdressed but felt most comfortable.

It took several months, but by the summer Arlington's leg had sufficiently healed so that now he could walk with a cane. Just before Edith returned home to Cincinnati she booked them into a little town called Port-des-Barques in southwestern France. It was a seaside resort in the Charente-Maritime department, not too far from Rochefort.

Sapia had been hired to do a series of sittings for a French psychologist and his colleague, a Polish psychologist named Julian Ochorowicz. Lucia had never heard of this Ochorowicz, but she did know of his companion, the famous Polish writer Bolesław Prus. She had read *The Doll* twice and admired the writer immensely. She practiced what she was going to say once they were introduced. However, when the time came for introductions, all she could do was murmur a few phrases in Polish. She didn't get to tell him how much she enjoyed his work until much later, at the end of the evening, when everyone was busy dissecting the sitting and by then her compliment seemed unimportant and easily brushed aside.

Sapia was not pleased with the arrangements. She did not like the little port town. It was too quiet for her. She said there was nothing to do but eat fish. She said the hotel was too small and her room was not comfortable and did not have a private bath. "*Primitif,*" she said, with a look of disgust. She used *primitive* to describe all sorts of unpleasantries. Arlington had to remind her in a heavy voice that this was not a vacation. Nevertheless, that evening he made sure they served rabbit, one of Sapia's favorites. Lucia went into the kitchen to supervise its preparation much to the ire of the cook. She ignored the woman and made a gorgeous Tuscan rabbit with pancetta, a recipe she had picked up in Italy. It had been months since she'd been in a kitchen and it felt like a homecoming.

Since Sapia preferred company, and preferred talking rather than listening, Lucia often looked for moments to get away. When Arlington was around he gave her that opportunity by occupying Sapia with a game of piquet. Lucia took advantage of this arrangement in the early evening before the second sitting when she announced that she was a little tired and needed to lie down. While Sapia played cards with Arlington Lucia slipped out the side door and went for a walk down the main road that ran along the port.

She followed the main street with its line of shops and hotels, past the official buildings, and finally onto a stretch of land covered in scrub oaks. From there she planned on following a causeway that led to an island called Île Madame, about two kilometers offshore. She had gone to this island on their first day and knew it to be a pretty walk. Still, it was nearly half past seven by the time she reached the road and she thought about turning back.

If it hadn't been so beautiful, with the sun lying low and voluptuous on the horizon, streaking the sky with red and orange streamers, she might've turned around and missed it all: the sunset, the shorebirds, the jellyfish, and the rising tide. As it was, she walked on, ignoring the sign that warned of flooding at high tide, not believing for one minute that the tide could be high enough to cover the causeway, perched as it was at least ten meters above the mudflats on top of a steep embankment made of boulders and stones. So, even though she could see a shimmering ribbon of water far off on the horizon, she paid no attention to it and kept walking at a comfortable pace, seeing no reason to hurry.

She had been thinking about Gabriel and wondering why he

had not answered her *bleu* when she stopped to watch a phalanx of returning pelicans gliding along the shore, the oystercatchers and red knots scurrying over the mudflats, the setting sun like a glowing bowl of custard. She thought he probably didn't get it or perhaps the reply had gotten lost. She pictured it stuck to the heel of a delivery boy.

She was not alone on the road that evening. She regularly passed picnickers and walkers all heading back to the mainland. One father picked up a dawdling child and strode off with her on his shoulders. Another man walked with a dog that scampered up ahead. A few glanced over at Lucia; one blocky woman called out to her, telling her that she was going the wrong way.

After a while Lucia found herself alone on the road, her eyes drifting out over the undulating mudflats to the horizon where the distant tide was wider now, more pronounced, and getting closer. She passed a couple too preoccupied to pay her much attention. The husband had hold of his wife's arm just above the wrist and was pulling her along despite her complaints that he was going too fast.

It occurred to Lucia how satisfied she was with her life now, how happy she was traveling with Sapia and helping people. Of course it was Sapia who mostly helped them; Lucia would occasionally contribute in some small way. The first time she asked a question of the spirits and got an answer it came as a shock, but by now she was used to it. She was even used to John King, that reprobate, who still presented her with a rose from time to time.

She thought she might have some kind of power. Sapia was always going on about it and Lucia was beginning to believe her. She did not know how that fit into her view of heaven and earth. It was still a mystery how spirits and séances could be part of the same world as God and church. She hardly spoke to Saint Lucyna anymore. She hadn't written to Babusia in weeks and she couldn't find her rosary, which didn't matter much because she hadn't been to Mass or confession in a while. Of course, she still had her mother's cross, hanging over her bed wherever that happened to be.

Lucia did not begin to understand the danger she was in until she saw the jellyfish. It lay there like a purple helmet halfway up the embankment, a jellyfish on the boulders. It could have been a hatbox or a piece of pie or an armchair; it was that incongruous. It surprised her to see it lying there, hard and impenetrable, baked by the sun into another kind of boulder, its tentacles stretching out with monstrous delicacy. Now it made sense why the others were hurrying back to the mainland. The ocean obviously came up that far. It would have to in order to strand the jellyfish. Still, it was on the slope of the embankment, not on the roadbed, so she didn't see any reason for alarm.

Further on she saw the rest of them strewn out on the road: large and small ones, baby jellyfish, giant ones too, like solid puddles of water. It had been a school of them swimming over the causeway, the roadbed far beneath them under the water. The tide had gone out so quickly that they didn't have time to swim away. Now it was coming back in and soon the causeway would be underwater again.

*I can't swim.*

Lucia turned back, tramping over the uneven road, stopping from time to time to check on the progress of her pursuer. The tide had already surrounded the island and was lapping at the embankment. She couldn't believe how quickly it rose. When it was halfway up the steep slopes she broke into a run. She ran past the bickering couple and a few minutes later the man and his dog. When she couldn't run anymore, she limped over the dusty road, pressing the cramp in her side, until she finally came to the entrance and safety.

"Isn't it a risk walking out there at high tide?"

She had just reached the main road and was bent over trying to catch her breath when she straightened and found Gabriel Richet sauntering over. "What are you doing here?" she asked. She suddenly felt hot all over.

"Looking for you." He handed her a red poppy that he had picked from a field nearby.

"How did you know I was here?"

"I asked for you at the hotel."

"No, I mean here, in Port-des-Barques."

"I'm a journalist, *mademoiselle*." He said this with a blithe half-smile. "We find people."

She tried not to show her pleasure. "And why did you want to find me?"

"Oh, I don't know. I thought maybe you'd sing for me." She gave him a look and he laughed. "What were you doing out there? Planning on swimming with the jellyfish?"

"I didn't know the tide was so high. I thought the road would be safe."

He looked at the sign that warned of high tides and raised an eyebrow.

"Yes, I know," she sighed. "Perhaps, I've been a little reckless."

"Perhaps. I hope you swim well."

"Not at all."

"Then it's a good thing you're a fast walker." He took her hand as natural as could be and they walked back toward the town.

"So why are you here, really?" she asked.

"I'm writing a story."

"What about?"

He shrugged, but instead of answering her he stopped to watch a chevron of birds gliding along the shoreline. "What are those?"

"Gannets."

"Are you sure?"

"Yes, gannets. Unmistakable."

He stopped to give her an admiring look. "It's safe to say, *mademoiselle*, that I don't know any other girl in France who could name that bird."

Lucia beamed with pride. He was right of course.

They were passing a café that catered to the fishing families. Through the curtained window Lucia saw two old men in stocking caps, their heads bent to their plates, finishing up their supper. Once she and Gabriel were on the steps of the hotel she thought about inviting him into the lobby. She was just wondering what

Marta would have to say on that subject when he turned to her and casually asked about Eusapia Palladino.

"Yes, we're here doing a series of sittings."

"Could you get me an invitation?"

"I don't know. It might be difficult. Monsieur Arlington is very strict about who attends. He doesn't like journalists."

"He knows me. And he knows my brother. Surely, he can make an exception."

"I'll ask. That's all I can do."

They agreed to meet the next day. Before he released her hand he brought it to his lips. "A bit of advice, *mademoiselle*. Read the warning signs. Believe it or not the locals know something about their tides."

She nodded and watched him go. When he turned back once to wave, she thought she should have invited him in.

•   •   •

Arlington came down the next morning moving surprisingly well for a man still dependent on a cane. He eased himself into a chair across from Lucia, careful to keep his leg straight out in front of him as he sat down with a groan. "The worst is trying to pull up my pants," he said, picking up a menu.

They had their pick of the tables since they were the only two guests in the room. It was early in the season and the summer rush hadn't started yet. Lucia had chosen a table by a large sunny window that looked out on the mudflats where a small fleet of fishing boats lay on their sides on the exposed sea bottom. Arlington put down the menu and gazed out on the bay. "I want you to stay close to Sapia during the sittings. Keep an eye on her."

"Why?"

He regarded her with irritation. "Just do it, please."

When the waiter came to their table Arlington ordered two café au laits, a plate of cheese, croissants, and fruit.

Once they were alone Lucia leaned in. "Why did you do that?" she asked quietly.

"What?"

"Why did you order for me?"

"I thought that's what you wanted. That's what you usually get."

"What if I wanted something else? What if I wanted smoked fish or an egg?"

"Do you want smoked fish or an egg?"

"I don't want you to order for me."

His eyes settled on her. "What is it, Lulu?"

She took a deep breath. "Why did you tell Madame Curie that I wasn't coming back?"

"You weren't coming back."

"But I didn't know that at the time. You told her weeks before I decided to stay."

"Yes, and then you made your decision and it was a good one. And now you're here with us."

She crossed her arms and looked out on the anchors of the fishing boats, brightly colored lead balls, deceptively nimble and playful in the fresh morning light.

He sighed. "Yes, all right. I shouldn't have done it. I should've waited for you."

Lucia pursed her lips and said nothing.

"I'm apologizing, what else do you want?"

Afterward, they took a short stroll along the sea wall to give Arlington a chance to exercise his leg. She thought that now that he was feeling contrite it might be a good time to bring up Gabriel.

"I ran into Gabriel Richet yesterday," she said, casually. She noticed that he grew starchy at the mention of his name. "He wants to come to a sitting."

"We don't allow journalists. I hope you told him that."

"I don't think he would be coming as a journalist. He's interested in spiritualism. He mentioned his brother."

"No, it's impossible. The table is full, in any case."

"He would only come the one time. We could make room."

He regarded her for a moment. "You like this fella?"

Lucia wavered. "I hardly know him."

Arlington's gaze drifted out over the flats. The exposed seabed looked choppy like the sea that had formed it. It was furred with green algae still soggy from a night under the water. "I think it's best if you don't talk to him."

"Why?"

"He's not exactly a friend of ours."

"But his brother—"

"He's not like his brother. His brother is a scientist who treats our work with interest and respect. This man is a reporter, and not a very good one at that. He wants a story. He wants to insult Sapia and make a headline."

"He's not like that. He is kind and concerned about science. He wrote a good article about the Curies and showed great care for their well-being."

"You don't know him, Lucia. You don't know anything about him. Please tell him you want nothing more to do with him."

"You're misjudging him."

Arlington leveled a look at her. "I want your promise."

She hesitated and then gave him a reluctant nod.

"Good. I don't want to have to tell you again."

Then a moment later Arlington brightened and said: "Let's go to that little shop you like. Sapia wanted you to pick out something nice for yourself. We'll put it on my bill."

•    •    •

When Lucia came off the causeway that afternoon, she saw Gabriel waiting for her under the oaks with a bunch of red poppies his hand. He looked glad to see her, hopeful and tense. The sun was still high in the sky, making the rivulets on the mudflats gleam like mirrors.

Black-winged stilts ran here and there on their stick legs, scooping up brine flies in their needle beaks. He greeted her warmly and gave her the poppies.

She hesitated, but only for a moment before taking them. "I'm not supposed to see you," she said, falling into step beside him.

"Who says?"

"Arlington. He thinks you're a reporter after a story. That you want to make mischief for Sapia."

Gabriel ran his fingers through his hair. "I always want to make mischief." He gave her his crooked smile. "Did you ask him about the séance?"

"He won't let you come. He doesn't trust you."

"Did you mention my brother?"

"Yes, but he said he has his rules."

"His rules," he muttered bitterly.

"He's worried about bringing negativity into the room. Madame Palladino finds it difficult when journalists are present."

"I'm sure she does."

"She says it muddies the aether. Makes it harder for her to contact her guide."

"That's convenient," he said, his mouth a rigid line of disappointment. "What does he think I'll find?"

"He doesn't think you'll find anything. He's merely thinking of Sapia."

He stopped to watch a group of children playing on the beach. "Haven't you ever been curious?"

"About what?" She didn't like his tone.

"It's not hard to make spirits appear out of thin air. Did you know that?"

"I don't know what you are talking about."

"They have tricks, you know. They're like magicians. They are very clever. It's nothing to make guitars float about and play by themselves. I have done it myself. I could show you how it's done."

"I must be getting back, *monsieur*. I'll be late. I'm sorry you could not be part of it. I think you would have been surprised. It might have gone a long way to answering your concerns."

"I'm not saying that your Madame Palladino is a fraud. I'm just saying that she could use a trick or two once in a while and you'd never know it. I thought you might be interested in seeing a few. Just out of curiosity."

"I do not like tricks, *monsieur*. Sapia uses her extraordinary gifts to help people. I have seen it with my own eyes, many times. If you do not believe that, then we have nothing to talk about."

Lucia turned and walked on with long, determined strides, skirting the puddles left by the morning rain. Her heart thrummed as she ran up the steps to the hotel, disappointment weighing on her chest. This was not how she envisioned their meeting. As much as she hated to admit it, Arlington was right not to let him into the circle. He would have polluted it with suppositions and suspicions. Now, she didn't know what to think of him. Her previous feelings for him had mutated into a welter of new ones, leaving her confused, disappointed, and restless.

•   •   •

The séance went late that night and Lucia was exhausted by the time they returned to the hotel. Sapia wanted to stay up and talk. She was hurt and indignant because John King had behaved so badly that night, throwing a fit and saying awful things about their host. "I am so upset with him. I cannot imagine falling asleep."

Lucia took her up to her room and listened to her complaints, nodding sympathetically. This apparently had a salubrious effect on Sapia, for soon she was yawning and ready for bed.

It wasn't long before Lucia was able to return to her own room, grateful for the time alone. She was just taking out her hairpins when a knock came at the door. It was the bellboy with a note. He said he was to wait for an answer. She tore it open and read it quickly. *Come out with me. It's a beautiful night. Not a jellyfish in sight.*

When she came down to the lobby, she found Gabriel sitting by the fire.

"We can't stay here," she whispered.

"Why not?"

"He might see us."

He got up and followed her to the door. The night was chilly, ruffled by a tangy breeze from the ocean; the streets were dark and deserted. They strolled along the sea wall and watched the tide come in, lit by a shimmering swath of moonlight. It had almost reached the shore when, one by one, the boats that had been lying on their sides in the mud began to right themselves in the water.

"I wanted to explain about what happened earlier," he said.

"You were horrible."

He laughed. "No need to mince words."

"You hardly know her. Have you ever been to her circles?"

"Once or twice."

"You should have seen the ones in Italy. They were wonderful." She told him about Rosalia, the snakes, the apparitions, and, in the last séance, a ghostly face glowing in the dark.

Here he stopped her. "Did you know that some mediums make it a practice of cutting out pictures from magazines? They paste them onto a mask that's been painted with phosphorescence. It's not hard to make a glowing head bounce around the room. I could show you how it's done."

"I'm telling you that she performs miracles and you talk about tricks? No trick could possibly explain the things I've seen. How could you know what I'm talking about when you haven't seen it for yourself?" When she told him about the writing on her arm, he gave her one his smiles and took her hand. He turned it over and began to unbutton her cuff.

"What are you doing?"

He didn't answer; instead he slowly pushed up her sleeve. She did nothing to take back her hand. She was more concerned about hiding her pleasure than making him stop. With the tip of his finger he pretended to write on her arm. She thought he was teasing her.

After that they walked back to the hotel and stood under the lamplight to say good night. She wondered if he was going to kiss her and what she would do if he did. Instead he took her arm again and pushed up her sleeve.

"What's this?" he asked innocently. He turned her arm so that she could see the one word written there. *Tricks.*

"Stop it," she said, rubbing it out. "Do you think it's funny?"

"It's a solution that acts with the oil on your skin. It's similar to invisible ink."

"It's a cheap trick. I know what you are trying to do. You are trying to hurt her. You're trying to discredit her so you can put her in your newspaper."

"Aren't you the least bit curious? Don't you want to know?"

"I do know. It is very clear. Arlington was right about you. You are not to be trusted. You have no honor, Monsieur. You are no friend."

She wasn't sure what she did after that. Even by her own admission she acted a little irrational, carrying on, shouting at him in Polish. She told him that she never wanted to see him again and if he came to see her, she would call the proprietor and have him thrown out.

"Calm down. I was just trying to help. I thought if you saw—"

"Go away."

"Yes, all right, I'm leaving. But listen, do me one favor. Ask them about Cambridge. Cambridge, and then you'll see."

•    •    •

Lucia never meant to ask about Cambridge. She told herself it wasn't important, that she should put it out of her mind. Nevertheless, she found herself thinking about it, mostly at night. Finally, at the end of the week, on their last morning in Port-des-Barques, it came to her that there was probably a simple explanation, and that if she asked Arlington about it, he would put the matter to rest. They were in the dining room finishing up their breakfast. Sapia was still asleep, so it was once again just the two of them at the table. Arlington sat across from her reading his newspaper, absently dipping his croissant into his coffee. When she asked him about Cambridge he looked up, the pastry dripping on the starched white tablecloth. He didn't answer her at first. He seemed to be sifting through a tangle of feelings that she could only guess at.

"Cambridge. Yes," he said, letting out a breath. "I suppose you read about it somewhere and now you want an explanation." He abandoned the pastry and looked over at her. "Well, what can I say about it? We were at the university. We were doing a series of sittings for the Society for Psychical Research."

His gaze flicked out the window to a one-legged newsboy selling papers on the corner and then came back. "They made such a big deal out of it at the time. They didn't have to do that. She was upset that night. A couple of blanks, and she gets desperate. You've never seen her like that. But take my word for it she'll do anything when she gets like that. She is a very talented and powerful medium. I believe this with all my heart. But, yes, on the third night she used a trick."

Lucia flared. "She cheated?"

"It was a clumsy attempt. They caught her right away. Why do you think I watch her so closely? Why do you think you're here?"

"And you still trust her?"

"She doesn't do that sort of thing anymore."

"How do you know?"

"I know. I've exposed the best."

"What if you are wrong?"

"I've never seen a medium like her before, Lucia. She is truly the white crow—the one that William James talks about—the exception, the honest medium. And she is honest for the most part. It's just that once in a while, when she's scared or impatient, there's a danger she might slip."

This was not the explanation that Lucia was looking for. It was not the one she was expecting. Still, once she thought about it, it wasn't too hard to understand. Hadn't she felt the pressure of having to perform? She knew well that plunging sick feeling. She supposed that she ought to chalk it up to a stupid mistake and leave it at that. It wasn't easy, it took some time, but eventually that's exactly what she did. Over the many months that followed, Lucia became adept at pushing away the nagging doubts. Mostly she focused on Sapia's prodigious talents, the mystery of her séances, and her generous spirit, and in this way she was almost able to forget that she had ever heard of Cambridge.

# CHAPTER 12

# April 1906

The office of *Le Matin* was located on the second floor of a bank building on rue de Rivoli not too far from the Hôtel de Ville. It was a large room filled with two rows of desks separated by a wide aisle. All the desks were being used, but only a few were occupied that morning, mostly by journalists. They perched on the edges of their swivel chairs and concentrated on the typewriters in front of them, poking one key at a time. Their desks were littered with overflowing ashtrays, notebooks, scribbled notes, and cups of cold coffee. The only neat desks to be found belonged to two female typists, aliens in this all-male realm, who had been planted across the aisle from each other at the front of the room near the inner offices. They hunched over their typewriters, their fingers flying over the keys, making a mockery of the feeble efforts of their colleagues.

Gabriel had been waiting for well over an hour on the bench outside Taillon's office. He had come that morning to try to sell three stories to his former editor in the hopes that he would be assigned at least one. The printer, a stocky man in an ink-stained apron, had just left. A reporter that Gabriel didn't recognize was called in. Gabriel had seen two reporters, a typesetter, and a secretary go in during the long while he had been kept waiting. A couple of them had been friends of sorts and asked how he was doing. In each case he told them that he was doing fine, that he had more work than he could handle, and that he had come by just to lend a hand.

Martin Taillon, the managing editor of *Le Matin*, liked to brag that he gave his reporters three mistakes. Gabriel's first mistake came when he failed to interview the flatmate of a *grisette* named Flora Bourget who turned up floating in the river. *Le Figaro* had gotten to the flatmate and she had led the reporter to the victim's boyfriend. The story had run on page two for three days.

His second mistake came when he falsely reported that one of the councilors in the 8th had been taking bribes. It turned out his source wanted the man's job. The paper ran a retraction. Even so, there was a lawsuit. The third and fatal mistake came when *Le Petit Journal* beat him to the story about mediums and their connection to the scientific community. The morning the story ran Martin Taillon called Gabriel into his office and gave him the sack. No explanation was needed. The meeting took less than two minutes.

That was more than six months ago, and ever since he had been looking for the story that Taillon could not refuse. It had to be big enough to put Gabriel back at his desk, which was currently being occupied by his replacement, a fat little toad from *L'Écho*. He knew it was out there. Once or twice he thought he had it, only to have the story evaporate when his source disappeared.

Taillon finally came to the door and waved him in. "What is it this time," he asked, puffing on a stub of a cigar to get it going. He was a rumpled man, once fit, now going to seed, who perpetually smelled of cigars. He usually had a smoking stub stuck between his teeth and liked to flick the ashes in the most unlikely places: coffee cups, envelopes, drawers, plants, and pockets.

Taillon's personality was an unnerving mixture of self-assurance and impatience. He was precise and curious, a swashbuckler when it came to uncovering stories. His insight led him unfailingly to the ones that would sell papers. Yet, when it came to his staff, he was wholly unaware of how his frequent outbursts affected them. Gabriel knew he didn't have much time before he would be asked to remove himself from the building. Taillon had little patience with reporters of the third republic, as he liked to call them, those who had earned his ostracism.

"I have a widow from the mine disaster," Gabriel said, leading with his best.

"I have three. What else do you have?"

"They have new evidence that will clear Coste."

"Wrong. We checked it out. He's going to hang. Next."

Gabriel had little faith in his last story. He knew what it would take to impress Taillon and this wasn't it. He took a breath. "Cambodian dancers at the Élysées." He pretended he didn't see Taillon's withering look. "A troop of young girls in a strange country, photographs of them in their exotic costumes, but they're homesick, just like little girls everywhere."

Taillon crushed out the spent stub of his cigar in a plate that had once held breakfast. "Richet, why don't you go out there and find me a story I don't have. Something new, something sensational, something that will make me regret I fired you. Right now I'm thinking it was the best decision I ever made."

Gabriel tried a few other papers that day: *Le Temps*, *L'Echo*, and *Gil Blas*. The editor at *Le Petit Journal* asked him if he could get one of his reporters an interview with Eusapia Palladino. "You know her, right? How about that girl, the companion. Can you get us in?"

For the rest of the afternoon Gabriel wandered the streets, not really having a destination. When it grew too cold and wet to stay out he returned to his flat, keeping his overcoat on because he couldn't afford the gas to heat it. He had saved some food from a family dinner the night before. His father had caught him in the kitchen with the cook, who was making him a package of leftovers.

"So, it has come to this?" his father asked, his lips curling in disgust.

Gabriel left without the package. He told the cook he didn't want it. But she ran after him and forced it into his hand. "You are not going hungry, *mon petit*. I have known you since you were a little piggy and I will not let you starve."

He laughed and assured her that he was not starving. He didn't tell her that it was because Charles was sending him money every month. He would never admit it to her. He barely admitted it to himself.

"All right, Zélie, I'll take it."

"Things will turn around for you," the kindly old woman said. "They always do." She gave him a hug. "I put your father's best in there," she whispered. "To keep you warm."

His father's best was gone by morning, the empty bottle on its side beside the bed, spilling its last drops on the sullen wooden planks. The food was still good though. He decided to save it for later. If he ate it now, he would have nothing for supper, and there was always a chance he would meet a friend who would buy him a bun or a cup of coffee.

When he came back that afternoon he checked his mailbox, hoping the money from his brother had arrived. He wanted to buy another bottle, and he had only a few sous left. The box was empty. So he went upstairs, ate the contents of Zélie's package, and then went back down to the corner to spend his last sou on a shot of indifferent whiskey.

He chose a table by the window, ordered, and waited for it to arrive. A few minutes later the man at the next table rose, threw down a few coins, and sauntered out, leaving his newspaper behind. Gabriel pocketed the few coins and snatched the paper. The man must've realized his mistake for he was back moments later looking for it, but by then the paper already belonged to Gabriel, at least in his mind. He shook his head when the man asked about it, saying he hadn't seen it.

He sipped the whiskey and read about the Courrières mine disaster. He was feeling a little better, warm and relaxed, and thinking about how he was going to raise the funds for another bottle when he turned the page and saw a picture of his brother standing with Pierre Curie, William Crookes, and Palladino in front of the Society of Psychology. The article was about the experiments that Charles and his colleagues were conducting on Eusapia Palladino's psychic powers. Words like *astounding*, *mysterious*, and *revelatory* were sprinkled throughout the piece.

Gabriel was about to order another shot when he realized he couldn't pay for it. Instead he studied the photograph more carefully.

Palladino's head was thrown back and she was laughing. His brother was standing next to her with that mischievous grin on his face, the one Gabriel knew well from his childhood. He must've said something funny in that dry manner of his.

A few pages later he came across another article. This one read: A SUNDAY WITH THE CURIES. The photograph showed a small gathering in the garden behind their house. Gabriel recognized Lucia sitting on a blanket with Madame Curie, Iréne, and two-year-old Éve, who looked nothing like her parents with her black hair and dark eyes. How happy everyone looked, how contented with their lives, and why shouldn't they be? Their lives were successful, easy, and predictable—free of hardship and defeat.

Gabriel went back to his flat to check his mailbox. The money had still not arrived and he still wanted that bottle of whiskey. It didn't have to be good, just good enough to not make him sick.

He decided to go out and earn the money. He waited for a couple of hours until the evening was well underway and then walked over to the Tête d'Orignal. The place was packed with students and a few well-heeled tourists, who came for the color.

He was always welcome at the café. The piano was always his to play. He remembered the night when he met Lucia here. She brought him the photograph of the Curies, and he was on top of the world. Taillon had told him he was running the story on page four and that he should go out and celebrate. He remembered thinking how beautiful she looked that night, how terrible her singing was, and how much he wanted to be with her.

He took a seat on the piano bench and began to play. The proprietor sent over a waiter with a whiskey and a plate containing a half franc silver coin. This was their bargain. The proprietor would loan Gabriel the coin to grease the crowd, knowing that at the end of evening it would be returned with a small percentage of his tips.

It was a good bargain, even if it meant that Gabriel had been reduced to begging—or at least that's how he saw it. He came to the café whenever he was in dire need, and played for several hours, anxious the whole time that his brother or some friends of his family would walk in and see him with his plate and his coins, a common musician playing for his supper. He could just imagine what his father would say if he ever found out.

The whole time he was playing Gabriel kept an eye on the door. He could tell at a glance if someone had money and if they looked the sort to part with it. A few people like that came in during the night and left a tidy pile on his plate. He was playing a popular song, one that his friends asked for so often that it became a joke between them. A gathering had formed around the piano; everyone was singing along. He was on his second whiskey and feeling much better when a gloved hand reached through the crowd and dropped a two-franc silver coin on his plate. Gabriel had never gotten such a big tip. He looked up and his stomach dropped.

"Gabriel." Lucia Rutkowska was as surprised to see him as he was her. She went on in a faltering voice. "Madame Palladino wanted you to have this."

It was then he noticed the famous medium sitting in the corner of the room.

He didn't thank Lucia. He couldn't say anything. He couldn't even look at her. She stood there a moment, her face flushed, then she muttered something under her breath that sounded like an apology and turned away. After that he ignored the protests of his friends who wanted him to finish the song. Without a word he got up and walked out the door, leaving the shot of whiskey and the plate full of coins on the piano.

•    •    •

Gabriel had few sources left, making stories hard to come by. Some had disappeared, others had died, but many required a little something in exchange and Gabriel no longer had access to the fund that Taillon kept in his bottom left drawer. So they all dried up, until he had only one or two left, mostly lower-level bureaucrats in the Town Council.

One of these was an ambitious clerk he had met at the Tête d'Orignal when they were both students. The fellow had risen up in the council and was now expected to be taken on by the prefect. He was a not-too-distant relation of the prefect, who needed men he could trust since he was perpetually under siege. Generally, this fellow's information was pretty tame, office gossip and wishful thinking, nothing to get the notice of Taillon, but Gabriel was grateful that he had some place to go that afternoon and that maybe, by some miracle, it would lead somewhere.

His mind began to spin out a warm fantasy. What if it was a good story, a brilliant story? He imagined a scandal in the council, bribery, embezzlement, something that would cause a stir. He could get his desk back, Taillon's approbation, and a series of articles. What if it was good enough to run on page one? It could even earn a headline, eighteen-point bold type, where Lucia was bound to see it. All of Paris was bound to see it.

The rain had turned into a downpour by the time Gabriel threaded his way through the afternoon traffic in the rue Danton. The street was noisy, as were most streets in Paris, because they were paved with wood or asphalt. The motors and the horse hooves set up a clamor and mixed with the cries of the peddlers and the jangle of the omnibuses. The sidewalk was so crowded that he had to take to the street several times just to get around. There he found himself dodging carriages and carts and trams rumbling by on their tracks. He was to meet this fellow at the Institute Library in the stacks where it was unlikely they would be seen. He got the idea his source liked the subterfuge, thinking it somehow lent importance to the meager information he was about to impart.

Gabriel was late and in a hurry when he glanced up and saw a crowd forming in the place Dauphine. Traffic had stopped. People were standing frozen on the sidewalk, gloved hands covering open mouths in an expression of shock and eager fascination. A few bystanders began moving tentatively closer to the accident that had occurred a moment before.

Gabriel's journalistic instinct propelled him through the crowd even before the import of the tragedy had time to sink in. The driver of a delivery cart piled high with military uniforms was trying desperately to calm his horses. The horses were snorting and whickering, rearing and throwing up their heads, their eyes wide with fear.

The crowd began to shout at the driver, accusing him of coming too fast off the bridge and recklessly knocking the man down. He was shouting back at them that he wasn't going too fast, that the man had appeared out of nowhere and had frightened his horses.

The man in question lay still under the cart; a rivulet of blood flowed into the street and mixed with a puddle of dirty water. Two gendarmes pushed their way through the crowd and helped the driver with the horses. Then they gently pulled the man out and that's when Gabriel could see that the wheel had crushed his skull. The man was beyond help despite the efforts of the gendarmes to get him into a taxi and rush him to a hospital. Gabriel was only vaguely aware of their efforts as the taxi drivers turned them down, one after the other. No one wanted the bloody mess in their taxi.

At first he was too stunned to react to the sight of the face, which he recognized at once. A great surge of sorrow washed over him as he bent down over the dead man. It was Pierre Curie, once alive and animated, now an inert body lying in the rain. His eyes open, his face still, peaceful, even gratified, as if the cart hit him just at the exact moment he had found the answer to a perplexing problem.

It was instinct, automatic.

By the time the gendarmes realized that no taxi driver would take the victim, Gabriel had filled up pages in his notebook with the horror of the crowd, the panicked horses, the cart piled with uniforms, the steady rain, the vein of blood in the street, and the dead man with his peaceful face and hideous injuries. Later, when he had time to think, he would realize what the precious notebook contained: the impressions of an eyewitness to the worst tragedy in a decade to strike the scientific community, the city, and the country at large.

# CHAPTER 13

# April 1906

F irst to go was the breath—coming as it did in ragged gasps, abandoning her lungs as fast as it filled them, leaving her weak-kneed and spent, as if she were laboring over an arduous task, which of course she was. She stood in the hallway, her legs threatening to buckle, her arms wrapped tightly around her middle, holding herself in, a tiny sliver of comfort found in the weight of her own arms.

"Is he really dead?" Even when she heard the answer she couldn't believe it. Not dead, surely. Not all the way.

She had been out to Fontenay-aux-Roses with Iréne, to the school, walking the grounds, fresh leaves, lusty buds, the narcissus had just unfurled their blossoms, cheerful mounds of yellow and white bordering the path, a whiff of their tangy smell drifting in the air. She had no idea that anything was wrong. She still could not grasp it, not even after she returned home and was told. Not even after they offered her his bloody cap.

She had talked with him just that morning. They lay in bed, his body pressed against hers, his arm around her waist, heavy and reassuring. She could feel his breath on the back of her neck as he whispered into her ear. They made plans to discuss his recent work with Eusapia Palladino. Lately, he had been more excited by his experiments with the medium than his work on radium. She became annoyed when he said he didn't want to spend the day with them, that he wanted to go over his notes. That was only this morning, less than eight hours ago. How could so much change so quickly?

They were out in the garden. She couldn't remember how they got there. The doctor was beside her on the bench, holding his head, rocking back and forth. "What was he dreaming of this time?" he kept muttering over and over again.

Somehow she got to her feet and began to walk into the field behind the Perrins' yard, first in one direction then another, stumbling over the uneven ground, her shoes sinking into the muddy channels left from the downpour. What was she to do? How would she live without him? And what about the children, now without a father? Her stomach heaved and pitched. She dropped to her knees. Her love was gone. Her life, and everything that was familiar and safe. The ground had given way and she was falling from a great height. With nothing to break it she would fall forever. Then someone lifted her up, wrapped a firm arm around her back, and held her close.

"What shall I do?"

"You will go on. You will work and you have Iréne and little Ève." It was Jean Perrin. He had his hand under her elbow and he walked her back to the house.

"How can I work?"

"You'll find a way."

"How can I work without Pierre?"

That night she sat alone in their room and wrote in her journal, telling Pierre about the accident, describing what had happened to his beautiful head, crushed beneath the wheel of the cart. She told him he was laid out in the back bedroom. She had wanted to wash him and lay him out herself, but they wouldn't let her. They kept her from him until he was ready.

She went on to describe their last days at the house in Saint-Rémy, taking walks in the countryside, picking a bouquet of blue wallflowers. She described leaving Paris with the girls. He had come to see them off and he nearly left them on the platform without saying good-bye. Then he joined them on that Saturday, and they went to the farm for milk. In the afternoon they went cycling with Iréne. He had to raise her seat because she had grown. He thought it strange that she had gotten so tall without him noticing.

The doctor came in from time to time and tried to get her to go to sleep, but she knew she never would. She would never sleep again. She sat on the rug before the fire, holding his bloody cap, bits of him imbedded in the material: red bits and white bits, scattered bits of his precious mind. No one would take it from her. It was hers now. It was all she had left.

Then Lulu was there, by her side. How did she know to come?

"The doctor sent for me. I came as soon as I got the *bleu*."

"He's gone, Lucynka."

"I know."

"How will I live? How can I go on without him?"

"You have no choice. It won't always be like this. You'll find your way." Lucia stroked her hair and held her in her arms. "It seems impossible now, but you will go on. You will never forget. You will always grieve, but you will heal."

Madame Curie laid her head on Lulu's shoulder and for the moment was comforted. *Zostań ze mną?*. "Stay with me."

"As long as you need."

Then Lucia saw what her former mistress was holding in her hands. "Is that his cap?"

She nodded.

"We have to get you into bed now."

She started to protest, but Lucia helped her to her feet and walked her over to the bed. Once Madame Curie was lying down it was nothing to take the cap from her. When Lucia saw what it held she waited until Madame closed her eyes, until her breathing was even, and only then did she step over to the fire and lay it among the burning coals.

•   •   •

A small gathering of family and friends arrived for the funeral. Madame Curie's sister, Bronya, and her husband, Joseph, had traveled from Warsaw. Monsieur's brother Jacques gave Lucia a start, because he looked so much like Monsieur. Ève ran through the rooms shouting nonsensical orders at everyone. Lucia brought her into the kitchen and gave her a good breakfast. Unlike her sister, Iréne, she ate everything on her plate, then asked for more.

The others knew Lucia only as a servant and didn't know quite what to do with her new station. When Henriette Perrin spilled her tea, she asked Lucia to get a cloth without thinking. Then, realizing her mistake, she colored and apologized, and looked helpless as she tried to mop up the tea with a handkerchief. Lucia assured her it was nothing and went into the kitchen for a rag.

Lucia sat with Madame Curie in the back bedroom where Monsieur was laid out. They spoke little, taking comfort in each other's presence while Madame Curie held Monsieur's hand. Occasionally, she would remember something that Pierre had been working on that she would have to complete: a letter to the Hôtel des Sociétiés Savantes summing up his views on legislation concerning accidents in the laboratories, his paper on the need for more science education, and his correspondence with Morris Arlington and other members of the Society for Psychical Research regarding his work with Eusapia Palladino.

Madame Curie lifted her eyes at the sound of the men arriving from the cemetery. Heavy footfalls in the parlor, hushed voices in the kitchen, and then, moments later, the doctor came in with a black cloth draped over his arm, ready to lay it over the coffin.

"No," Madame Curie said in alarm. "I don't want it. I want flowers."

"We don't have flowers, Marie. And they're waiting. Everyone is waiting."

"I don't care. Let them wait." She rose. "Help me, Lulu. Hurry, before they take him away."

She led the way through the kitchen and out into the yard where they went to work picking a basket of daylilies and early lilacs. They brought the flowers back in, made bouquets, and covered the coffin with them. When Madame Curie was satisfied, Lucia helped her with her hat and veil, took her hand, and led her out to the parlor.

The funeral was supposed to be limited to only those close to the family, but word had gotten out and a large crowd had assembled in the cemetery waiting for the proceedings to begin. Madame Curie hid behind her veil and leaned on the arm of Dr. Curie on one side and Jacques on the other. They brought her down to the grave site where a secular official in a black robe presided over a simple ceremony.

Afterward, friends got up to speak, offering testaments to Pierre Curie's achievements, his dedication to science, his authenticity and generous spirit. During the remarks Lucia's mind wandered. She remembered the day Monsieur taught her how to ride a bicycle on a summer holiday in Le Pouldu. They rode along the Brittany coast, her front wheel wobbling, alarming at first, but then when she got the hang of it, she understood the appeal—the freedom, the sea stretching out to the horizon, a flat blue plate bordered by rocky beaches, the women working the oyster beds, their skirts tucked into their waistbands.

Toward the end Lucia looked up and saw Gabriel Richet standing halfway up the slope, among a group of journalists. She turned away, hoping that he had not seen her. She did not want to talk to him, not after the story he wrote about the accident. It made the headlines and was reprinted around the world. It wasn't anything he said in the article. He was kind to Monsieur. It was the fact that someone had profited from Monsieur's death, and that person happened to be Gabriel Richet.

After the remarks, after the coffin was lowered into the ground and friends and family had gathered around the widow, Lucia walked back up the grassy slope with Madame and the doctor toward the waiting taxi. When they passed the clump of reporters on the hill, she glanced over and found Gabriel watching her with a look of concern and possibly even contrition. She held his gaze for a moment or two, until it seemed as if he wanted to come over, and then she let her eyes drift away.

•   •   •

That night Lucia stayed with Madame Curie until she fell asleep. The whole house was sleeping. Even from the landing she could hear the doctor snoring in the back bedroom. She went down to the kitchen and lit the stove. She put the kettle on and while she stood there waiting for the water to boil she glanced around the room. Even though she had been back to this kitchen many times in the past two years, for some reason, that night, she came to it with a fresh eye. There were the pots and pans hanging on their hooks, their shapes outlined on the wall. There was the stained sink smelling faintly of bleach, the cracked linoleum floor dull from hundreds of washings, the saltshakers she had bought in the market, all the utensils she once took for granted: bent measuring spoons, a food grinder, chipped mixing bowls, and a broken whisk that still worked if you weren't in a hurry.

She brought her tea over to the table and blew on it. The doctor must have turned over in his sleep for the snoring had stopped. The house was quiet.

Then she heard a woman's voice calling out from the front garden, sharp and woeful.

"Pierre!"

It was Madame Curie standing on the path, shivering in her nightdress. "Pierre. Come home, Pierre." She was calling up to the stars in a voice awash with grief and longing.

Lucia grabbed a shawl off the hook and ran out to her, wrapping it around her shoulders, rubbing her arms to warm them.

"He isn't here, Lulu. I thought I felt him, but he isn't here."

"Come in. It's cold."

She shrugged off Lucia's hands. "No. I want him to come back.

I want him to walk through the gate." She kept her eyes on the stars as if she could find him there among the constellations. She called out to him again.

Lucia followed her gaze up to the Great Chariot. There was the box; there was the shaft. There were the two stars Merak and Duhbe—Merak on top, Duhbe pointing the way to Polaris. She could see the Great Chariot and most of Ursa Major, but Monsieur Curie was not among them.

After she put Madame Curie back to bed she went to her old room in the cupboard off the kitchen. She had been staying there ever since Monsieur died. She did not want to go back to Sapia's, not yet. It felt like home here with the Curies, like returning to her childhood bed. She lay there thinking about Babusia, Poland, her father and her siblings. She said a prayer for Madame, for the girls and the doctor. It had been a while since she had spoken with God. It felt awkward, like a pose. She liked it better under the stars, their blue light shining cold and mysterious, yet tangible, an observable expanse, a tapestry of knowable phenomena just up there in the sky.

• • •

She woke in the middle of the night to the sound of someone pacing the house. She heard padded footfalls and for an instant her mind brought her back to the nights when she lived here, when Monsieur stayed awake roaming the house because of the pains in his legs. Then she remembered that Monsieur couldn't possibly be wandering the house, that he was gone, and that she must have been dreaming.

She lay back down and closed her eyes. She was nearly asleep when she heard it again, shuffling in the kitchen, right outside the curtain. It sounded like stocking feet on the linoleum floor. She smelled something acrid, like burning electrical wires, and froze when she heard a tendril of breath near her ear. She told herself not to be frightened. Still, she felt a cold stone in her stomach.

She parted the curtain with trembling fingers and looked out—
a sliver of moonlight cast a wedge on the tablecloth. It wasn't much,
but it was enough to show her that the kitchen was empty. She
wanted to ignore the presence, to assign it to the juddering leaves of
the sycamores, but she knew it was there and that, somehow, it was
meant for her.

She heard or thought she heard a string of whispered utter-
ances difficult to make out. It might have been the leaves in the
night breeze, except for the undertone of urgency. She waited until
the stone in her stomach melted away, until her fingers stopped
trembling, and her breathing grew regular.

She felt strong. She wasn't afraid after that, because she knew
what he wanted.

She swung her legs over the edge of the bed and stood up. Then
to the corners of the empty room, to the space over the stove, to
the air all around her, she said: "Don't worry, Monsieur. I will look
after her."

# CHAPTER 14

# May 1906

A few weeks later Lucia strode into Madame Curie's room and opened the drapes. Sunshine flooded the room, teasing the dark corners and flashing off the mirror. This time there was no protest. There was no greeting either, no attempt to be cheerful. In silence they both got down to their tasks. Madame Curie climbed out of bed on her own. Lucia was already at the armoire pulling out one of the two black dresses that her former mistress owned. Lucia did not like to compare Madame's things to Sapia's. There was something so fragile and helpless about Madame's old corset and plain cotton shift. Especially when compared to Sapia's long straight-fronted corset with the line of pink rosebuds on the bodice and embroidered silk shifts.

Lucia helped her dress. First the heavy cotton stockings, then the shift, the corset, and finally the dress along with its plain cloth belt. She pinned up Madame Curie's hair and brought over her shoes. Finally, at the front door she helped Madame with her coat, gave her a moment or two to collect herself, and opened the door.

The weather was on their side that day. It was cold, but fine. Buds lined up on the hydrangea branches awaiting their turn to open. The garden smelled of loamy soil, mold, and wet bark so sweet that Lucia could taste it in the back of her throat. They walked to avenue d'Italie to find a taxi. Lucia knew Madame Curie couldn't manage an omnibus filled with people. One of them was bound to recognize her, and there would be a flurry of whispers and long, sympathetic faces. Lucia held her up as they plodded along, Madame leaning on her arm, putting one foot in front of other, her features a mask of endurance.

They found a taxi and Lucia helped Madame Curie inside. Then she climbed beside her, leaning forward to give the address to the driver. He nodded once and eased the motor out into traffic. As they traveled up the avenue Madame Curie sagged against the cushions, her cheeks ruddy from the cold, her eyes dull and somber. Lucia was glad that most of the black bunting had disappeared from the lampposts. It had been weeks since Monsieur's death, and the city had moved on.

They traveled up to avenue des Gobelins and onto the bridge. It was odd to see the world continuing as if nothing had happened: a patron at an outdoor café raising a hand to signal a waiter, *nounous* gossiping in the park, an argument between two shopkeepers. It all seemed unreal to Lucia, like a moving picture show, like observing the world from inside a glass bowl.

When they reached their destination Lucia paid the driver and helped Madame Curie to the sidewalk. There were stairs to climb, a lift just big enough for the both of them, and then a long hallway, footfalls ringing off the Moroccan tile, and a door at the end. It opened as they approached.

"I've been waiting for you," Eusapia Palladino said, stepping aside to let them in.

Sapia brought them into the parlor and gave Madame Curie the most comfortable chair in the room, the one she usually sat in. She and Lucia took the sofa. Sapia had arranged for tea and had been to her favorite bakery for cat's tongues. It was all laid out on the best lace tablecloth. At first no one spoke, no pleasantries, just a few questions. "Cream? No? Lemon?"

Sapia did not ask how Madame Curie was doing. Over the years her experience with widows had taught her not to ask that. Instead she sipped her tea and ate her cat's tongues and talked a little of the weather and a bit about their recent trip to Genoa. Sapia's voice was generally loud, but today she spoke just above a whisper. Lucia kept an eye on Madame Curie in the overstuffed chair, looking small and vulnerable, like a wintering animal in its den, the cushions billowing up around her, sheltering her, keeping her apart and numb, or so Lucia hoped. Withdrawn and silent, obediently holding her plate of uneaten biscuits.

"I can help you," Sapia said at last.

"I don't think anyone can help me."

Sapia smiled. "He is not gone."

"He is dead."

"But he is not gone. You have felt him near you, yes?"

Marie Curie looked up sharply, her face fixed with astonishment. "Yes, I have," she whispered. "I have felt him." Her eyes flooded with tears, but this time they were tears of relief. "How is it possible?"

"I only know that it is." Sapia rose and held out her hand. "Come, I think it's time we begin."

She led Madame Curie into the little room she used for séances. Lucia followed them until Sapia stopped her at the door. "I won't be needing you today, *dolcezza*. Madame Curie and I should be alone."

Before Lucia had a chance to respond, the medium shut the door.

•   •   •

Lucia had made plenty of cakes over the years, pies too, pastries of all kinds, but she had never bought one from a bakery. This was an inferior confection to Lucia's way of thinking, a butter cake with too much sugar and too little invention. However, it was Sapia's favorite, mainly because the icing was blue, and blue was her favorite color. She loved the rosebuds and the butterflies made out of pink sugar. If it had been a dress, the medium would have worn it.

Lucia had just left the shop when she encountered Gabriel Richet. She was looking right at him without seeing him because her mind was preoccupied with keeping the cake box dry in the rain. They met crossing the street.

"Mademoiselle Rutkowska, what have you got there?"

She was holding the box in one hand and her umbrella in the other. The umbrella was Italian. Sapia had bought it for her in Venice. "Something I want to keep dry."

"Then we must get you out of the rain," he said, walking her to the curb where they stood under an awning. "I saw you at the funeral. I wanted to come over."

"I know," she said. She kept her eyes on the passing crowd, her expression cool and indifferent.

He studied her for a moment or two. "Still angry I see," his lips bunching in irritation.

"No, I am not angry. I do not know you well enough to be angry." She wished him a good day and tried to walk on, but he didn't step aside for her.

"How is your Madame Palladino?" he asked, making no attempt to keep the edge out of his voice.

Lucia gave him a brief smile. "She continues to help people."

"I'm sure she does. I'm working on an article that may be of interest to you. Mediums in Paris, their methods and talents. I'm including many secrets of their craft."

"Craft? I did not know there was a craft."

"Oh yes. There is a craft."

"Well, no doubt there are some who would find this interesting. I'm not one of them. Good day, Monsieur Richet."

She went around him and walked on. She quickened her pace, but he matched it. "Do you know how they make guitars play on their own?"

"Isn't there some other tragedy in the city you could exploit? The death of a child perhaps, another mine disaster?"

"A music box in a hidden compartment. They have lots of hidden compartments. In their clothing, in their boots. They hide all kinds of things in them, netting for robes, ectoplasm made out of cloth. I think my brother will find that interesting, don't you agree?"

"I do not know what your brother will find interesting. And I wish you would find another place to walk."

He stopped in front of a toy shop and called after her. "Someday you may want to know the truth, *mademoiselle*. And when that time comes, I hope you'll be ready for it."

•   •   •

Madame Curie often came to rue Hérold, sometimes for a sitting, sometimes just for a visit. Lucia, who was once again living in Sapia's apartment, was never allowed in the séance room but she would sit with them beforehand and listen to Sapia's stories, which Madame Curie seemed to find interesting. Madame usually arrived distracted, dour, and hectic, barely holding herself together, but then in a little while she would relax some and even seemed to be consoled by the time she spent with the medium. Sometimes their sittings would last for an hour or more, sometimes less. Lucia would wait for them in her room or in the parlor and then she would see Madame Curie down the lift and make sure she got a taxi.

One night when it was raining Sapia decided they would stay in. They had a fire going in the stove, which Lucia would feed from time to time while she read out loud from the latest installment of a *roman-feuilleton*. Sapia had brought over a lamp to the table by her chair so she could better see the pillowcase she was embroidering, a bluebird perched on a branch covered in dogwood blossoms. Sometimes she commented on the story, but more often she liked to guess what was going to happen next.

"Your Madame Curie is getting better, yes?"

"She is working again in the laboratory."

"Good. Monsieur Pierre was very stern about that. He said you must work, Marie. You must go to the laboratory. She listens to him, eh?"

"She always has. What else did he say?"

Sapia looked up and then shook her head. "No, Lucia. Some things are just between a husband and wife."

"So she speaks with him?"

Sapia went back to her embroidery. "Mostly, she remembers."

•   •   •

Lucia rose early the next morning and threw back the drapes, stepping out through the French doors to the little balcony with its wrought iron table and chairs. She put on a heavy coat and warmed her hands around the steaming cup of café au lait. She ignored the chill in the air and slid into her chair, stretching to get a view of the street over the railing. She loved this time of the day when the maids were out washing the stoops and polishing the brass doorknobs and knockers. The tradesmen trundled by in their carts or on foot, delivering eggs and butter, milk and cream, and ice to the larger flats along the avenue. Her former life looked so appealing from five floors up, so regular and ordered, that she almost missed it. She gave a wave to the little kitchen maid across the way, who waved back with her polishing rag. This had been their ritual for months now, even though they had never spoken to each another.

Sapia was not an orderly person and was used to leaving her things lying around the sitting room or wherever she happen to drop them. Even though they employed a girl, Lucia was used to picking up after her.

Later that morning, after Sapia had left for the *salon de coiffure*, Lucia picked up a scarf and a pair of shoes by the sofa and a jar of rouge on the mantel and brought them back into Sapia's room where she put the scarf back in the drawer and the rouge on the dressing table where it belonged.

She was about to put the shoes back on the rack when she stopped to admire them. They were well made, black, and they buttoned up the side. They looked comfortable, the leather being of the finest quality, pliable and soft. They were light and had mother-of-pearl buttons. She placed them on the shelf next to Sapia's evening slippers, the ruby-red ones with jet beads on the toe and ribbons for straps. She often admired Sapia's collection of shoes. There were so many lined up on the rack, ones for every occasion, that she wondered how the medium found the opportunity to wear them all.

By early afternoon Sapia returned looking well coiffed and chatting about the gossip she had heard in Madame Capillissima's. It had turned into a warm day, so they decided to have lunch out on the balcony. They talked about what they would do that evening and their upcoming trip to Genoa, where Sapia was scheduled to do a series of sittings. Madame Curie wasn't expected until two, which gave Sapia time for a nap.

She unbuttoned her boots and kicked them off. She slipped out of her dress and dropped it on the floor before padding off to her room. Out of habit Lucia picked up the dress and laid it over a chair. She picked up the shoes and was about to put them by the dress when she stopped to take a better look.

They were different from the other pair. These were black with white uppers. She always wanted a pair with white uppers. She noticed that the little buttons up the side were abalone, like drops of oil swirling on water. She turned the heel this way and that, admiring the fine stitching, and that's when she felt a button on the inside of the heel. She was just thinking that it was odd to have a button there, on the inside of a shoe, when she found that she could press it like a doorbell. Instead of chiming, it clicked. It was surprising how easily the heel of the shoe opened—designed on a hinge, so it would be wide enough for the foot to slip out, quiet and smooth. As if by magic.

•     •     •

That afternoon Madame Curie arrived at four o'clock and she and Lucia waited in the parlor for Sapia to join them. During their tea and conversation Lucia kept a sharp eye on Sapia's shoes. She was wearing black boots, but Lucia could see only the toes peeking out from under her long skirt and couldn't tell if they had white uppers.

Finally, when Sapia ushered Madame Curie into the séance room and shut the door, Lucia decided to look for the boots. She had to be sure that Sapia wasn't wearing them, that she hadn't smuggled tricks into the séance room for the purpose of deceiving Madame Curie. She went to the obvious place first: the rack in Sapia's armoire. It took only a moment to see that both pairs of boots were missing. She dropped to her knees and looked under the bed, then in the bathroom, and finally under a pile of clothes in the corner. She searched the parlor, the kitchen, and even the balcony. They weren't there.

Lucia placed her hand on the doorknob to the séance room and was about to turn it when she happened to glance back at the mirror over the mantel. There in the corner she saw the reflection of one shoe, a shoe with abalone buttons, a black boot with a white upper, lying on its side and half hidden under the armchair in the corner. She paused and then deliberately lifted her hand off the doorknob and returned to her seat.

Since Lucia usually saw Madame Curie down after the sittings, it was only natural that she would accompany her on that day. They stepped out of the flat and walked down the long hallway to the lift. Lucia pressed the button, and they waited for it to arrive. Madame Curie looked better for the time she spent with Sapia. She was energetic and preoccupied, no doubt having a think. That could change once Lucia told her. She might lose Monsieur all over again. Then there would be nothing but a corpse in the ground, nothing to bring his wife relief, to give her a little peace from the unremitting loss and loneliness.

When the lift came, Lucia slid back the gate and followed Madame Curie inside. She pressed the down button, causing the gears to complain as the tiny box began its slow descent to the street. The funeral came to mind. Gabriel's look of contrition. His words on the street. Did she want to know the truth? She did want to know.

More than anything she wanted to know before the lift reached the first floor. By the third floor Lucia decided that Madame had to know. To keep the evidence from her would have been unthinkable. She had devoted her life to the pursuit of empirical evidence. Truth was the driving force that animated her, this need to know. She would want the truth. She would want to draw her own conclusions, no matter what the consequence.

Madame Curie kept her eyes on the passing floors. She seemed comfortable if impatient. Lucia stood behind her, shoulders rigid, her features set in an attitude of grim helplessness. She stared straight ahead, not daring to look at her former mistress, solemnly counting the floors as they glided by. She was just thinking that she ought to begin when the lift bumped to a stop, and Madame Curie struggled with the heavy gate.

Lucia hadn't counted on a taxi waiting there at the curb. She thought she would have a little more time. Madame Curie was delighted at her luck. She said she had to get back to the laboratory; there was so much to do. She climbed in promising that she would be back soon. She squeezed Lucia's hand and thanked her, as she did each time.

Lucia hesitated with her hand on the door. After a moment or two Madame Curie looked at her with uncertainty. The driver turned to see what was causing the delay.

The shoe did not have to be important. It could be a misstep, an occasional detour. It didn't have to be any more of a problem than Cambridge. She managed to put Cambridge in its proper place. It had taken some time, but she was able to do it. However, she wasn't sure if Madame Curie could do the same, especially in her state. She might lose perspective, overreact. She could lose everything.

Lucia remembered her promise to Monsieur. She smiled down at Madame Curie and leaned in to kiss her on both cheeks. "Take care," she said. "Do not work too hard. Remember your health."

Madame touched Lucia's cheek with her fingertips, shiny and taut, destroyed by the work.

Then Lucia gave the driver the address and shut the door. She stood there in a little patch of sunshine watching the taxi take its place in the street. She shivered, gave a quick smile to a passing neighbor, and turned back to the apartment.

# CHAPTER 15

# June 1906

I t was true Marie had no proof that Pierre was there. She couldn't measure his presence like she could levels of radioactivity. Yet, she knew when he was with her. The difference between an empty room and one that he filled. The empty room was just a collection of things, heavy and dull, ordinary objects, cluttered, that provided a function. Then the air around them became charged with energy. She felt it on her arms, at the back of her neck. The aether came alive with his presence and so did she, especially at night in the laboratory, after the others had gone home. She thought of it as their time together and stayed late every night hoping that he would come to her, which he often did.

In this way they would continue their work together.

She spent that day working on the effects of gravity on radiation. Pierre had become preoccupied with the subject before he died. She would go home soon, spend what was left of the night writing in her journal. She would tell him about the day's work, about her desolation. She would remember pieces of their life together, a ramble in the countryside, gathering oysters on the Île d'Oléron, cycling in the Port Royal Valley, the banks of periwinkles and violets, the streams and ponds.

That night she felt his presence as a tingling at the back of her neck. She sat up, tense and still, listening for signs of his presence; alert to every sound; hoping for confirmation, even though she didn't need it. She already knew he was there.

"Pierre?" She rarely spoke out loud to him. "Pierre?"

A fluttery breath blew across her cheek. She wiped away the tears with the palm of her hand. She heard a faint rustling at the back of the room near the instruments. Was he checking them? Was he checking to see if she had calibrated them correctly?

The hair on her arms stood up. The tingling had spread to her scalp, down her back, her whole body was humming. She wondered if she was matching his wavelength. Was it electrical in nature? She couldn't imagine the physics of the phenomenon, yet it comforted her to think they were in concert as they were in life, that their connection had somehow survived even death. Relief settled on her like a down counterpane. She felt his love as a physical presence.

"No words, Pierre."

He was alive again.

# Acknowledgments

For Judi, Meredith, and Jeannine, my constant stalwarts. For the women of the Santa Cruz writing community, the Abbeyites, and my other group that has no name, who opened their doors and fed me in all the important ways.

For my sons, Justin and Ryan, my galloping knights. And my intrepid editor, Dan Smetanka, who wades in with unfailing insight and a mighty red pen.

Finally, a very special thanks to my first reader and go-to idea man, Ryan Peckner, creative genius and son extraordinaire.

With gratitude and appreciation to you all.